A Heart Set Free

by

Janet S. Grunst

SMITTEN

HISTORICAL ROMANCE

LIGHTHOUSE PUBLISHING OF THE CAROLINAS

A HEART SET FREE BY JANET S. GRUNST
Published by Smitten Historical Romance
an imprint of Lighthouse Publishing of the Carolinas
2333 Barton Oaks Dr., Raleigh, NC, 27614

ISBN: 978-1-946016-01-0
Copyright © 2016 by Janet S. Grunst
Cover design by Elaina Lee
Interior design by Karthick Srinivasan

Available in print from your local bookstore, online, or from the publisher at:
www.lighthousepublishingofthecarolinas.com

For more information on this book and the author, visit: JanetGrunst.com

Brought to you by the creative team at Lighthouse Publishing of the Carolinas: Eddie Jones, Kathryn Davis, Shonda Savage, Brian Cross, Payton Lechner, and Lucie Winborne

Library of Congress Cataloging-in-Publication Data
Grunst, Janet S.
A Heart Set Free / Janet S. Grunst 1st ed.

Printed in the United States of America

Praise for *A Heart Set Free*

This is a tender, heartfelt novel about new beginnings and love blooming in unexpected places. *A Heart Set Free* weaves rich history and romance together into a beautiful tapestry of faith sure to find a special place in readers' hearts!

~**Laura Frantz**
Author of *The Mistress of Tall Acre*

Fleeing a painful past of betrayal and humiliation, Heather Douglas will do anything to leave her Scottish homeland—even indenture herself as a servant in the American colonies. While she survives the dangerous ocean passage, Heather is faced with fresh fears in Virginia. She knows her new situation will be a challenge. But she is unprepared for life with her master, who bought her indenture … and then stole her heart.

A Heart Set Free is Janet S. Grunst's debut novel, and it is a treasure. Heather is a likeable yet flawed protagonist. Bent on forgetting her past, her new life brings her face-to-face with her own shortcomings, forcing her to confront her lack of forgiveness toward those who have hurt her.

Grunst has done a laudable work of weaving Heather's spiritual growth into this historical romance. The reader observes a young woman emerging from her cocoon of denial to be freed to face who she is, while seeing herself as worthy of love. A sweet historical romance that will beg to be on your bookshelf.

~ **Elaine Marie Cooper**
Author of *Saratoga Letters*

A Heart Set Free is an absorbing tale of one woman's quest to hide from her past. Janet S. Grunst has skillfully woven faith elements and a compelling love story into colonial history to produce a novel not to be missed. The reader will be captivated from the first page.

~ **Ann Shorey**
Author of the Sisters at Heart series

With a love for, and knowledge of, all things colonial, Janet Grunst brings to life both the setting and her characters and their story.

~ **Carrie Fancett Pagels**
Author of *Saving the Marquise's Granddaughter*

Forgiveness and the healing power of love are at the heart of this touching debut, set amidst the verdant farmlands of colonial Virginia. Author Janet Grunst will delight fans of historical Christian fiction with this emotionally-charged story of faith, painted in beautifully vivid scenes and with engaging characters that will keep readers turning the pages. I was truly inspired after reading *A Heart Set Free*, and look forward to more works from this talented author.

~**Kate Breslin**
Award-winning author of *Not by Sight* and *High as the Heavens*

Janet Grunst's debut novel is a sweet historical romance filled with hope and touches of humor. Readers will identify with her richly drawn characters, Heather and Matthew, as each must learn that freedom has more to do with God's grace than their own actions. *A Heart Set* Free conveys timeless spiritual truths of forgiveness and redemption while drawing the reader into the finely detailed world of colonial living. Ms. Grunst has written a satisfying inspirational romance that will leave readers with a sigh and a smile, looking forward to her next book!

~**Kathleen Rouser**
Author of *Rumors and Promises*

A Heart Set Free is a very worthy debut for author Janet Grunst that will have readers eagerly awaiting her next book. Heather Douglas' shadowed past in her Scottish homeland has driven her to seek a new beginning as an indentured servant in the American colonies. A young farmer, Matthew Stewart, needs a caretaker for his young son and daughter, who have been living with close friends in distant Alexandria, Virginia, since his wife's death. He purchases Heather's indenture, but in the confusion of making the necessary arrangements, he neglects to explain that they will have to marry for the sake of propriety. Thus when the parson arrives, Heather faces an unexpected and stark choice: marry a total stranger who seems to be kind and mother his children . . . or take her chances on finding another master.

Grunst integrates the historical setting of 1770 Virginia into the story so naturally that one learns a great deal about the colonial era and society without realizing it. In this period leading up to the Revolution, the colonies are in turmoil, as are the hero's and heroine's lives. Heather and Matthew are appealing characters who are torn between a deep attraction and the very personal secrets, conflicted motivations, and fears that are powerful barriers to each fully trusting the other. Grunst's portrayal of their faith journey had me rooting for them to finally open their hearts fully to each other and to God. The conclusion of *A Heart Set Free* is heartwarming and inspiring, and I highly recommend it to readers!

~**J. M. Hochstetler**
Author of the American Patriot series and the Northkill Amish series

Dedication

To my husband, Ken, an unexpected gift from God.

Acknowledgments

To my parents, who passed on the love of reading to their children.

I am so thankful for the encouragement and tenacity of Linda Glaz, my agent with Hartline Literary Agency. Her patience and guidance helped to make this a better story. Thank you to Lighthouse Publishing of the Carolinas—Kathryn Davis, Payton Lechner, Shonda Savage—and the rest of the team who made this story a reality.

My appreciation to the friends and family who supported, prayed for, and mentored me. For the friends who took the time to read the story and offer helpful suggestions.

To my husband, Ken, who encouraged me to never give up on my dream to write stories that communicate the truths of the Christian faith that will entertain, as well as bring inspiration, healing, and hope to the reader.

I am most grateful for my Lord and Savior, Jesus Christ, for His provision, mercy, and grace in my life. He put this story in my mind and gave me the heart to write it.

CHAPTER 1

1770

Heather Douglas stood on the dock, shivering in disbelief. Her heart skipped a beat as she touched her wrist. It was gone. How had she forgotten? The gold bracelet her mother had given her was gone. She had sold it two days before. She sighed. There had been no other choice. She would not beg for charity from family acquaintances. Besides, the gossip about her had already begun amongst neighbors and the patrons of her family's shop.

Her family had been fabric merchants, mercers, in Perth for many years. The Douglas name was well established and respected. Stories of indecorous behavior were prone to travel, so she had to do the same. She had thought Edinburgh would be far enough away to save her family's honor. It was not, but it was a starting place. It was in Edinburgh that she learned of a way to leave Scotland and find a new beginning.

Some new beginning. She shuddered.

She had left a life of comfort for a warehouse filled with others like herself who were leaving Scotland for the colonies.

Like many of the other indentured servants, she had spent the frigid night in the barren warehouse on the wharf, waiting to board the ship before dawn. Now, outside and exposed, she shivered as the icy rain penetrated her woolen cloak. Her toes were so cold she could hardly feel them. The emigrants had formed a queue to embark the merchant vessel, *Providence*. Her churning stomach reminded her it had been too long since she had last eaten.

A flurry of activity on board the ship drew her attention to the sailors hanging from the tall masts, readying the vessel for the transatlantic voyage. The men shouted to each other while weaving through the rigging like giant spiders. She spotted a tall man with authority, possibly the captain of the *Providence,* standing on the gangway, going over with the agents what she assumed was the passenger manifest. Like her, most of the passengers were indentured servants, but she had learned from an agent that there were also redemptioners making the crossing—emigrants who had paid for a portion of their passage and were expecting friends or family in the colonies to lend or give them the unpaid balance.

Unlike the redemptioners, she had no one to help her once she arrived.

She shook violently, one hand clutching the hood over her head to fend off the wind and rain, her other hand clinging to the embroidered satchel. In it was everything she chose to take with her. She should have taken more, but getting away from Ross had been her primary concern. Now thoughts of her brother only irritated her, and that served no purpose.

The wind carried bits of conversation. There were a number of families with small children and others like herself who appeared to be solitary travelers. Behind her, a tall, attractive woman tried to console two young girls. The freezing rain crystallized at the woman's hairline. What had driven her to make a decision like this for herself and her girls?

"I cannot imagine it will be much longer until we are allowed to board, Emily. Do try to be patient. I know you are still tired."

One of the girls tugged at her mother's skirt. "I am hungry, Mama."

The woman pulled something from one of the portmanteaus she carried.

"Here, Katie, have some cheese and bread. Remember, I asked you to breakfast with Emily and me."

The tall woman glanced up, made eye contact with her for the first time, and smiled. Her large brown eyes, arresting against so creamy a complexion, invited friendship. "I had to wake the bairns up early this morning to arrive in time. Now there is nowhere to go."

Heather nodded. "They will surely have us go aboard soon or allow us to return to the warehouse to keep out of the weather."

Some of the other passengers in the queue also seemed restless about the delay. The captain stood on deck giving orders to the agents. Two of them went ashore and motioned to the emigrants to begin the climb up the oak gangway. Each one stopped briefly to allow a ship's officer to make an accounting on the manifest.

Waiting her turn on the ship, Heather drew the satchel to her for warmth. All the activity on deck awed her. The icy fog and muffled sounds made an eerie scene. Passengers walked precariously around what appeared like miles of coiled hemp ropes. The crew, though busy preparing the ship for sail, appeared quite intent on the emigrants, particularly the women. One rather swarthy sailor standing near them licked his lips and winked at her. He grinned at the tall woman behind her. It made Heather's skin crawl.

She turned away from him and whispered to the woman, "Keep your girls close."

The woman's face turned anxious. "I wish he would be about his business and leave us be."

Heather raised her chin and glared at him, but he ignored her. His eyes rested on the smallest girl.

The woman frowned and drew her daughters close to her full skirt. "Aye, I shall be glad when we get through this checkpoint and can go below."

The sailor, reeking of tobacco and spirits, brushed against Heather and mumbled something as he made his way aft.

Her eyes followed him as he disappeared from view into the fog. She glanced again at the small girls. They would need to be protected in the weeks ahead.

Once accounted for, she headed for the ladder leading below, as the others had before her. Impatient, some of the crew pushed and shouted as they herded the remaining passengers to the "between-the-decks" area below. There, the men were steered to one side, the women and small children to the other. Heather squinted to try and make out shapes in the darkness ahead. Her eyes watered, and her nostrils flared at the caustic air. Had they even bothered to clean the ship before funneling the passengers aboard?

The ceilings in the cramped, poorly lit quarters were so low that standing upright was impossible for all but the children. The bunks, covered with straw pallets and positioned next to each other throughout the musty area, smelled of mildew and urine. Trunks or bundles had to be placed at the end of the children's smaller bunks. This arrangement allowed for only a few narrow aisles for moving about the compartment. With such crowded conditions, privacy would be nonexistent. Desperate for a place to sit, Heather quickly chose a bunk and clutched her bag. The others fought over what they must have perceived to be the choice locations.

"Good day, again." It was the woman she had first noticed on the dock. Hers was the first sign of friendship Heather had witnessed in days. How she longed for a friend.

"Allow me to introduce myself. My name is Sara Macmillan, and these are my daughters, Emily and Katie. Have these pallets been spoken for?"

"Nay, I do not believe so. I am Heather Douglas. Pleased to make your acquaintance."

Sara set her portmanteaus on a pallet and motioned for the girls to climb onto the smaller one. "Quite extravagant accommodations we have." Her sarcasm was softened by a smile. "Are you from Edinburgh, Miss Douglas?"

"Nay, I … I am from Perth."

"Ah, you had a bit of a journey. We were a mite more fortunate in that sense. We have been staying with my aunt in Edinburgh these past two months."

She smiled at Sara and removed her cloak, which was heavy with rainwater. "It is so dark and close in here, and the peculiar odor makes it difficult to breathe."

Sara shook out her cloak and placed it on the pallet. "I heard someone say they use vinegar to wash down the walls and deck. I suspect they are not overly concerned about our comfort."

"It would appear not. Is your husband aboard also?"

Sara lowered herself onto the pallet, and her expression grew pensive. "John, God bless him, passed on six months ago. The girls and I are going to Virginia to his brother's home. Andrew and his family live some miles south of Alexandria. It was John's dream to settle in Virginia. Now it is ours."

Heather studied Sara's sad brown eyes and those of the two little girls. Her heart filled with empathy for them, and for a few minutes, she forgot her own pain.

"Do you have family or friends in the colonies, Heather, or are you indentured?"

"Nay. I have no one there. I am indentured."

Sara continued to watch her as if waiting for her to continue. "May I ask why you indentured yourself? I have never known anyone who did that."

She hesitated a moment, knots forming in the back of her neck. Could she trust Sara with her history? How much worse could things be? "My father died recently, and our family circumstances required I seek employment … preferably far from home. I believed this was an answer."

"Well, fresh starts are always good. This is a new beginning for all of us."

Heather glanced about. *Fresh start, indeed.*

❧ ❧

In the days that followed, Heather enjoyed the times when she and Sara talked about anything and everything. Sara often referred to her faith in Jesus and how much He had helped her and the girls, particularly in the months following John's death. Sara prayed with the girls and read her Bible regularly. Heather rummaged through her satchel for her own Bible, something she had only thought to bring at the last minute before she left home. After a few minutes of thumbing through the pages, she glanced at Sara.

"Do you mind if I ask you about your faith, Sara?"

"Of course not."

"Please do not misunderstand me. I can see you are a very religious woman. It is, well, you speak of Jesus ... it is as if He is your friend, someone you converse with ... right here." She waved her hands in front. "I think of Jesus as the Son of God, and someone I worship and pray to, but not here."

Sara's smile was like a balm. "I understand what you mean, Heather. Years ago, I believed what I was taught about God and Jesus. I attended services, prayed, and tried to do and say the right things. But whenever I fell short of my expectations, I suffered guilt that I was never good enough. When John and I married, he explained to me that believing in the Lord was but one part of faith—that I also needed to receive Him in here." Sara patted her chest. "He became more than my Savior, who would forgive me my trespasses when I died. He forgives me whenever I go to Him with a repentant heart. It is the Holy Ghost that I carry with me everywhere. He brings my sins to my conscience when I have erred. He is my comforter, teacher, and yes, my friend. My faith has changed from being a religion to a relationship." Sara reached over and squeezed her hand. "Does that help to answer your question?"

There was such peace in Sara's face, something Heather had experienced little of lately. "Aye. You have certainly given me much to think about."

"If you have more questions, I am here."

❧ ☙

The conditions below deck were abysmal. It was crowded and offered little privacy. The air was musty and the stench nauseating. The passage seemed never-ending. Days turned into weeks, and the abundance of time without activity allowed Heather's mind to wander. At night, when talking ceased and sleep was elusive, painful memories and fear replaced the boredom.

She needed to focus on the future. Freedom. It would be seven years before she would experience it again. There was no way to turn back. Nay, she did not really want to go back. Whatever awaited her had to be better than what she had left behind. When she signed the indenture, the agent told her that upon completion of her seven years of service, she would be free and receive a small parcel of land for her own. Aye, it was a wise choice to leave Scotland and her past, with all its losses, behind.

A rustle interrupted her musings. The dim light of a nearby lantern accentuated the peaceful expression on Sara's face as she tucked the blanket around her girls, now sleeping soundly. "It will be grand to finally reach Virginia. Andrew says we will love living there."

"As much as I want to get off this ship, I fear what lies ahead for me."

"Heather, was what you left in Scotland so bad? When you told me why you indentured yourself, it almost sounded as if you were trying to escape something. Did I misunderstand you?"

Heather's stomach clenched. "I needed to leave. I was without resources, and there was an unjust scandal brewing about me." As close as she had grown to Sara, she was not ready to reveal more about her life or her mistakes. "Now, tell me again about John's brother. You said he and his family live south of Alexandria. Does he live in town, or in the country?"

Sara's smile suggested she saw through the ploy. "Andrew and Rebecca live in Fredericksburg. He is involved with commerce along a nearby river. Living with John's family in Fredericksburg will provide the best possible situation for us."

❦

The following day, a violent storm engulfed the *Providence*. Heather grasped the edge of her pallet to keep from rolling off each time the square-rigger pitched and rolled. Fierce winds and torrential rain thrashed the creaking vessel. The sound of ill passengers shouting and screaming from the violent buffeting made her cringe. The stench turned her stomach. She held a handkerchief to her nose, but it did little good. She prayed her dry heaves would not return.

Earlier that day, the crew member who brought their daily ration of water indicated that the captain and his mates were struggling to keep the ship upright and on course. Some passengers only stared at him. Others shouted pleas or hostile words.

Bile filled her throat. The sick relieved themselves wherever they could, and any sense of modesty had long been lost.

Her stomach heaved again, and she covered her mouth. She closed her eyes, trying to mentally escape her present circumstances. If only she could change the events that had brought her to this merchant vessel. But the past would not be altered.

Was it seven or eight weeks now they had been at sea? It was difficult to keep track. She had counted the days at first, but once so many people became ill, she stopped. What purpose did it serve?

She scratched herself and picked what she suspected were weevils from the hardtack. *Think about something else, Heather, not about the desire for a decent meal, or for a drink of cool, clean water—and certainly not for a bath.*

She recalled those last days at home filled with hurt, confusion, disillusionment, and the need to escape. Indenturing herself had been an impulsive decision, and she was not an impulsive person. But she had found no work as a seamstress those few days spent in Edinburgh. She had no prospects of employment and no money, and the scandal was sure to become known. It had seemed the wisest choice at the time. All her hopes rested in the life she would find in Virginia. It was foolhardy to dwell on matters she was powerless to change.

When the rolling of the ship finally subsided, she folded her legs under her. She glanced down to her soiled woolen dress. Pathetic. It had been a handsome frock once. Now it needed more than thread to mend the tears. The calico dress in her satchel was just as filthy.

Her eyes burned from the acrid air as she gazed around at the other passengers. At the onset of the voyage, they numbered ninety; now only seventy-two remained. They moaned in agony. The foul stench of so many—their sweat, waste, and vomit—was enough to turn any stomach, even in a calmer sea. Heather looked forward to the days when the passengers were allowed on deck to walk about, enjoy the sunlight, and breathe fresh air.

※ ⁂ ※

As Sara and her girls climbed off the ladder to the deck with Heather, the wind whipped at their cloaks and skirts. The children were steered to an area amidships where they could play safely. The adults were grateful for the opportunity to walk upright. She and Sara drank in the fresh cool air but did not allow their gazes to stray far from the girls.

She tapped Sara's arm when she spotted the sailor in the blue patched shirt ogling them.

Sara turned her way. "Ignore him, Heather. Smell that fresh sea breeze. I was beginning to wonder if we would ever get out here again."

"Aye. My thoughts also."

Sara's brow furrowed. "The deaths of the Maxwell children were heartbreaking. My girls played with them, and I am concerned that they might take ill." Sara bit her lip and pulled her cloak tighter across her bodice as she glanced in the direction of the girls. "Katie has been so quiet today."

Heather placed her hand on Sara's back. "The turn around the deck will do us all good. Exercise and sunshine have always perked us up before."

Fighting the wind, Sara gathered her hood around her face. "I had no idea how we would be berthed and fed or how confining it would be for the girls. I fear for them above all else."

Heather squeezed Sara's hand and pointed to the sailor approaching them. "He is following us again." She shuddered, and a lump formed in her throat. She took Sara's arm and steered her toward the area where the girls were seated with the other children. The youngsters were enthralled by three sailors playing on wooden hornpipes. But far too soon, they were ushered below to what had become their prison.

The next day, the crew began to ration water as the demand for it grew. Below deck, people were growing restless and worried. Hostility and fear were becoming as virulent as the fever among the passengers. Each day, more of the passengers were taken ill with dysentery and fever. The disease was taking its toll on all, particularly the children. A few days before, two more children had died after days of suffering from a rash and fever. Day after day, bodies were given up to the sea. Even the crew appeared anxious about the spreading calamity. Some of the sailors who distributed the hardtack and water and removed the slops were overheard saying that there had been more fever on this trip than they had seen on other crossings.

❦

Once again on deck, Heather stared out on the green swells. The breeze against her face revived her after days and nights of grieving. The last week had been the worst of the voyage. *Why, oh why, Lord?*

Katie had taken ill like so many others onboard. While Sara nursed the feverish child, Heather had kept Emily as distant as possible. On the second day of Katie's illness, the pestilence also struck Emily. To bring down their fevers, the two women bathed the girls day and night with their meager supply of water. Weak and exhausted, Sara, too, finally fell ill. Heather faithfully cared for her friend.

Emily and Katie died within two days of each other. Sara lingered two more days before dying.

I will miss you so, Sara—your wisdom, your kindness, your unwavering faith. We prayed, Lord. Where were You?

She would not dwell on it now. It was too painful. She had to think about the future. Land had been sighted low on the horizon, and now she saw it too. Gulls squawked as she took one last glimpse at the sky before heading back to the hold. It would not be long now. They were in the Bay of Chesapoyocke, close to the Potomack. Ahead, somewhere out there, was the port town of Alexandria and her future.

CHAPTER 2

The horse-drawn wagon picked up speed as it turned off the dirt road and onto the cobblestone street. Every time Matthew Stewart came to Alexandria, he was reminded of the constant activity that surrounded this busy river port. The sounds of carriages, commerce, and voices here were such a contrast to a mere twenty miles west, where his small farm was one among many that dotted the rolling, wooded countryside. His spirits picked up. They always did when he came to town. Adam and Maggie Duncan were more than friends, and seeing them was exactly what he needed now.

The days on the farm were filled with work. It was the evening hours that brought on despair. The emptiness and silence of the farmhouse became unbearable then. He could remember days when it was filled with love and joy—a wife and children. For a moment, he closed his eyes in an effort to push back memories of Elizabeth. He shook his head. *No, do not think about what is lost. Be grateful and focus on today.* He would see Mary and Mark again, if only for a short time.

On a footpath to his left, a family laughed and chatted as they climbed the steps to a large brick home. Heaviness rose in his chest. Seeing his children occasionally was not enough. He wanted his children with him. But how? It was foolhardy to try to take care of children so young without help. He turned the wagon onto Fairfax Street.

The sun climbed higher in the sky, and the heat intensified. Spring had arrived with a vengeance. The thunderstorms of the past few days, and now the heat, made the atmosphere oppressive and muggy. Warm days like this were rare in early spring. The freshly washed osnaburg shirt he had put on that morning was already soaked with perspiration. He wiped his brow and placed the black three-cornered hat back on his head. His hair was damp despite being tied back in a club. A common planter, he dressed more simply than many of the gentlemen in town.

The jug of water he brought had been emptied miles ago. He longed for Maggie's cooking and a cool drink. He missed the delicious home-cooked meals he had once enjoyed. "Oronoko Street and the 'clan' are just around the corner, Honey." He tugged the reins to the right, steering the old horse ever closer to their destination. It would not be long now.

He pulled the wagon up in front of the modest brick house just as the Duncans' oldest son, Donald, bounded out the front door. Not far behind was his mother, Maggie, now heavy with child. Smiling and waving, she carried Cameron, the youngest of the three Duncan children, straddling what was left of her hip.

"Matthew Stewart, what a joy to see you. Adam is around back. Wait till I tell him you are here. And the children … oh, how they have been missin' you."

Maggie's enthusiasm always charmed him, and this time was no different. But her tired appearance brought on a twinge of guilt. It was no wonder. She cared for a home and five children and now had another on the way. Homemaking and childrearing required effort and energy. He had become well acquainted with such tasks in the weeks following Elizabeth's death.

"Maggie, you are a sight, but a good one." He climbed down from the wagon. The sound of running feet and a little girl's voice made him turn.

"Papa, Papa. I hoped you would come today!" Mary ran toward him with outstretched arms.

He knelt on one knee and wrapped his arms around the child. The touch of her warm, soft cheek and small arms encircling his neck both warmed and saddened him. It was not easy to let her go.

"I have missed you so, Mary. Here, let me see you." He held

her at arm's length.

The last year had brought a marked change in her. She was no longer the giggling little miss with dimples and chubby arms. Mary, now nine, had grown into a taller, thinner, and much more mature girl. In spite of her serious nature, she could still apply her charms when it suited her.

She smiled. "Papa, come see my duckling in back. Mark has one too."

He stood. At that moment, a small boy of four shot out from behind the house, grinning and shrieking. "Papa, Papa, Papa, you are here!"

He leaned down and tousled his son's dark, wavy hair. "How is my fine boy? Have you been good for Mrs. Duncan?"

"Oh, yes, Papa. We have ducks." Mark's eyes and voice filled with mirth. "Come see them."

"Let me give Honey some oats, you two, and I shall come around back."

He smiled and turned once more to the woman still at his side. "Thank you for being so good to them, Maggie. They seem to be faring very well."

"Aye, I think so too. Now do not tarry with the nag, Matthew. There is a meat pie inside waiting for you."

"I will see to Honey, wash the road dust off, and join you."

"Aye, but not before I get my hug." She shifted the child in her arms and gave Matthew a gentle squeeze as he leaned down to buss her cheek.

"Are there goings on out here, and with my wife, in the middle of the day?" Adam's jovial voice came from around the side of the house.

He smiled at the portly, balding man. "Adam, were it possible to steal your wife and get away with it, I would surely try."

"Sure. Sure you would, Matt, and me bairns too? And would it not be a fine joke, us fighting over them? I may not match you in height, but I daresay I outweigh you. You are gettin' too thin, man." Adam glanced from his friend to his wife. "Maggie, be the love that you are and fix dinner for this starved, scrawny bag of bones."

"Aye, it will be ready shortly, so do not be chattering out here long." Maggie turned and lumbered up the steps, children following.

Matthew laughed and watched them parade inside, the mother duck followed by her ducklings.

Adam reached up and patted the horse's neck. "Matt, we can go down and put your supply order in after dinner. I would enjoy the walk, and besides, you must see all the ships in port. I am sure that you will find anything you might want among all the wares being peddled there."

"I sensed that there was something astir as I came into town." He saw to the horse, took a wooden crate from the wagon, and handed it to his friend. "Here, a few things from the farm that you might use."

"That is mighty good of you. Maggie will be pleased too."

"Good of me? It is hardly enough for all that you and yours are doing for me, Adam."

As they walked into the house, he smiled at Maggie. "Mmm, something smells delicious in here. Feed me like this and you may end up with me a boarder too." He handed Mark the damp hat as he sat at the table that dominated the room.

Mark pranced around the room. This was what a home should be: a man, a woman, and rooms filled with the sounds of happy children.

Mary crawled up onto his lap. "Oh, Father, would you stay?"

"No, dear, I shall be leaving again after I pick up the supplies, same as usual." He brushed the loose strands of hair from her face. If only she understood.

"Papa, please stay." Mark, with his dark hair tied back in a club, was a smaller version of his father.

"I have told you before. I must work the farm, and the animals must be cared for. I cannot be gone too long."

"Please, may we go home with you?" Mary tugged on his shirt.

Mark snuggled in beside him. "I want to go home. I want to be with Papa too."

He stared at Mark for what seemed a long time. Heaviness filled his chest. How might he make them understand how he ached each time he left them? He had no choice. The children had to be cared for, and the Duncans' offer to take them in had been a blessing.

He and his children joined the Duncans gathered around the table for dinner. How would he ever repay Adam and Maggie for all they had done for his family?

As they bowed their heads and folded their hands, Adam began the blessing. "We thank You, Lord, for all You have given us. We ask for Your blessings on our food and time together. May it nourish our bodies and strengthen us for Your service. Amen."

Adam devoured the meat pie on his plate. "Ah, this is tasty." He reached for the basket of bread. "Maggie, my dear, Matt and I will leave for the wharf and Brady's after dinner. May I get you anything?"

"Nay, I shall be going down there tomorrow. The merchants have so much that is new, and I must see it for myself."

When dinner was over, Adam walked to the mantle and picked up his pipe and bag of tobacco. "One of the ships has a cargo of indentureds to be sold off."

"Ah, now that is what you may get for me, my dear. I can surely use the help around here." Maggie's voice was playful as she arranged her husband's steenkirk scarf. "Find a healthy one who can chase after these wee ones, and of course, one that enjoys scrubbing and carrying the slops. Shall I go on?" Maggie smiled.

"You have said more than enough." Adam's expression and words were like a warning.

Matthew pushed away his plate. "I fear my children have been an added burden, Maggie."

"Nay, Matthew. I was only teasing." A curious expression suddenly emerged on Maggie's face. She put her hand to her chin, and a sly grin formed as she glanced first at him, then back to Adam. Maggie handed Mary a bowl holding the remnants of the meal. "Please now, children, all of you, take this out to the ducks."

"Matthew, dear." Maggie faced him once the children had left. "Would you consider purchasing a bondswoman? It might solve your problems. She would care for the children, cook, clean, and help you around the farm. Your wee ones could be home with you again."

Matthew's mouth dropped open. He stared at Maggie before turning to Adam.

Adam nodded his head in agreement.

"If the children are too much for you, Maggie—" Matthew started.

"Nay, it is not that, Matthew Stewart. I love them. I am trying to think of what is best for all of you. The children miss you, and each visit you tell me you want the wee ones with you. Is that true or not?"

"Maggie, some of those people are criminals that the agents have gotten from the streets. The women—what information will be provided on them—what they have done or where they have been? I am not so desperate that I would take an unknown woman into my home and leave my children in her care."

"How proud you sound, Matthew. Perhaps some of the women are only seeking a way to leave Scotland or England. I understand the agents promise them much—land, clothing, livestock, and their passage for five, six, or seven years of labor. Some of those people are trying to start a new life to escape the poverty over there. It may be that they are not all of such questionable character." She paused, and added, "Having another person, a woman, helping on the farm might be good for you, also."

Adam grabbed the pipe from his mouth. "Maggie Duncan, you do amaze me, woman." Chuckling, he patted Matthew on the arm.

"Well, there is always the widow Mackenzie. She would relish the chance to help you, Matt."

Choking on his tea, he stuttered, "Nev—never mind. Do not even jest about that." He wiped the spilled tea from his chin.

It was common knowledge that Hattie Mackenzie had set her cap for Matthew Stewart. Not finding the talkative, domineering woman to his liking, he avoided her as much as possible whenever he came to town. Was he desperate enough for Hattie? *No. No, not that*.

"I must admit, I shall experience true joy the day that the widow Mackenzie snares herself another husband. It shall not be me." He shook his head, ending the discussion of the widow.

As they sat sipping their tea, he reached over and placed his hand on Maggie's. "I am not seeking a wife. No one can take Elizabeth's place." These days he spent less time dwelling on thoughts of his beloved wife and the babe who also perished, but the conversation brought back the memory. He held the child partially responsible for her death, but to a greater degree, he blamed himself for her being in the country and far from help during a difficult pregnancy and birth. His palms grew damp, and sweat speckled his forehead. If only he had been able to get her help in time.

Adam tapped him on the arm. "Matt, we had best be off."

"Let me check on Mark and Mary before we go. They wanted to show me their ducklings." He regretted spending so little time with his children on these infrequent visits. To have them home again would be a blessing indeed.

The men went behind the house to admire the small yellow and brown creatures. Jean Duncan and Mary played with their dolls on the brick stoop while Cameron and Mark chased the ducklings, almost running into them.

"Whoa there, lads." Adam reached down and put his arms around his son. "You are going to chase the life out of the wee quackers. Where is Donald, Jean?"

"He has gone off to the Lamonts', Papa. You told him he could go after dinner."

Adam grinned, and he poked Matthew in the side. "Twelve years old, and he has an eye for the wee Lamont lass."

Matthew studied Mark and Mary. "We are off to town. What shall I bring back for you?"

All eyes turned toward him. "Sweets." "Ribbons." "A ball." "Beads."

"I shall see what I can find. It will be a surprise."

The men walked around the house to the footpath.

"Matt, what do you think will happen if Parliament does decide to impose the taxes? There are enough people around here that will not be takin' that sittin' down." Adam grew agitated as he spoke.

"We will experience the effects of it, of course. But away from town, we do not bother ourselves about politics the way you do here."

"If it comes to a fight, Matt, it will be difficult not to get involved."

"I suppose what you say is true, but I cannot imagine it coming to a fight. We are British subjects, and loyal to the Crown."

When they turned onto Water Street, he stopped. The small port was filled with an array of sailing vessels.

"That is quite a sight—all those ships in or near the port, Adam. The motherland has already invaded the Potomack."

While they walked along the quay, he shook his head. What an amazing variety of goods were being sold off the ships to the local merchants: china, fine fabrics, spices, and other luxuries the colonists yearned for.

Farther down the dock, Adam pointed to a group of men lined up behind a table. Among them sat a man who appeared to be the captain of one of the ships handling some documents. Adam pointed toward the motley passengers. "Those are the indentureds. Aye, they are being sold off like cattle. I wonder if their destination will be any better than whatever they left behind in their mother countries."

Matthew swallowed hard. "What a sad sight." A filthy line of humanity shuffled from the ship's gangway. "They certainly are a shabby and sickly looking bunch. I remember Thomas Reed, the smithy, came over on one of the ships a few years back. He said that the conditions were frightful and that many died before reaching us."

Adam laughed. "It seems you have a source of gossip other than my Maggie."

"I may live out in the woods, Adam, but we are not totally out of touch with the goings-on in town."

They stayed a few minutes longer and watched the group of men barter off several of the weary travelers. As each man's indenture was purchased, he shuffled off with his new master. Matthew shook his head. Who would not empathize with these people? Most of the men and some of the women would labor in the fields of the large tobacco plantations in heat they had never before experienced. How many would survive? It was a hard life for someone in good physical condition, but these people needed a miracle.

CHAPTER 3

From her elevated perspective on the deck of the ship, Heather viewed quite a bit of the waterfront of Alexandria. The landscape was wooded and dotted with clapboard, brick, and stone buildings. Peaked roofs were visible all around. It lacked the antiquated and well-established appearance of home, but it was only a young and growing colony.

Watching the people walking about took her mind off her present circumstances. A few of them seemed intent on their destinations while others appeared to be on a leisurely stroll. Some men were clearly occupied in the port trades. The women beside her on the deck, fellow indentureds, observed the activity below them on the quay. A small woman on her right shuddered in fright. Heather understood—fear coursed through her own stomach. What might she say to comfort the woman, and would her reassurances bring any peace?

She smiled at the woman. "This seems like a nice town, not so different from what we are accustomed to seeing at home."

"Will they speak like us?" The woman's brow furrowed and her lips pursed as she rubbed a quivering hand across the bag she carried.

"It is a British colony, so they are bound to speak English." Heather wiped the perspiration from her face. "The weather is warm. The women wear lighter fabrics and colors, but all else seems the same. We have traveled so far from home, yet the people here cannot be that different than they are in Scotland."

"This heat and mugginess is nothing like Scotland."

It was impossible to relieve the dampness saturating her

chemise underneath the lightweight green wool. She glanced down and rubbed at the tear in the seam at her waist. Mending and washing were immediate requirements. Had she more than two dresses in her possession, she would have relished burning this one. She stroked her tattered skirt and shuddered. She smelled like a fellmonger. *Mind You, I am not complaining, Lord. At least I can finally breathe fresh air, hot and damp as it is.*

Again, she scrutinized the platform adjacent to the ship, where the men, her fellow passengers, were being taken away one by one. The reality of her circumstances made her heart race. It blotted out the town, its citizenry, and her physical discomfort. Soon, she would be sold. Terror rose in her throat, and it choked her.

"Me fine ladies, it is time to go to the platform." The agent waved in their direction.

❦

Adam pointed to the deck of the ship. "Over there, Matt. There are the women. They will bring them out after the men."

Matthew's focus shifted to the women leaving the ship and walking onto dry land. They appeared to be in worse condition than the men. He could not remember seeing women in such a disheveled state. How would they appear if they were clean? And why would they ever leave their homeland to travel under such miserable conditions?

His eyes surveyed the women as they drew closer. One stood out among the rest. The other women moved and spoke among themselves, but she stood alone and still. Only her head moved. She scanned the dock and beyond to the town. Was she searching for someone? His gaze slowly dropped from the ivory cap partially covering her light sandy-colored hair to her face. She had such a sad expression, but beautiful eyes. Most likely they were blue or possibly green, the same color her dress might once have been. And her skin was so fair. The more he studied her, the more curious he became. Her garment was of fine quality, though soiled and torn and hanging loosely on her frame. The green bodice and skirt were set off by the ivory of her chemise, pulled up to fill in the round neckline and ruffled below the sleeve. He might be mistaken, but she appeared to be a woman of some refinement. Why would such a woman be here on the auction block?

Adam tapped his friend's arm. "Matt. Where are you, man?"

"The tall woman over there, in the green dress. Do you see her?"

"Aye, she is a comely one, she is. Seems a bit proud, though, for one that is about to be sold off."

"Perhaps not pride, Adam, just fear. There is a certain quality about her—dignity, not arrogance." And yet, through the filth and squalor, it was difficult to tell.

They watched the sale of the human cargo for a few more minutes before they continued down the street to Brady's Shop. Upon entering, they stopped to talk with two other men of Adam's acquaintance. After a short time, Matthew broke away from Adam and his friends and approached the shopkeeper, now finished with another customer.

"Good day, Mr. Brady. All is well with you, I pray?"

"Very good, Mr. Stewart. It is good to see you in town again. I see the children on occasion, and they seem to be doing very well."

"Yes, the children are fine, thank you." He handed the merchant his list. "The Duncans have taken excellent care of them. I will return in about two hours for the supplies if that is agreeable with you?"

"They will be ready, Mr. Stewart." The shopkeeper turned and began gathering the items listed.

With arrangements made and favors for the children purchased, he stepped outside to join Adam, who was in the midst of a conversation with a mutual friend.

His gaze and mind wandered back to the ship carrying the indentured servants. Perhaps Maggie was right. Purchasing an indentured would certainly enable him to bring Mark and Mary home. *But how do I bring a woman into our home?* No ... yet he imagined how he might make it work.

"Matt, I have been talking to you, and you have not heard a word. What has gotten into you, man?"

"I am sorry, Adam. What were you saying?"

"I was telling you that I am worried about Maggie. She has not carried the baby well this time. She has pain and does not sleep well, so I asked Lamont if his oldest girl, Sally, would help out a bit. I am only telling you this because you think that you have burdened her with Mary and Mark. The girls and Sally will be all the help Maggie needs, so stop worrying about the children being a problem."

"For heaven's sake, Adam, I have imposed." Maggie should have been enjoying her own young ones, not taking care of his. And now she needed help.

He stared again toward the city dock. He could not bring a woman into his home unless she was his wife. But could he marry a stranger? *If this is Your will, Lord, show me, and I will resolve to change the situation.*

The men continued their discussion as they walked back the way they had come. When they once again were near the ship, they stopped to watch the women.

"Is it that fair lass from the ship that has clouded your mind, Matt?"

"She is hardly a lass, though I wager that she is younger than me by a few years." As they talked, he spotted George Lamont approaching.

"Mr. Lamont." Adam put his hand out to the newcomer. "Matthew Stewart and I were commenting earlier on how occupied you have been lately with the law."

The solicitor, bewigged and smartly dressed in a matching buff coat and waistcoat, smiled and paused to chat. "Good to see you, Adam, and you also, Matthew. Busy as ever. I am not at my desk now because Mrs. Lamont coaxed me to accompany her here while she perused some new fabric. I have no doubt that within the next few minutes too much of my wages will find its way into that silk merchant's pocket."

They were interrupted by the sound of a woman's voice shouting in Gaelic. Lamont laughed. "There is one little lass that will give her master a handful. But she shall not do badly with Thomas Reed as her keeper."

Again Matthew studied the tall, fair woman. She now stood with the others behind the table. Seeing the terror in her eyes, his stomach tightened. Blue eyes—yes, definitely blue, like cornflowers. He was startled when she surveyed him for a moment before she glanced away.

It would not be like it was with Elizabeth. He was not searching for love, only a way to keep his family together. It was the only answer. He turned to the solicitor.

"Lamont, I want to engage your services for a business transaction. Would you please inquire into the background of the tall bondswoman in the green dress?"

As Mr. Lamont walked to the table where the bargaining was proceeding, Adam laughed. "Maggie will be pleased as pie. She always is when someone takes her advice to heart. But, Matt, are you sure? It would be the four of you living together in that small cottage."

"Well, if Lamont does not find out anything too objectionable about her, and if he will stake me until I can get him the funds, I shall take her and marry her right away. That is, if she agrees. It is the only way we can live together in the same house."

Adam wore a quizzical frown. "Matt, it is not at all like you to be impulsive. We can take care of the children. Wait and find someone you want to marry."

"Adam, I have no time for courting, nor a desire to wed, but I have been away from my children too long as it is. It is no good. It was impossible for me to care for them and work the farm. I tried that, and we nearly lost Mark to the pond. No, I must make this work. It certainly is not the first time a man took a wife for convenience's sake. And really, Adam, can you imagine the likes of that one being burned up working in the fields all day?"

Adam had a discerning yet cynical expression. "Somehow, I suspect she would never make it to the fields. Here is Lamont now."

"Well, it seems that there is not much information about her except that she boarded at Edinburgh and that they are not aware of any criminal record. Her name is Heather Douglas, age is twenty-eight, and she can read and write. My guess is that she is running away from something or someone." George Lamont stood silent for a moment before continuing to convey what he had learned. "She is unmarried, more genteel than most, and healthier. They want fifteen pounds, granting a seven-year indenture for her. What would you have me do?"

"Will you stake me until I can get you the funds?"

"Your credit is good with me, Matthew."

"I shall buy her indenture now." *Lord, please make this work for all our sakes.*

Heather's tense fingers clutched her satchel. Standing upright on dry land proved as challenging as adjusting to the ship had been. During the weeks at sea, she had tried to imagine what this day would be like, but nothing prepared her for this degradation. She watched as the crowd of spectators grew. Less than forty feet away stood three men staring directly at her. Her face grew very warm in the bright sunlight. *Do not faint. Focus on something else and not your fear.* She scanned the crowd before her gaze returned to the three men. One was a gentleman in a fine buff-colored broadcloth coat and waistcoat, and the other two wore plain waistcoats, breeches, and lightweight shirts with ordinary steenkirks. The taller of the two had a bold expression on his face. She glanced away but continued watching from the corner of her eye.

People milled about like scurrying ants. *Watch the people, not those men.* It was to no avail. Her eyes kept glancing back to the dark-haired colonist. *Why does he stare so?* She would show him. She lifted her head and returned his gaze. He was now deep in discussion with the gentleman in the fine suit, pointing at her. The women were like caged animals on display. Her eyes followed the gentleman when he walked to the table.

She had done this to herself, and there was no one else to blame. Taking a deep breath, she loosened the grip on her satchel and pushed her shoulders back and her chin up. She would have to accept whatever came. The urge to scratch the chafed area where the boned bodice rubbed at her waist plagued her. *Whatever the future holds, please, dear Lord, may it include a bath soon.*

The woman standing next to her poked her gently. "I think that gent is going to pay your bond price. Cheer up, lassie. No doubt it'll be a fine house you find yourself in. At least that big and burly chap left after buying crazy Millie Munro."

Heather shook her head. "Poor Millie was probably sane before this nightmare of a voyage."

The tall stranger seemed very sure of himself when he addressed the better-dressed man. Now, again he studied her, and it was far too long a moment before she glanced away.

"Douglas! Come this way," the captain shouted.

Standing perfectly still, she stared at the captain. Was he addressing her?

"You, Heather Douglas, come here."

Head held high, she slowly walked over to the table where the captain sat conversing with the three men. Was the gentleman purchasing bondservants? It surely would not be the plain-dressed man, the tall, intense one with the piercing brown eyes.

"Miss Douglas, this is Mr. George Lamont, solicitor for Mr. Matthew Stewart. Mr. Stewart has purchased your indenture. You are to go with him now." The captain waved her forward; his authority was the final word.

She braced herself to gaze into the face of her new master. The intensity of his dark eyes and the serious set of his mouth did nothing to quell her anxiety. Still holding the satchel, she stretched her fingers. Her hands had grown clammy.

"You have rights." The captain's bellow drew her attention back to him. "If you are mistreated, you have the courts. Is that not correct, Mr. Lamont?"

"Yes, yes, but she shall not have need of them with Mr. Stewart." Mr. Lamont threw the captain an impatient frown before he turned to face the man who had purchased her.

Mr. Stewart tipped his hat to the solicitor. "I thank you, Mr. Lamont, for your assistance. I trust you will take care of the other matter?"

"Yes, certainly, I shall see to it right away before we return home. Good luck to you."

Her gaze traveled between the men as they continued to speak to each other, their words now inaudible. Why would he want her indenture? Many indentured servants went to the large plantations to work, some to be ladies' maids, seamstresses, or governesses. This man did not appear to be a man of wealth. Perhaps he was a plantation overseer or a tradesman, for his rough hands had the telltale signs of a laborer. She fumbled with her satchel. Perhaps she should ask. Nay, that might not be appropriate. What should the demeanor of a bondservant be? Obedient and loyal was how good servants acted, not unlike a child to a parent. Her confidence was momentarily buoyed. Loyalty was something she understood only too well.

"It is this way, Miss … uh … Heather." The man motioned to a walkway.

The Stewart chap seemed a bit unsure of his place too. He must not have many servants.

He continued speaking to his companion before turning toward her. "I am Matthew Stewart. This is Adam Duncan. My children are at his home. Later, we will be off to the farm." He noticed her traveling bag. "Is that all you have?"

"Aye, sir."

The three walked briskly on their way, the two men in front. She fought to keep up on her still weak and wobbly legs. *If only they would slow down!* Her breathing grew rapid as she made an effort to stay with them. At the same time, she tried to take in everything about her new surroundings. Were those crushed shells on the path? Some of the structures they passed were Georgian style, with intricate bonded brickwork, while other houses were in a Manor style with extended wings. A few more modest homes were clapboard. These were nothing like the many gray buildings, all with smoking chimneys, she had seen in Edinburgh.

She was exhausted and not recently accustomed to this much exercise. Try as she might, it was a struggle to keep up with the men, and it was difficult to hear all that they said. When they finally stopped, she nearly ran into them. "Pardon me."

"This is my home." Mr. Duncan faced her before turning to his friend.

She glanced up at a narrow plain brick residence with a small front porch.

"Matt, let me go in and speak to Maggie." Adam made eye contact with her. "You can rest on the stoop."

She needed no extra coaxing. Grateful for a chance to rest, she dropped onto the brick steps, panting. Mr. Stewart stood on the far side of the steps, mute. Relieved, she gathered her thoughts and caught her breath. The voyage she had considered so interminable was now replaced by quickened events far from her control.

"Are you feeling ill?" Mr. Stewart appeared concerned. "You are quite pale."

"I am a bit unsteady yet on dry land. And a mite weary and hungry from the voyage."

"Of course. I should have realized that."

There was a long silence. The sound of children playing somewhere nearby was a welcome interruption.

Glancing his way, she caught him studying her. No doubt he was noticing her disheveled appearance. How would she divert his attention elsewhere?

"You have an interesting town, Mr. Stewart."

"Yes, it is a well-planned and growing community." He gazed off into the distance, appearing like he wanted to hide his awkwardness.

"Do you live near here?" Her fingers tightened on her satchel.

"No. My farm … our home is west of here."

Silence.

"Maggie will have some food for you inside." His eyes traveled slowly down her slender, ragged, and soiled form. "Maggie is Adam Duncan's wife."

She shivered and took a deep breath. This was her fresh start. She would make it work.

CHAPTER 4

The door opened, and a stout and smiling woman surveyed her. "Well, Matthew Stewart, it would seem you have outdone yourself. Come in. Come in."

Mr. Stewart stood back waiting for her to enter, and Heather waited to follow him. They started toward the door at the same moment, colliding with each other. The Duncans, standing to the side, shook their heads and smiled.

Once they were all inside, and the proper introductions were made, Heather did not miss Mr. Stewart's comment to the mistress of the house: "Maggie, she is quite hungry. Given the sight of her, she may not have eaten in a while. Have you anything you might give her? I need to talk to the children. Are they out back?"

"Aye, to both your questions. Now go. Adam, would you fetch some more cider?"

Heather sat at the table and glanced about. It was a simple yet inviting home. The cleanliness and the aroma of baking appealed to her more than anything else, as her stomach growled. A large hearth dominated one side of the main room. Several pots and a kettle hung from hooks inside the fireplace. The large table sat directly in the middle of the room, and there was a sitting area at the opposite end of the room. The furniture was a combination of a few quality pieces and other rather rough-hewn ones.

Turning her head, she sensed Mrs. Duncan was scrutinizing her. No doubt the woman wondered if she was worth the fifteen pounds Mr. Stewart had paid for her.

"Where do you hail from, Heather? My husband said the ship sailed from Edinburgh."

"Aye, we sailed from the port of Leith, not far from Edinburgh. I am from the Perth area. Is it always so hot here?"

"Nay, this is warm for this early in the season."

"Mrs. Duncan, might I please have some water to wash my hands and face? I would go for it myself if you would direct me. I am so dirty from the ship."

"Aye, I can see. There is a bowl and pitcher of water over there." The woman motioned to a table near her. "Please call me Maggie."

She nodded as she poured the clear water into the bowl. "It has been so long since I have tasted clean water." She quickly scooped a handful and drank, not caring about the noise she made.

When Maggie rested a hand on her back, she glanced up and saw a sympathetic face. Maggie poured water from the pitcher into a cup and handed it to her. She smiled. "Go on. Enjoy our good well water. It is cold and delicious."

"I am grateful." She took it with tears in her eyes. After drinking another cup of water and washing her face and hands with the cloth Maggie handed her, she sat down to a hot meat pie and vegetables. Loud, angry voices came from behind the house, but it was difficult to tell what all the fuss was about. Besides, she wanted no distractions from the delicious meal in front of her. She shoveled the food into her mouth, making only a slight effort at proper manners. The woman seated across the table staring at her probably thought her very rude.

The door opened, and the two men entered. Mr. Stewart was red faced and appeared quite disturbed. He turned to Mr. Duncan. "Thank you, Adam. I needed a few minutes alone with Mary. Mark will be easier."

At this point, five youngsters rushed in, all staring in her direction. Mr. Stewart introduced the children to her.

Mary, the man's daughter, shuffled from foot to foot, a frown planted on her face. "Is this the surprise you brought us home from the shop, Father?"

"I did not forget, Mary." He sounded exasperated and reached into a parcel and pulled out candy and ribbons. "Here, the ribbons are for you and Jean, and there are enough sweets for all of you. Now, go and gather your things. We shall be leaving within the hour."

When the children went back out the door, the farmer placed his hat on his head. His penetrating brown eyes caught hers. "Lamont has arranged it. I shall go for the parson now, and then we must be off. The afternoon is waning, and I have yet to pick up the supplies."

What did he need with a parson? Did one bless indentured servants? A quaint tradition, indeed. Or did he think she needed baptizing? Her cheeks grew hot as indignation rose from somewhere deep inside her. She glanced at Maggie. "I am not a heathen. I have already been baptized."

Maggie's eyebrows were raised, and her husband had a sheepish grin. He got up and made preparations to leave also. "I have tasks to do out back, Maggie." Adam gave his wife a sympathetic smile before turning to Heather. "He should have spoken to you, but I suppose his mind is a bit scrambled right now." He put his hand on his wife's shoulder. "Maggie, be a sweet, and do the deed, will you, my love?"

Maggie's eyes narrowed, and her hands went to her hips as she watched her husband walk out. She turned to Heather and smiled. "I have tea. Would you be carin' for a cup?"

"Oh, aye, ma'am, aye. I have not had any tea for so long."

Taking the kettle from over the fire, the woman muttered, "Lord, give me wisdom in my words, and this one wisdom in hearin' them."

Heather breathed in the almost forgotten aroma of tea.

"Matthew Stewart is a man of honor, so he would not be bringing a lass out to his farm to live alone with him and his wee ones. Well, his dear Elizabeth died a year ago and left him with the two. So there you see—he is needin' the help of a wife."

It took a moment or two for her to understand the meaning

behind the woman's jumbled words. Nay, she had to be mistaken. The food she had eaten threatened to return to her dry throat. She drew quivering hands up to her cheeks. "A wife. I am to be his wife? Oh, merciful God, what have I gotten myself into now?"

Maggie brought the teapot and two cups to the table and searched her face.

"But Mrs. Duncan—Maggie, surely there are many fine, young, unmarried women around here. My indenture is for seven years. After that, I am to be free."

Maggie set a cup of the hot liquid down in front of her. "Is there a husband back in Scotland you are runnin' from, Miss Douglas?"

"Nay." She sat back in the chair, frowning.

"Well, it seems to me that you should be thankful for a husband. You are not young anymore. And, I might add, you can count your blessings that it is him who bought your indenture and not another. Your lot does not have an easy time of it during your indenture. When it is all done, what have you got? Those agents promise you what is rarely delivered." Winded, Maggie sat down to a cup of tea.

"I am to be free when my indenture is over. How can I be free if I am married to him?" She wiped the tears from her eyes.

Maggie's voice was gentle but adamant. "Look, lass, I can see you are frightened, but you need not be. Matthew is a kind man. There are all kinds of freedom, Heather. What makes you think you would not be free with a good husband? It is the best and safest state for a woman."

She gripped the edge of the table and leaned toward Maggie. "I cannot believe that he is bringing clergy here and not even … not even asking me if I would marry."

Maggie reached for her hand. "Matthew should have said something to you first, but in his zeal to bring his wee ones home, he got the cart before the horse. I suspect he is as anxious as you are and just forgot. Heather, you do not have to marry him, but it would be difficult to hold your head up here if you were living in such close quarters and not wedded. Be sensible. Perhaps this is

God's provision for you."

"But I do not know the man, nor he me."

"Let me tell you, lass, you never know a man till you are married, and even then it takes time and trying."

The children returned, interrupting the conversation, and sat at the table, staring at her.

Maggie got up. "Now, I must pack up the children's clothes."

Heather needed air and a chance to think about this disturbing change of plans. She walked to the service yard door.

Maggie followed and handed her an empty water pitcher. "Would you please fill this from the water barrel?" She reached out and tenderly touched her arm. "Think, lass. Even if you go back to be sold again, you do not understand half of what might happen to you. You shall be safe with Matthew. He is a godly and considerate man."

Outside in the yard, overwhelmed by exhaustion, she filled the pitcher and sat on the back step. *What should I do now?* She reviewed all Maggie had said. There was really little choice. She lowered her head and wept, shoulders shaking, tears flowing.

Her mind drifted back to Sara. If only her friend were here to advise her. Sara, with her ready smile, her cheerful manner amidst trouble, and her words of faith, would calm her. What was it she had said? "Seek God's will. Let Him direct your path." Sara truly believed God was able to bring good out of every situation.

"Is this Your will, Lord?" Her words startled a cat sleeping nearby. Voices in the house caught her attention. She took the pitcher inside and handed it back to Maggie. The heaviness in her heart permeated her entire body.

Matthew Stewart had returned with an older man in clerical garb, whom he introduced as the Reverend Mr. Northrup. The man evidently was already acquainted with the Duncans and Matthew Stewart.

After a few minutes of exchanged pleasantries, the clergyman addressed her. "Might we go out to the water barrel, Miss Douglas?

I am a bit thirsty and would like a few words with you."

"Aye, sir." She hesitated, stared at the others, whose eyes were all fixed on her, and followed the clergyman to the door. When she glanced over her shoulder, she noted a compassionate smile on Maggie's face.

Outside, she filled a tankard of water and handed it to the parson.

"Thank you." He paused and motioned for her to join him on a nearby bench. Was he searching for the right words? Reverend Northrop had a sympathetic yet resolute countenance.

"It is a bit unusual, not posting the banns. But under the circumstances, it will do. I have been acquainted with Maggie and Adam Duncan for several years, Matthew Stewart almost as long. They are good Christian folk. Matthew has told me a bit about your situation, and that you, the Duncans, he, and the children would all be best served by his marrying you, and your returning with his family to his farm. Before I ask you what your opinion is on this, I want to tell you that many of the indentured servants have a far more difficult time once they get to the Colonies than they ever did crossing the sea. Many are treated very poorly. I shall not go into all the ills that can befall you. What I would say is that there is many a woman who would count herself fortunate to have Matthew Stewart as her husband. He is a man of strong faith, and I believe he has your best interests as well as his own in mind. If there is some reason that you should not be wedding him, please tell me now."

She got up from the bench and walked back to the barrel. Turning, she faced the parson. He had kind but questioning eyes. *You dare not lie to a man of the cloth. Besides, what options do you really have?*

"Nay, Reverend Northrop, there are no legal reasons I cannot wed Mr. Stewart. I realize my choices are few, and what may become of me if I do not wed him may be far worse. I have learned that love and marriage oftentimes have nothing to do with each other."

The parson nodded. "Many a marriage has begun with little knowledge between the partners, but with work and faith, love can grow."

Reverend Northrop took her hand in his and prayed for her and Matthew.

Tears ran down her cheeks, but when she opened her eyes, a peace came over her that she had not encountered in a long time.

When they returned inside, Mr. Stewart was waiting for her in the kitchen. The parson glanced at him before leaving in the direction of the main room.

The sheepish look on the farmer's face would have been laughable under other circumstances. "My apologies, Miss Douglas … Heather. I should have said something about the marriage … I mean asked." Mr. Stewart's gaze was penetrating. "I hope you will agree, this is best for all of us."

She studied his face and the way he held himself. Dared she trust her instincts? She had erred before. Might this be part of God's plan that Sara had spoken of? "Mr. Stewart, you do not lack for advocates. I will agree to marry you and care for your children."

They returned to the parlor, and Matthew Stewart urged the parson to proceed with the ceremony. The children were off gathering their belongings, leaving only the five adults standing in front of the hearth. The ceremony was quiet and quick, not at all what Heather had dreamed her wedding would be. She gazed down at the same filthy, green dress that was almost becoming a second skin, and wanted to cry. She never imagined this rag would be her wedding gown.

Mr. Stewart shook the clergyman's hand. "Thank you, sir, for coming on such little notice. May we take you home on our way out of town?"

"No, thank you, Matthew. You are in a hurry. Besides, I want to stay and try to talk Maggie out of some of that apple pie I see over there. God's blessings on you both."

Heather sat at the table, silent, numb, and emotionally drained.

In a daze, she watched the activity all around her. While Maggie placed items in a basket, some of the children began carrying parcels to be loaded into the wagon. Mr. Northrop had settled into a Windsor chair in front of the hearth when Adam and Matthew left. There, in a corner, sat Mary, with damp, red, angry eyes. The girl was no more than nine or ten. Heather sympathized with the unhappy child. The recent events seemed out of her control as well.

Maggie placed the basket in front of Heather. "I have put a few items in here you might be needin' and may not have handy when you first get there."

The aroma of the freshly baked bread was intoxicating. She glanced at the round woman standing over her. "Thank you, ma'am. You have been kind and generous."

"We shall see each other again before too long. Adam and I pray you and Matthew will both find peace, Heather."

Heather smiled, took the basket and her satchel, and walked outside to the others. Was it peace she had experienced earlier or resignation? Would she ever have genuine peace?

The Duncans said their good-byes and promised to see them soon. Adam helped Heather up to the seat in front and walked around the side of the wagon to Matthew Stewart. "Good-bye, friend, and remember, give it time."

With a slap to the horse's back, they were on their way home.

CHAPTER 5

Heather grasped the side of her seat as they traveled the bumpy road. A brief glance confirmed that Mr. Stewart was focused on the path ahead. It mattered not. It was more interesting to observe Alexandria's fine homes, buildings, and shops. This was so different from the centuries-old buildings and well-established neighborhoods of home, and she found it fascinating.

They stopped briefly at a merchant's shop to pick up some supplies. The shopkeeper was speechless when Mr. Stewart introduced her to him as his wife. The situation was as amusing as it was embarrassing.

"Sir, you had not mentioned taking a wife."

Mr. Stewart briefly glanced her way, eyes wide, and cleared his throat. "Well, it uh, developed very suddenly this afternoon."

"Oh, I see." The shopkeeper appeared even more perplexed. He smiled and nodded in her direction. "I offer you my best wishes … Mrs. Stewart."

At that, Mr. Stewart nodded awkwardly and cleared his throat. "Thank you." He tipped his hat. "Good day, Mr. Brady."

Before climbing back up on the wagon, Matthew Stewart glanced at her. "You might be more comfortable in back with the children. You can stretch out and rest your back against one of the sacks."

"Aye, I shall." Was it that she had not bathed in months or her weary demeanor that brought on the suggestion? She stepped up into the back and seated herself amidst the parcels. Crowded with the bundles and children, she was spared his silence and their conversation, both quite awkward. At least she was no longer trapped in the hold of the *Providence*, with its misery, the smells, and the agonizing sounds. She tugged at the bodice of her dress and hoped the occasional breeze would relieve her of some of the clamminess and stench. *Perhaps the odor offends him as much as it does me.*

Underway once again, she gazed back at the thriving city. When might they return? It was just her misfortune to be taken off into the wilderness by a farmer. So many uncertainties lay ahead. Now seated in the back of the wagon with the children, she tried to ignore their constant stares. The girl sat with her arms crossed, glaring. Well, it was better than sitting next to a stone-silent Matthew Stewart.

The terrain was hilly, with many more trees and far fewer homes as they traveled west. As the dwellings became less frequent, she suddenly remembered stories she had read when she was a child about the natives in the Colonies. Her muscles tensed. The hair on her arms and neck rose on end. Some of the tales of the savages had been terrifying. Could there even be some nearby, perhaps in the woods? But surely Mr. Stewart would have mentioned if there was any danger. She relaxed again.

The wagon continued along the well-traveled road. In the late afternoon, the sultry stillness broke when Matthew Stewart called to them over his shoulder. "It shall be a few hours before we are home. We should stretch our legs a bit. The horse needs some water so we will stop in a while. Until then, you might get some sleep."

"The wee ones' heads are nodding as though they will drop off any time."

"No surprise—it has been a long day for all of us."

"Aye, that it has." A long and bewildering day—and it was not over yet.

She turned in the wagon to better see the direction they were traveling in and straightened the brim of her bonnet to shade the sunlight from her eyes. Mr. Stewart had purchased it for her when they stopped at the merchant's shop. It was a nice gesture—and it hid her filthy hair, for which she was grateful.

She glanced at the children, thankful that they had dropped off to sleep. While the wee lad had been cheerful and friendly, his sister was quite the opposite. Mary's continual glare intimidated her. Sleeping, the girl appeared bonnier, with soft brown hair framing her face.

Overwhelmed by the day's events, Heather shook her head. Leaving the ship provided momentary relief. But that was cut short by the reality of being sold, wedded, and now heading into the woods. It had been an unbelievable day.

Turning her head, she peered at the back of the man who purchased her and made her his wife. He carried himself well, more refined than his common clothing suggested. His appearance was not unpleasant—a tall chap, reserved, but too lean. There was a rugged but sad look about his face. What was most unsettling was his quiet, intense nature, which made him difficult to read.

Matthew Stewart turned his head to address her. "This nag seems in no hurry to be back in her own pasture."

She shifted and turned toward him, her voice low so as not to disturb the children. "Thank you for the bonnet, Mr. Stewart, and for the chance to rest. I am tired." When he did not respond to her remark, she shrugged and closed her eyes. The rhythmic motion of the wagon and the steady sound of the horse's hooves made her drowsy. Sleep was inescapable. She leaned her head back on one of the sacks, only to be jarred awake a short while later when he brought the wagon to a stop.

Matthew Stewart stepped down from the wagon. His voice, no more than a mumble, sounded irritated. "I cannot believe I was talked into purchasing you, Honey. You are not worth half of what I paid. The day will come when I will have to replace you with something a little younger and livelier."

Her stomach clenched, and she gasped. She was wrong to think the man was refined. If only she had the energy and courage to respond. Instead, she stewed, scratching her side where her filthy chemise irritated her skin.

As he came around to the back of the wagon, he smiled at the sleeping children and then whispered to her, "It will be a couple more hours before we are home. I am going down to the creek over there to get some water for the nag. You may want to get out and have a drink yourself."

"No, thank you." She refused the hand he offered in assistance. His bewildered expression did little to ease her irritation.

Once they were underway again, she rested her head against one of the sacks and stared up at an almost cloudless sky. It was not the first time she had misjudged someone's character. He may not be the gentleman he was touted to be by his friends. Nay, other than her mother and Sara, the people she should have been able to trust had all disappointed her. Her mind traveled back to her mother, gone these many years. She sighed as she closed her eyes and surrendered to sleep.

Faces from the past haunted her dreams. Her mother, a once beautiful woman, now wasted, was dying. Her father, his silver hair shining in the dim light, was seated on the bed, holding his wife's hand in both of his. In all Heather's twelve years, this was the first time she had ever seen her stoic father brought to tears. Their gentle voices moved her.

"Angus, please go. I would speak to Heather now. Bring Ross and Eileen in when we are done, dear." She was so weak.

"Rachel, stay with us." Her father leaned down and kissed his wife. He appeared reluctant to leave the room without that.

Her mother's pleading blue eyes brought a lump to her throat.

"Heather, oh, Heather, I am depending on you so."

"Mama, hush. Do not try to talk. Please save your strength." Fear pressed in on her chest, making it difficult to breathe.

"Heather, you must take care of them now. Your father cannot, and Ross will not. They all need motherin', but mostly wee Eileen. Girl, you are so strong and carin'." She squeezed her hand. "You will not fail me, lass? Promise me."

Her throat tight, she nodded affirmatively.

Her mother's voice was weakening as she motioned her to come nearer. "I am asking much of you, lass … and they shall demand more. But they will need you, even if they show little appreciation. Your blessing may never be from them." After a few shallow breaths, Mama waved her hand. "Bring the others."

With tears in her eyes, Heather leaned over and kissed the face she loved and tiptoed to the door to call her brother and sister.

She would never know if Ross and Eileen's time with their mother was also instructive, for within moments, the woman they all loved breathed her last.

Heather shook. Or was she being shaken? "Aye? … oh … I … I—"

Mr. Stewart's voice brought her back to the present. "You were thrashing and moaning. I feared perhaps you were taking ill. Are you sick?"

Concern was written on his face. She remembered his recent comments. *He thinks he made a bad bargain in purchasing a sickly servant.* "Nay, you need not fret. I am not ill, Mr. Stewart. I suppose I was dreaming. Are we near your farm yet?"

"Yes. We shall be there shortly." The children began stirring and peering around.

It was much darker now. How long had she slept? The children, fully awake now, were being playful yet somewhat shy in her presence. All around them were open fields or woods that stretched off in the distance. Revived after her nap, she took a deep breath, grateful again for being in the open and no longer in the hold of a ship. The woodland sounds and mild temperature appealed to her senses. It reminded her of the lowlands of Scotland, except that there was no noticeable breeze. It was different by far from the howling, chilly winds of the moors. Aye, it would take some time to get used to this new land.

She repositioned herself again to see the trail better and glanced at the man she had just married and at the children who were now under her care. The course of her life had been dramatically altered in just hours, and nothing would ever be the same again.

Matthew Stewart guided the wagon off the main road and onto a narrower path. The full moon lit up the sky, enabling her to still see a bit. There were fields to the right, woods to the left. Up ahead, she made out a small one-story clapboard frame dwelling nestled in among some tall trees. To one side of the cottage, a way off, was another larger structure that resembled a barn.

Mr. Stewart finally pulled the wagon to a stop. "We are home, children. Home at last." He sounded jubilant as he lowered himself from the wagon, went up the stairs, opened the door, and entered the house.

Within minutes, she saw a light through the windows. He came back and lifted Mary and Mark down from the wagon.

"Wait." He handed them each a basket. "You can help carry things inside."

As the children cautiously followed their father into the cottage, she climbed from the wagon and trailed behind them, carrying her satchel and a basket.

He had lit candles and an oil lantern, making the main room appear shadowy. Still standing in the doorway, she studied her new home.

"Come in. Come in, Heather. I shall light another lantern and finish unloading the wagon. The animals can wait a few more minutes."

As her eyes adapted to the light, she noticed plastered walls, glass windows, and a wooden floor. It was warm and inviting, not as primitive as she had feared. There were blue cloth-covered cushions on the furniture around the hearth. Curtains framing the windows were of the same fabric. Close to where she was standing was a handsome oak table, a bench, and two ladder-back chairs. Several pieces of pewter, silver, and pottery lined the shelves of a hutch against the far wall. To her left, the kitchen area of the room had a cabinet and a small worktable under the window. It was surprising how tidy the house was when only a man had been in residence. And it was evident that a woman had at one time made this house a home.

The children explored every inch of the cottage as if they had not been there in a very long time. Mr. Stewart opened shutters and windows to bring in some fresh air. The room was hot and had a stale smell from having been closed up.

"Do you need help, Mr. Stewart?" She wanted to be useful.

"No. Feel free to wander around and become familiar with the house while I go outside to unload the supplies."

As she stared at the door behind the departing man, she mumbled, "Feel free, he says. Fine words, considering the situation."

To the right of the front door was a ladder leading to a loft. Underneath it was a small alcove. The alcove, with its bare bunk, was probably where the wee ones had slept at one time. The children climbed the ladder leading to the loft.

The young boy stepped on the first rung of the ladder.

"Take care you do not fall off."

"Yes, ma'am." Mark grinned while Mary's eyes narrowed.

Directly across from the front door and next to the sitting area was another room. Upon going through the door, she noticed a large frame bed with a quilted blue and white coverlet on it. A handsome wardrobe and an elegant claw-footed, high chest-on-chest of drawers suggested they had once been in a prosperous home. What had the woman who had occupied this cottage been like? Glancing at the bed again, she jumped back, clutched her bag to her chest, and withdrew from the room. When she turned, there was Mr. Stewart. "I … um." A warm tide rose to her face.

"You are welcome to put your things in there, Heather." He motioned to the room. "I see Maggie sent a basket. Would you see if there is something in there for Mary and Mark to eat? I will put their pallet back on their bunk so that they can sleep when they are finished eating. I will be in the barn and see to Honey and the animals, so you need not wait up if you are tired."

Honey? She covered her mouth with her free hand. *Oh, my.* Honey was the name of the horse. Perhaps it had not been her he had referred to earlier, but the horse. She shook her head.

"Sir ..." She twisted the handle of the bag as her face grew warm.

Matthew Stewart turned and waited for her to continue, his eyes searching hers.

"Sir, you have not mentioned where you will be bedding down." She was determined not to lower her eyes, though the urge to run, and even lose the contents of her stomach, weighed on her mind.

He was still studying her when he responded, "I shall get my things and sleep in the loft." When he reached the bedroom door, he turned. "Tonight."

Reprieve. But for how long? He had purchased her indenture to be his housekeeper and care for his children. It was likely that he would want his comfortable bed back after tonight, and she was more than agreeable to take a pallet up to the loft and give him his room and privacy. She had no reason to think he fancied her.

Heather removed her hat and placed it on the oak bench. She scratched through her matted hair. When she picked at her filthy garment, she laughed. He would have to be mad to find her desirable.

Maggie Duncan had packed a bounty in the basket. Along with the freshly baked bread were some pickled vegetables and smoked meat. There were even some sticky sweet rolls with a spicy smell. Her mouth watered.

She studied the two small faces eyeing her as well as the contents of the basket. "Come here and sit down for a bite to eat." Mary and Mark hurried to the table, seeming to be quite at home again. She set out a wooden trencher of food and let them choose what they wanted to eat.

After eating some of the bread and meat, Mark thumped his hand on the table. "I am so thirsty."

"Well, of course you are." She placed two cups of water in front of the children.

Mr. Stewart returned, carrying a small pitcher of milk. "George Whitcomb did the afternoon milking and left some in the springhouse. It is not cold, but fresh." He smiled and seated himself at the table beside his children. His expression communicated pure pleasure as he looked from one child to the other. "It is so good to have you both home again. I cannot begin to tell you how pleased I am."

"Me too, Papa." Mary's smile was disarming before it turned down in a frown as she glanced Heather's way.

Mr. Stewart got up from the table. "Now, it is off to bed with you two as soon as you are finished."

"Yes, Papa."

He went back outside, and Heather helped Mark get into his nightclothes and listened as they said their prayers.

When the children were tucked in their bed, she went back to the table to clean the dishes and finish unloading the basket. *How will I manage to fit into this family? The girl already sees me as an intruder.* She sighed. How would she have responded in Mary's place? Perhaps the same. She would give her time. They were all tired and did not know each other yet.

Exhausted, she walked outside to the water barrel and filled the large pitcher she found in the kitchen. She peered back at the cottage. With the light shining through the windows, the scene was pleasant, and it brought her a modicum of peace. *Tomorrow I will explore and see what this farm is all about.*

Back inside, there were things still to be put away. When everything was in its place, she wet a washrag and began wiping her face, neck, and arms. Seeing how futile the task was, she threw it down. There had to be a washtub somewhere in the cottage. She began searching every corner, but after a fruitless foray, she gave up. Tomorrow she would find it. Relieved, she sat in what seemed to be a comfortable chair across from the hearth.

Tomorrow. I will have a bath tomorrow and no longer be filthy and smelly. With a newfound hope, she would do her part to make this newly constituted family work out. The movement of the beautiful clock sitting on the mantle over the hearth fascinated her, and the pressures of the past weeks subsided as fatigue brought sleep. Whatever lay ahead, right now she was thankful for water to drink, food to eat, a decent place to sleep—and the promise of being clean tomorrow. How was one day filled with so many changes? And the day was not yet over. There was much to ponder—a new country, a new family, so many new experiences. Sighing, she leaned her head back, bit her lip, and closed her eyes. Aye, and a new husband.

Matthew carried a lantern to the barn and lit another one inside the door. He looked around. With the moonlight shining through the door, there was plenty of light to take care of Honey. "ready for a good rubdown, girl?" He picked up the brush and began. "When we left this morning, would you have ever believed we would be bringing the children home?" He smiled when the horse whinnied. Looking into Honey's face, he shook his head. "And then there is the woman … a wife. That was a surprise." His well-established rhythm of brushing and giving a rubdown invited reflection. "I did pray about it. It was impulsive, and I do not act impulsively … usually." *Talking to a horse. I have been alone too long.* He filled the water trough and used the pitchfork to give the horse some hay.

He strode to the barn's doorway and gazed up at the sky. The moon was bright and so were the stars. The storm he anticipated must have dissipated. His glance shifted to the house, lit and inviting, and a home again with the children inside. It would take a while for them to get used to a new mother. Heather was a stranger, not even from the colonies. *I should have asked her if she has ever been on a farm.* She was old enough to know her way around a house. It was not like she was gentry and unfamiliar with housework.

The woman carries herself like a lady, despite being so dirty and poorly clothed, but people of means do not indenture themselves.

He picked up a rag as he left the barn and walked to the well to wash. The cool water felt good against his skin. Her reserve was not surprising. She had not expected to get married. What was it Adam said? Give it time? *I will give it as much time as it takes. This has to work, Lord.*

It was quiet inside the cottage. He looked into the alcove; the children were already asleep. That was to be expected. It had been a day out of the norm, full of unforeseen events. He closed the curtain separating it from the main room and glanced to the door leading to the bedroom. It was open. He took a deep breath. *I did not expect an invitation.* Barely making a sound, he looked into the room and shook his head. It was empty. Where was she? A glance toward the hearth answered that question. He could see the top of her head over the large, cushioned chair. A closer look explained the silence. She was fast asleep. *What now? Do I leave her there? No. Best get her to her bed.*

CHAPTER 6

Heather slept fitfully. She dreamed she was back aboard the *Providence*, being buffeted by the movement of the ship. Sara was slumped over Emily, worry etching her face as she held a damp cloth to her daughter's forehead to bring down the fever. The two women bathed the girls day and night with the little water they had. Despite the constant attention, the girls' fever and delirium persisted, and their health continued to deteriorate.

On the third day, Katie died. Sara's weeping lasted throughout the night, and she could not be consoled. In the hours that followed, Heather and Sara intensified their efforts in nursing Emily, but she succumbed the following evening.

"No! Not my babies! Please, not my babies, too." Sara collapsed onto her pallet with uncontrollable sobs, her eyes red with exhaustion and tears.

"I am so sorry, Sara. I wish there was something I could say to lessen the pain."

"I know."

"Sara, the sailor said that he would place her body with Katie's and that the service for them—and the others—would be tomorrow." She heaved a sigh and moved to Sara's pallet, where she wrapped her arms around the grieving woman. So much loss, where days before there had been hope.

Sara's voice was low and filled with grief, her skin pale. "Thank you for all your help and for your friendship, Heather. What would I have done without you?"

"Please do not thank me, Sara." She held the friend she had come to love and trust.

"First John, and now my girls; I cannot bear it."

They both cried and prayed for strength and comfort.

In her dream, Heather tried to make sense of it all. Sara took ill the same day the girls' bodies were committed to the sea. It was a muddle in her mind.

Heather's stomach clenched as she wiped Sara's feverish skin with a damp cloth. She was so sick. How much longer would she last?

The day's meager ration of putrid food had been passed around hours ago. She had grabbed a few of the dry, weevil-infested biscuits for herself and the ailing woman reclining beside her. Their meals lately were only hardtack with a bit of molasses. The brackish, foul smelling water would be given out later.

She sat on the edge of Sara's pallet and searched for words, hoping to comfort her friend. A low moan drew her attention back to the frail woman. "I am right here, Sara. Please keep fighting."

"God bless you. What would I have done … without you … these past weeks?" Sara gasped or coughed with almost every word.

"Please do not give up, Sara."

Sara's voice was barely audible. "So wanted … to reach John's family."

She leaned forward. "You shall, dear. Please do not despair. We both will be far better off in Virginia than we ever were at home … or on this squalid ship." Hope. Sara needed some words of hope. "We shall have good, fresh food to eat, and clean water, too. We shall bathe, have clean garments, and comfortable places to sleep. And you shall begin a new life with John's family. You have everything to live for." She feared her voice lacked the conviction of her words.

"Do not be sad on my account, Heather. You find happiness there. Put aside your past." Her voice grew weaker, but she seemed intent on saying what was on her heart. "Do not lose faith or hope. God loves … He forgives … He has plans for you." Now it was only whispers.

"Do not exert yourself, Sara." She scanned the dark, damp hold. Despite all Sara had lost, she remained hopeful and even gracious. How did she maintain her faith in a loving, forgiving, and generous God? If only that trust would sustain her and give her the will to live.

Heather searched the gaunt faces of her fellow travelers. Cries filled the air. Strangers begged to be released from their torture. Why did these people go to such great risks, endure this deprivation and humiliation, merely to get to the colonies? What promise did that land hold for people willing to sell themselves into years of servitude? Or were some of these sick and weary people just like her, simply running away?

❧ ❧

As she struggled to wake up, Heather sank deeper into the folds of the quilt. The ship's pallet had never been this soft or still before. Her waking dreams were interrupted by the sound of children laughing in the distance. Slowly opening her eyes, she gazed about. Her heart racing, she sat up with a start.

"Where am I?" It took a couple of moments for her to remember the events of the previous day. By that time, there were three other people staring at her from the doorway of the room.

"Do not fret, children." Mr. Stewart broke the silence. "I fear our noise woke Heather up. Go back to the table and finish your breakfast."

Now fully awake, she realized she was in the large bed amidst the pillows and the blue-and-white quilt. But she had no recollection of going to bed. The last thing she remembered was sitting in front of the hearth. Although her shoes were off, she was still in the filthy green dress.

The man stood smiling in the doorway, seeming to enjoy her confusion. "When I came in last night you were in a deep sleep. So I carried you in here, removed your shoes, and loosened a few stays. I hope you slept well and were comfortable."

She glanced down to her bodice where, in fact, the stays and lacing had been loosened.

"Thank you—I am sorry you had to trouble yourself." Heat rose to her face.

"No trouble at all." He turned to leave. "There are biscuits from Maggie's basket out here if you are hungry. I shall be going out to the fields soon."

As she put on her second shoe, a thought flew into her mind. She must not let him get away without telling her where there was a tub or someplace to wash.

She dashed out the bedroom door to find the man before he left, only to see him sitting at the table with the children. He had removed his shirt and was shaving. Startled by his half dressed appearance, she backed into the doorframe, hitting her head.

"See, Father, I told you she was strange."

"Quiet, Mary. Finish eating and go get dressed." Mr. Stewart's focus was still fixed on her. "Is something wrong?"

"Nay. Nay. I, ah, came for the biscuits." She raised her eyebrows and smoothed her skirt.

His quizzical smirk was as annoying as his familiar and casual demeanor.

Seating herself at the table with the rest of them, she finally settled into a more reserved manner. She picked up a biscuit and focused on the bowl of water in front of him on the table. "Mr. Stewart, what would you have me do today?"

His eyes followed hers to the dish. "Well, to begin with, you can call me Matthew."

"I mean, would you care to list my duties, so I shall not have to continually disturb you?" The biscuit crumbled in her hand. This was not going as she had hoped.

"I see. Well, Mary and Mark need supervision, and the regular household chores, cooking, cleaning, wash—"

Quickly leaning across the table, she nearly tipped the bowl of water into his lap. "Have you a tub for washing? I mean for clothes and bathing?"

They all looked astonished.

He wiped his face, put his shirt on, and settled back in the chair. "Yes. There is a tub on the side of the house." He looked her over. "Large enough to bathe in. Wait, I think I still have—" He got up and went into the bedroom. Within minutes, he was back, carrying a small parcel.

"I had forgotten we had this. This soap is from England. I gave it to my wife on her birthday." A momentary frown passed across the strong face as he opened the wrapper and held the soap to his nose. "She loved sweet-smelling things." He carefully rewrapped the treasure. Very deliberately, he reached across the table and placed it in front of her.

The fragrance of violets permeated the air. Her throat tightened at his tender expression and gesture. Swallowing, she took a moment to respond.

"Thank you. I—I shall use it for the wee ones, also."

The corners of his eyes lifted in a smile. Kindness lingered in his expression. *He is attractive, no denying that.* Her pulse increased.

Mary broke the spell. "We had baths two days ago, Papa. Tell her we do not need to bathe today."

Matthew glanced at his children. "Mary, Mark, Heather is here to take care of you and assist me with chores around the farm. Please try to be helpful. Though we do not know her well yet, she seems to be, well, a reasonable sort. Mary, do you understand what I am saying?"

"Yes, Papa. But, she is not my real mama, and she never will be." Visibly upset, Mary ran from the table to the small alcove.

A worried frown formed as he got up and followed his distraught daughter, leaving Mark shaking his head.

The boy resumed eating, and Heather returned to the bedroom and sat on the edge of the bed. She had no intention of taking the place of the girl's mother. Opening her satchel, she set about emptying it onto the bed. *They can have all the time they need to get used to me.*

The few items were but a meager reminder of what her previous life had been. The Douglas men had certainly made an adequate living. In her twenty-eight years, she had acquired many nice things, all left behind by her sudden departure. Studying her few remaining possessions, she shook her head. How little she missed what she had abandoned. What she did regret were the illusions, now shattered, and the desires, never to be fulfilled.

She shook out the blue muslin and calico dress. Ah, the wrinkles in it and the petticoat would be remedied simply enough by letting it hang out in the sultry weather. The shift would do as nightclothes. She would wash all of these garments later, as they were barely cleaner than what she wore. Thankfully, she had brought another pair of shoes and stockings. She had been foolish not to bring more.

She clutched a soft blue and green tartan shawl to her. No longer a Douglas; now a Stewart. Nay, she would always be a Douglas and wear the tartan. She was a Stewart in name only, certainly not in her heart. After placing her worn Bible, hair comb, and cap in one of the dresser drawers, she went back to the main room to see about locating the tub.

Matthew Stewart was near the door, ready to leave. "I will be in the south field." He pointed in the direction of the door. "The henhouse backs up to the barn. You might get the eggs and feed the chickens. Kindly has been milked, so you need not bother about that."

His directions made little sense.

A slow smile crept over his face. "Kindly is our milk cow. I will be back mid-afternoon for dinner. Oh, and about Mary." His embarrassment was evident. "I told her she is to show you the same respect she would any adult. If she is rude again, I want you to tell me. I think she is out of sorts with all the changes."

"I understand, Mr. Stewart. I will do my best to calm her fears."

He studied her for a moment, nodded his head, and walked out the door.

He was an unnerving individual, but there was no use fretting about it. He was gone. Now, to find the tub and finally bathe. But first, she would see that the youngsters were occupied.

They were sitting in the alcove on their pallet, playing a game.

"I will be outside for a bit, children. I need to do some wash." With a clear conscience, she went to the side of the cottage and searched under the porch. Not there. She soon found it on the other side of the well. She pulled the large, pitch-coated wooden tub to the stairs. How was she to get it up the steps and into the house? It was a warm day, so she decided to bathe outside. To fill the tub faster, she dragged it to where the water barrel was located, near the well.

With cool water in the tub, she added some steaming water from the hearth. Everything she needed was assembled nearby. She gazed in each direction, assuring herself no one was around. Peeling her clothes off, she lowered herself into the tub, moaning in utter delight. Aye, an answer to prayer. She smiled and completely submersed herself. With the soap Matthew had given her, she began lathering and scrubbing from head to foot with a vengeance. No lingering when the job was done. She did not want to be caught by the children in her immodest state.

Once dry, she put on the blue muslin dress, feeling more invigorated than she had in weeks. As she hummed an old Scottish melody and began lacing up her shoes, she glanced up to see Mary watching.

"You surprised me. I was unaware you were there." She pointed to a basket. "Please bring over that pile of soiled clothes. I will wash them with my own."

"You look different." Mary gathered the items to be washed.

"I imagine I do." She laughed and wrapped a cloth around her long, wet hair. "When I finish the wash, would you like to help me with the chickens?"

"No, I think not." Mary pointed down the hill. "There is a pond over there that I have not been to in a long time. It used to have ducks on it."

Heather shaded her eyes from the morning sun and glanced in the direction the child indicated. It was inviting and beautiful, particularly the way the large trees draped their long thin stems of lacy leaves down to the water. Delicate trees with creamy white blossoms grew amidst tall oaks and pines. Three deer stood sheltered at the edge of the woods. She smiled at Mary. It might be an opportunity to become better acquainted with the child.

"Mary, the three of us can go down to the pond after the chickens are taken care of. We can take some bread along in case we do find some ducks."

"No. I want to go down there now." Mary stamped her foot on the ground, staring straight at her. "I shall take Mark and watch him. You do not need to come."

This was not going well. "I, too, would like to see the pond, and I will be happy to go with both of you when I am finished with the chores. It would be dangerous for the two of you to go alone, so please wait."

The angry child turned and stomped back to the cottage.

Heather soaked the soiled garments, unconvinced she had won the battle. Discouraged, she sat on a stump and combed out her hair so it would dry in the sun while she finished the wash. Befriending the child would take time. Both of them would need to make adjustments.

Once the laundry was washed, she draped everything over the nearby boxwood hedge. The chickens needed addressing. "What do I know about live chickens?" She marched toward the henhouse. "Nothing. All I have ever done is cook them. Well, how difficult can gathering eggs be?" Inside the small dwelling, she looked around at all the cubicles. *Most animals sense when you are tentative, so act like you know what you are doing.* She reached under a hen and felt with her fingertips until she located the egg but jumped when the chicken started clucking. Several other hens began to voice their concerns. Ten minutes later, when she left the henhouse, she spotted Mary not ten feet away. "Look." She grinned and held out the basket to show her bounty.

Mary's lips were tightly closed. She shook her head. "You made the chickens nervous. They can tell when you are scared of them." The child's self-satisfied remark and sneer tried her patience.

"Let me put the eggs inside, and we can go to the pond."

❦

The pond was indeed lovely, and the children's laughter cheered her. As soon as they started scattering pieces of bread, ducks and geese came from the water and under low-lying shrubs along the bank, where they had either been sleeping or nesting.

"I will sit up here on the bank while you feed them." She sat below a large tree. "I have had enough pecking and feathers for one day."

When they headed back to the cottage, she gathered the dry laundry from where it was draped on the boxwood and put it into a basket. No matter where one lived, one would never be free from chores.

Later, as Heather folded the clean clothes by the hearth, she thought back ten years to when she was but a girl of eighteen. That day, her resentment had gotten the better of her. She had spent the morning cleaning the house. It was Eileen's chore, but she was nowhere to be found. Eileen was never around when there were chores to do. When her father chastised Heather for not helping in the shop, she had barked at him and left the house, slamming the door.

She ran to a slope overlooking the Firth of Tay. This spot, high on a bank that overlooked the estuary, was her haven when the pressure became unbearable. Her mother had understood her children's differing natures, yet she had extracted from Heather a promise and laid on her duties that sometimes seemed like a prison sentence.

She was responsible for overseeing the house, caring for her father, and maintaining some control over Eileen. Now she was also being called on to help in the shop. There was no end to her obligations. It was not fair. Ross was free. He had taken off to sea that month. He had walked away from the shop and the family, with Father's blessing. What would she do if she were free? As she gazed at the steady waves, her irritation subsided. As always, when the anger departed, the guilt intensified. She should be back at the shop, figuring the inventory, or upstairs, taking care of the house or preparing dinner.

There were fences to mend after losing her temper with Father. Remorse filled her as she rolled over onto her back and gazed at the cloudy sky. She must go home to make amends with Father and speak with Eileen about being more reliable. Eileen was twelve now and should very well take over some of the duties.

She must not put off going home and preparing the mutton and barley stew any longer. Those folks were always hungry and ready to eat.

Her reminiscences were interrupted by a masculine voice. "Is dinner ready?"

Heather looked up. The sight of Matthew Stewart brought her back to the present.

She stood and faced him. "Nay, sir. I was folding clothes and I, ah … was daydreaming. I will … the dinner will be on the table in a quarter hour." Was the flush on her face noticeable?

He stood there for a moment, eyeing her from head to foot. "Fine. The children are out front. We will wash and be back in a few minutes." A smile slowly formed on his face before he walked out the door.

Why did his gaze make her heart race?

CHAPTER 7

Heather quickly set about putting something together for dinner. She sliced some ham and bread while she listened to the children questioning their father about friends they had not seen in awhile. Once seated, Mr. Stewart prayed before they started eating. She glanced up from her plate and noticed the man studying her like a hawk eyeing a chick. Was it because she had forgotten to prepare dinner? The children, immersed in their own conversation, did not appear to have noticed. When the meal was over, she rose and cleared the dishes. Another brief glance his way caught his eye, and his gaze held hers too long. The heat rose from her neck to her face before she turned away.

"I see you found the tub."

"Aye, sir, clean at last. Thank you again for the soap."

Mark giggled. "You smell better, Heather."

The youngster's coy remark made her laugh. "I daresay, lad."

She glanced at Mr. Stewart. His lips were pressed tight together as if trying to stifle a laugh.

When Mr. Stewart returned to the field, she suggested to the children that they go for a walk. Mark was delighted to be out in the warm sunshine. Mary, however, seemed hesitant.

"Would you show me around, Mary? I have never lived on a farm before."

Mary glared as she picked up her bonnet and led them out the door.

The first place they surveyed was the barn. But, as it was a warm day, the foul smell and flies drove them out quite quickly. Continuing along the path from the cottage, Heather spotted their father working in the field to their right. He had the field more than half plowed, and as he guided the plow behind Honey, shirtless, she noticed he was a fine-looking man. He was a bit thin, but she would work on that. As Mary led them on, there was a small gully to their left that ran along the path, a natural barrier to the field and wooded area beyond. Cattle grazed on the grassy slope. Pines towered over trees now coming into leaf or blossom. It was not unpleasant here in the Virginia countryside.

Her thoughts turned to Mary. How might she engage the girl? "Mary, what sorts of things do you like to do?"

Silence. The girl seemed intent on the trail that stretched before them.

"I will need your help, Mary. I am unfamiliar with country living. In Scotland, I lived in town."

Mark pulled at her skirt. "Do you have any children?"

Startled by Mark's question, she sat on a nearby rock and seated Mark next to her. "Nay. Though I did help to raise a child."

A glance at Mary confirmed the girl's interest was piqued. Heather would open the door to her past, but only a bit.

"I was a wee lass when my mother died, and I had a sister who was about your age, Mary." She had caught the girl's attention, so she continued her story. "Her name was Eileen, and she was a bonny lass like you."

The girl sat on another rock and furrowed her brows.

"I understand how difficult it is to lose the mother you love."

The children seemed to digest what she was saying.

Mary's eyes widened. "Did your father marry again?"

"Nay. He did not marry again, but I believe I would have been pleased if he had taken a wife. I would have had someone to share the work with, and he would not have been so lonely."

"What happened to Eileen?" Mary's inquiry was encouraging.

"She married when she was still quite young."

Mary moved to a closer rock. "Why did you not marry?"

"My father took ill, so I remained at home to care for him." She cleared her throat. *No need to address this particular matter with the children.* "Now, I think it is time we returned to the house. I still have chores to do."

These children had suffered tragedy much as she had experienced. Perhaps God did have a purpose in her being here—to help them heal. She needed to be patient, more so than she had been with Eileen.

The children waved to their father and raced back toward the cottage. Following at a distance, she reveled again in all the beauty around her. There was an appealingly fresh smell to the air despite the warmth—such an improvement from the sweltering, stale, odiferous confines of the ship. At least she had survived that miserable experience.

Lord, may I never forget what it was like to do without, to live in fear. May I appreciate every day of relative peace You give me. She bent over to pick a weed with a blossom not unlike the thistles of her native land. *Why must people experience the devastation and terror life holds before they genuinely appreciate its blessings?*

The remainder of the afternoon flew by quickly. The children played quietly in front of the cottage. She found a sewing basket, and she brought the family's mending, as well as her own, to the porch so she might watch the young ones. Her eyes on occasion wandered to where the children's father was planting—so much work for one man to do alone. How lonely it must have been for him out here all those months without his family. No wonder he was desperate enough to buy a wife so he could regain his children.

"Mary." She got up. "It is time to go in and start supper. Would you help me, please?"

The little girl stared at her awhile as if assessing her options. With some hesitation, she got up and followed her inside.

Heather prepared a pastry filled with meat, onions, and the pickled vegetables Maggie had sent. What was left of Maggie's bread had been eaten earlier. She would make more after the dishes were cleared away.

Working in a kitchen again satisfied her after being gone from one so long. With patience and effort, she might get used to this new life. Perhaps, in time, she would reconcile herself to the loss of her family, and even find the peace she sought. But she would have to be careful to not allow her daydreams to interfere with her work again.

❧ ❦

After supper, Heather settled into a chair in front of the hearth. The day's chores were behind her, and Mary and Mark were finally in bed. Refreshing breezes changed the warm day to a cool but pleasant evening. At last, she would have a chance to relax and reflect on the first full day in her new home.

Matthew Stewart opened the door and came inside. She stiffened and moved her feet off the footstool to the floor. Perhaps he would go out again. When he reached the hearth, he took his pipe and tobacco down from the mantle. Her hopes were dashed. It was evident he was there to stay.

The flickering light from the lanterns highlighted the profile of his face, now focused on a painting over the mantle. "Strange, to share this home again after so long." His arm leaned against the mantle. He stood silently.

She wanted to escape to the solitude the bedroom promised, but he might think her rude since he had only now returned to the cottage. *Nay, I had best stay for a short time, perhaps even offer him back his room and suggest that I would prefer the loft. Then again, this might not be the best time to address that subject.*

The only sound was of an owl nearby.

Still, she felt she should say something to fill the void. But what? More silence.

She shifted her gaze between him and other objects in the room. "I hope you do not mind my taking the wee ones down to the pond today. They wanted to go. I insisted that I be with them, although I believe Mary would have preferred that I not go along."

His focus drifted from the painting to her now, yet his mind seemed elsewhere.

She shifted in the chair. "I am sorry I was late having your meal ready."

Silence.

Perhaps he had not heard her. She leaned forward. "Mr. Stewart?"

He sat down in the chair next to hers, his expression confusing. He briefly rubbed his hands together before leaning back. "You were wise to go down to the pond with them. Not long after the children's mother died, Mark fell in that pond, and we nearly lost him, too." His voice cracked with emotion. "The accident made me realize I dare not try to care for the children while managing the farm. They were too young and needed constant watching. Maggie and Adam very generously offered to help with them. As difficult as it was to give them up for a time, I feared what would happen if they stayed here without someone to see to their needs."

His candor touched her. "It must have been so painful to part with your wee ones, and so soon after losing your wife."

"Maggie and Adam offered them more than I was able to." His earlier reserve returned and his vulnerability, exposed like a fleeting breeze, was once again hidden. "I am thankful to have them home. Having you here makes that possible." His eyes fixed on hers.

She sat very still, watching his eyes take in all of her. The fire's low light added to the intimacy of the room and keeping her mind on the conversation took considerable effort. Heat rose to her face. Could she excuse herself without his taking offense? "Anyone can see you care deeply for your children, Mr. Stewart. I am sure you are meant to be together." She arose. "And, now, I will be—"

"Heather, I have been reluctant to question you about your background, but I find it odd a woman of your apparent breeding chose to indenture herself." His scrutiny arrested her and demanded a response.

She kept silent.

"I would have guessed you to be a tradesman's or merchant's wife, possibly a landholder's. But never a bondservant."

She turned, not wanting to gaze into those dark, probing eyes. This conversation needed to end now.

"Why did you choose to leave your homeland?"

She turned her head and forced her eyes to meet his. "I desired to come to the Colonies, Mr. Stewart, so I indentured. I am a bondservant—nothing more. And now, may I be excused? I am still very tired." Not waiting for his reply, she retreated to the safety of the bedroom and closed the door.

Once inside, she began to shake. She paced back and forth in the room. The door to the past was closed, and she certainly did not want him or anyone else knocking on it.

A few minutes later, she sat on the edge of the bed, unfastening her hair. Would she ever be at peace living in this house with him, or less ill at ease in his presence? Her fingers unwound her hair with practiced precision. Hopefully, once routines were established and they were more comfortable around each other, perhaps the silences would seem less awkward, and the tension would dissipate. *The man has spent too much time alone in this place.*

She combed her hair with ferocity. *My past is none of his business.* The fragrance of the violet soap still lingered. His expression when he gave her the soap came to mind, and she softened. He was not really a bad sort. He obviously loved his children, and he had been generous to her. Was it his voiced observations of her that had made her bristle? She would need to be more on her guard and keep her distance.

She heard him in the other room as she removed her dress and shoes. She could not make out what he was doing from the muffled sounds. Soon, he would go out to see to the animals before returning for the night. When the door closed, she padded to the window and pulled back the curtain a couple of inches. Between the moonlight and the lantern he carried, she could observe his comings and goings. Matthew Stewart was a handsome chap. And he certainly seemed a likable one, no denying that. When he looked at her, she knew he genuinely wanted to know what was on her mind and in her heart. He was serious, yet he could also see the humor in situations. *Oh, Heather. Do not be so quick to trust him. People are not always what they seem.*

She saw him leave the barn and head toward the house, so she darted for the bed. *Have I sunk to spying on the man?* Her job was caring for his children, not snooping on his whereabouts and activities. So why did he continually creep into her mind?

As she drifted off to sleep, her thoughts were no longer on Matthew Stewart. It was questions about his wife that raced through her mind and piqued her interest. What had Elizabeth been like? Did Mary resemble her in any way? Would Elizabeth approve of her being here, caring for her family and sleeping in her bed?

CHAPTER 8

Heather walked through the garden, pulling weeds, pruning, and assessing what work was still required to make the overgrown kitchen garden useful again. For now, it needed water. She surveyed the area, but the children were not in view.

"Mary, Mark, where are you? I need your help to water the garden." Where had they gone? She walked around to the front of the cottage, peering in every direction. How was she to watch over them and accomplish the many tasks demanded on a farm? She spotted the boy coming around the side of the barn. "There you are. Where is your sister?"

"In the apple tree."

"What is she doing in the apple tree?"

"Trying to hide from me."

She smiled as she took his hand and retraced his steps to the far side of the barn.

"Mary, how did you get up there, and how are you going to get down without tearing your petticoat or gown?"

"I stood on that crate and used the branch to pull myself up. I think I have already stained my skirt." She grinned sheepishly.

"When you and Mark wander off on some new adventure, I do not know where you are or what you are doing. That makes it very difficult for me to complete my tasks because I must search for you. I need the two of you to help me water the garden."

The girl hesitated and looked as if she was weighing her choices. "Would you help me down, please?"

Heather gingerly climbed onto the crate and extended her arms to aid in Mary's descent, which ended with them both falling to the ground. They brushed the soil off their skirts and burst into laughter.

"Mary, young ladies should not be climbing trees. Now, help me get the buckets and water the garden."

After pouring water onto some reseeded herbs and new plantings, Mary caught her eye. "I forgot how much of the day Papa spent caring for the animals and working in the fields."

"Spring is a busy time of year for farmers. He does return to the cottage for dinner, Mary, even though it often means working later into the evening."

❦

Over the next several days, the operations of the farm and household began to take on a normal pattern. The attitude and behavior of its members, however, were still anything but warm and harmonious. Matthew observed Mary's icy stares and condescending manner toward Heather more than once. Mark's genial nature was in complete contrast. And there was Heather herself. Why did the woman bristle so when he questioned her about her background? Was she hiding something?

One early morning, nearly a week into their coexistence, they sat around the table, sharing the breakfast Heather had prepared. Matthew studied Heather's and Mary's pensive expressions. "Tomorrow is the Sabbath, and we will be going to service at the Turners' home."

All eyes turned to him, but Mary was the first to respond. "The church has not been rebuilt yet?"

"No." Matthew glanced at Heather, who seemed to be waiting for an explanation. "Our church burned down in February, so we have been meeting at two different neighbors' homes every other week since then. Folks decided to wait until after the harvest to rebuild."

Mary tugged on her father's sleeve. "Will we stay for dinner afterward?"

"We usually do." He noticed a frown on Heather's face. "Neighbors each bring something to share, whether it is bread, soup, stew, or a dessert. Perhaps we could take something simple."

Heather took a deep breath. "I could make some bread or soup for you to take. Am I to go with you?"

"Certainly. It will be a good opportunity for you to meet some neighbors." Why was she so resistant? He glanced out the window to the early morning light. "Well, I need to get a start on the day. I usually do not hire on this early, but I am getting behind. If I cut out the midday meal, I would have another good hour of daylight."

Mary, amber eyes flashing, got up from the table with a start. "No, Papa. We do not see you very much now. We are left here all day with *her*. I miss the Duncans. We had other children to play with there."

He turned to his daughter. "Now, Mary, even if it is only for a short time each day, you see more of me now than you have in almost a year. There is a great deal of work to be done around here, especially at this time of year. It is natural that you miss Maggie and the children. But, Mary, I will not have you showing so little respect for Heather. Honestly, you have no reason to dislike her."

"Well, she is very strange, and she is not at all like Maggie. She makes me do too many chores. She is forever washing and wanting everything clean."

Matthew studied his daughter and stifled a grin, but said nothing.

"Papa, she is too tall and skinny. And have you noticed all the freckles on her face? Yesterday she was down by the pond, crying. We do not need a servant, Papa. Send her back, or make her work in the fields so you can be here with us." Mary pointed to her. "She is not like Maggie or Mama." Out of breath, she appeared to be finished with her evaluation.

He shook his head. Mary's remarks were hurtful. "Do not be so critical of Heather. Of course, she is different from Maggie or your mother. She comes from Scotland and life here is new to her."

Heather's face revealed her embarrassment, and Mark's eyes were wide as saucers.

Be patient, man. "And since when have you not liked freckles? I never knew you to find Donald Duncan's thin frame or freckles offensive. As to helping with the chores, Mary, a farm involves much more attention and work than living in the city, and you are old enough to do your share around here."

Mary crossed her arms, her lips pressed together.

"Come here, child." He took his daughter's hands in his as he drew her closer. "Finding fault with Heather's desire for cleanliness is silly. I, for one, have appreciated having clean clothes to wear. Perhaps it was your treatment of her that brought her to tears."

Heather averted her eyes.

"And about this servant business, I never told you she was a servant. Where did you hear that?"

"Donald Duncan said that you bought her off the dock and that she is our bondservant." Mary pulled her hands from her father's and placed them on her hips.

"Mary, she ... Heather is my wife." Matthew looked at his daughter intently. "I needed someone to take care of you and Mark and to help with the house. That is why she is here. We must learn to live peacefully together. Did you ever stop to think that she might be lonely also? You have Mark, but Heather has no family here."

"Yes, she does. She has you."

Matthew glanced at Heather to gauge how she had taken the child's careless remarks. The woman looked embarrassed. Her eyes were downcast as she got up and began clearing the table. How mistaken Mary was if she believed that they shared anything more than this small cottage. "We need to bring some sense of peace back to this situation. Mary, do you remember the Whitcomb family, over the hill?"

"The Whitcombs? Tobias, Martha, Timothy, and Teddy?"

"Yes. We may see them tomorrow, although they often forgo services. I know you miss Maggie, but she does not need us around right now, being so close to having the babe. You have friends here."

Mary's lips were pursed, but her hands were no longer on her hips. "Mark, do you want to go outside? May we, Papa?"

"Yes, but do not wander off."

"Yes, Papa."

Mark jumped up from his seat and joined his sister. The children nodded to him before going through the doorway.

He turned to Heather, who was holding a rag in one hand and grasping the back of one of the chairs with the other. "I am sorry about Mary's rude behavior. I think she needs some time to get used to … the changes."

"I understand."

How long would it take for Mary to accept Heather? At least the woman did not respond in anger. She must have had some experience with youngsters. He got up from the table and prepared to go out again.

"Mr. Stewart."

He stopped, turned toward her, and leaned against the hutch. "Yes?"

"You should not have to be going without a meal. I can bundle up some food and bring the wee ones out to wherever you are working. That way you would not have to come all the way back here, and you and the children would still have some time with each other."

He studied her face while she spoke. She was considerate, but with her fair coloring, more hours of sun every day meant more freckles, much to Mary's woe.

"Is something wrong?"

"No. Of course not." He laughed.

"Then why do you keep staring at me?"

"Well, for one thing, I was imagining how many more freckles you would have if you worked in the fields, as Mary suggested. About the offer to bring a meal out to me, are you sure it is not too much trouble?"

"Nay, it is no trouble, and the fresh air and walk will do us all good." She began twisting the rag in her hand. "There is something else, Mr. Stewart."

"What is it?" Something had the woman on edge. She was an enigma, but she seemed to have a kind nature.

"Well … well …"

"Well, what, Heather?"

"I wondered if you would like me to be reading to the children. Yesterday, when I was reading my Bible, Mary asked if I might read it to her. I can teach her to read and write if you wish."

"I would like that, but I wanted you to get used to all of us—and this place—first. I appreciate your willingness to work with the children. Perhaps that might encourage a more cooperative attitude in Mary."

"I can read to them from the Bible, or something else if you prefer."

"You received an education in Scotland?"

"Aye, sir. The Scots place great value on such things."

"Remind me to pick up a primer the next time we go into Alexandria. I believe Mary may have left hers at the Duncan home, and with their brood, they are welcome to keep it." He put his hat back on his head and turned to go outside.

"Aye, there was one other thing."

He stopped at the door and faced her. She did not strike him as a timid person, so why was she so apprehensive? "Yes, Heather?" He watched her wring her hands together.

"I, well, perhaps you would want your room back."

It took all his effort not to grin. *Do not read too much into this. She is all business.* "What did you have in mind?"

"I would be quite satisfied with the pallet in the loft, sir."

"I think we will keep the sleeping arrangements the way they are. For now."

CHAPTER 9

After completing chores on Sunday morning, they set out in the wagon for the Turner farm a few miles away. Riding beside Matthew, Heather held a basket with the two round loaves of bread she had made. A knot formed in her stomach. Would the neighbors welcome her? Or would they question Matthew Stewart's marriage to an indentured servant?

Mary and Mark chattered in back as they bounced on the rutted road. The silence in front of the wagon only put her more on edge. Was this as awkward for him as it was for her?

He glanced her way. "They are good people, Heather. You need not worry about how you will be received."

Their eyes met. How had he read her thoughts? Was she that transparent? "We shall see."

When they arrived, Matthew introduced her to Aaron and Amelia Turner, a clergyman, and two other couples, as well as ten children of varying ages.

Amelia Turner took the basket. "I am delighted to meet you, Heather. We had no idea Matthew had remarried." The woman had a warm smile and seemed sincere.

"Thank you." Heather glanced about the room. Would more people arrive soon?

"Those are our children over there." Amelia pointed to two boys around Mary's age and two small girls who were obviously twins. "Cole and Logan are eleven and ten, and Emily and Ellen are three."

"You have a fine family, and your children are not far in age from Mary and Mark." Heather smiled, watching the twins pursue

Mark as he attempted to avoid them.

Amelia motioned for her to be seated. "It is wonderful for Matthew to have his family home again."

Aaron Turner spoke up. "We may as well get started. Pastor Jones will lead us today."

Matthew and the children sat with Heather as the service proceeded. It was less formal than what she was used to at home, but it was not unpleasant.

Afterward, she joined the women serving the dinner in the kitchen.

Betsy Edwards, the oldest woman, approached her. "A pity not many folks came today. It would have been nice for you to meet more of the neighbors. Sometimes we have as many as ten adults and two dozen children."

Heather silently sliced the bread and listened to the conversation, answering the women's questions when necessary.

Patience Morgan ladled the stew into bowls. "You do not sound like you are a native Virginian, Heather."

"Nay. I have recently come from Scotland." *No more questions, please.*

Patience grinned. "It must have been Matthew's Alexandria friends, the Duncans, who brought the two of you together. I think their families came over from Scotland a generation past."

"Aye, they were our witnesses when we married." Heather shot a nervous glance at Matthew, but he was in the midst of a conversation with Aaron Turner.

Amelia handed her a trencher for the bread. "I thought that might be the case. I imagine you have met your closest neighbors, the Whitcombs."

"Nay, not yet." Heather did not miss the knowing look the ladies gave one another.

The next hour passed quickly as the families ate and visited. When they parted, well wishes were given with the promise of seeing each other again soon.

As they rode home, Heather sighed. It had been easier than she had anticipated.

"I told you it would go well." Matthew's countenance confirmed her thoughts.

"So you did."

※ ※

Matthew joined Heather and the children for breakfast the next morning. "Children, I have neglected your religious education and your reading and writing too long. I have no time right now to devote to it, so I have asked Heather to spend some time each day reading with you." He looked around. There was no resistance—good. "This will be an excellent opportunity for you to gain the skills and knowledge you need." He got up from the table, gave Mary a squeeze on her shoulder, and tousled Mark's hair.

"Heather, if you have no other plans, I think we might have chicken for dinner. That old lame one will be getting tough if we do not eat her soon. The axe is hanging on the wall inside the barn door."

"Chicken sounds good." Mark's eyes lit up.

Heather glanced up from cleaning the iron skillet. "The axe? Kill the fowl? I, ah, I never—"

"You have never killed a chicken?" Clearly, this was all new to her. "Would you prefer that I kill it this time?"

"Oh, would you, Mr. Stewart? I will be happy to cook it and bring it out to you this afternoon for dinner."

He grinned and headed to the barn for the axe. The woman must never have lived on a farm before.

Heather was still putting dishes away when he returned with the dead chicken, minus its head. "Here." He laid it in the basin.

"But … the feathers." Heather peered down at the bird, and then searched his face.

"That is the way they come, Heather, with feathers. You can

dip it in a bucket of very hot water to make plucking easier." He pulled a few feathers to demonstrate how best to accomplish the task. "It is best to pluck it and gut it outside—less messy that way."

"Gut it?"

"Cut the rest of the neck off. Open it up here." He pointed to various areas of the fowl's body. "Then you need to remove all the innards. I bet you are a quick learner. Think of it as part of *your* education—an opportunity for you to gain the skills and knowledge you need."

❧

Heather sat on the porch, concentrating on plucking the chicken, which entertained the children. By the time the job was done, she was covered with the plumes. She stepped off the porch and walked a distance from the cottage. There, she shook her entire body and flapped her petticoat, hoping to be free of the feathers clinging to her skin and garment. In her wild dance, she did not hear the horse and rider come from around the side of the barn. When she glanced at the children, Mary and Mark stared beyond her. She turned to find the object of their attention and cringed. A rider surveyed her while fighting back laughter.

"George Whitcomb. I have the farm over there beyond the trees." He twisted his torso in the saddle and pointed past the barn. "I came over for Matthew. Is he around?" He got down from his mount and extended his hand.

"I am Heather." She wiped her hand on her petticoat before extending it. "I believe you will find Mr. Stewart in the south field."

The portly man spotted the children and grinned. "Mary, how fine it is to see you back home. You too, Mark."

"Thank you, Mr. Whitcomb." Mary grinned and curtsied.

"A pleasure meeting you, Heather. I will go find Matthew." He lifted his cap, remounted his horse, and was off.

She turned and retrieved the chicken. "Come on. We had

best get you gutted and cooked." She stalked back to the cottage porch and took a breath before picking up the knife to practice the next new skill. "Wretched critter." The churning in her stomach removed any appetite for chicken. All she wanted to do was wash up to her elbows.

Once the chicken was roasting on the spit, they began reading. She had only read the first few verses of Proverbs when Mary looked up at her, bewildered. "I do not understand a lot of it. What does it mean?"

"Aye, it can be difficult to comprehend the meaning, even for a grown person. But like so many things, the more you read or hear it and think about it, the more you will understand what is meant. These proverbs speak to us of the importance of seeking wisdom from God. They instruct us much the way a father or teacher would, telling us that we have choices. We can choose to follow God's ways or our own ways. Listen to the seventh verse: *The fear of the Lord is the beginning of knowledge, but fools despise wisdom and instruction.*"

A twinge rose in her throat. How was she to instruct the children on the Scriptures and the wisdom of being under authority when she had resented being under her own father's authority? She closed the Bible. "It may be difficult to comprehend now, but I am sure that as we read more, we will gain greater understanding."

Mark grinned from ear to ear. "I like your reading, Heather."

"Your papa said that he would get a primer in town so that we can read from that also. Now, Mary, we need to tend to the biscuits, and I must check that chicken."

"Yes, ma'am." While Mary's voice sounded hesitant, she did follow Heather to the kitchen, where the two of them prepared the meal.

"Your father has done a good job of keeping this place tidy, Mary, but I think it needs a thorough cleaning. It needs dusting and sweeping out, and the rugs need a beating. The windows also should be washed. Will you help me?"

"I suppose I might do the dusting." Mary bit her lip.

"Thank you. That would be a big help." *Why the melancholy look on the girl's face?* "What is it, Mary? You seem troubled."

"Why did God let my mama die?"

Heather took a breath and wiped her hands on a towel nearby. How might she communicate what the child needed to hear? It was important not to minimize the girl's heartfelt concern.

"Everyone kept saying it was God's will." Mary's voice grew increasingly agitated. "Except Papa. I heard Papa tell Maggie it was his fault that she and the baby died, but I do not believe that is true. Papa loved Mama. Why did Papa say that, and why would God let her die?" The child's voice was filled with emotion as she turned and fled the room to her pallet.

Heather pressed her hand against her stomach to relieve the uncomfortable sensation. She stared as the curtain that shielded the children's sleeping alcove swayed. Still stunned by Mary's painful outburst, tears formed in her own eyes as her throat tightened. *Poor child. What can I say to comfort her?* She walked to the alcove, pulled the curtain back, and sat down beside Mary.

"I am sure your father did everything possible for your mother. I cannot tell you why she died." She smoothed back Mary's hair from her damp face. "Each day of life we have is a gift. None of us understands how many days we will enjoy that gift. We just need to live each day that God gives us in a way that honors Him and those we love. Think about all that you learned from your mother and loved about her. That was what comforted me most when I lost mine."

Mary sat up on her pallet and wiped her eyes, all the while watching and listening.

"God understands our sadness when we lose someone we love. Think of the pain He experienced when His Son Jesus went to the cross. Life is filled with hardships. As we learn to live with—or in spite of—our difficulties and disappointments, we can grow stronger, Mary. Enduring trials also equips us to aid and encourage one another."

"I want my mama back. Seeing you always reminds me that she is gone."

"Of course, you miss her. I am truly sorry." She sat on the pallet and rubbed the girl's back. *Lord, please comfort this unhappy child.* A few minutes later, she hugged Mary and returned to work at the table, choking back her own tears. Poor Matthew. How horrible that he believed himself responsible for his wife's death. Surely he had done everything within his power to save his wife and babe.

᭖

They picnicked in the shade of a large oak tree, but Mark was the only one who seemed to be enjoying it. Heather hoped to break the gloomy spell.

"Did that chap who came by this morning find you, a Mr. Whit … Whit—?"

"Whitcomb." A grin replaced Matthew's pensive expression. "George Whitcomb. Yes, he commented on meeting you."

"Aye." She laughed. "No doubt he had plenty to say about the sight he saw."

"He may have mentioned you were fully committed to the task at hand. The Whitcombs have invited us all for dinner tomorrow, a way of welcoming you and celebrating the return of the children. Hannah is no doubt anxious to make sure everything is fine over here." One of his eyebrows rose, giving him a cynical appearance.

She could not make out his mood. He did not seem at all pleased by the invitation. Was he embarrassed that she was included?

"It will be good for Mary and Mark." His gaze followed the children. "They have missed the Duncan children, and they do need other youngsters to mix with occasionally. The Whitcombs have four children."

She gathered the remnants of the meal. The children had long since gone off to gather wildflowers.

He turned to her, still looking serious. "You should not have come out here without your bonnet this time of day. You have nothing to shade your arms and face. You are likely to take a bad burn."

"I realized too late that I had forgotten it." Surely it wasn't her sensitivity to the sun that troubled him. "Mr. Stewart, while it is good for the wee ones to mix with other children, perhaps I should stay at the house tomorrow while all of you go to the Whitcombs'."

Matthew stood up, brushing the grass from his breeches. Towering over her, he put his cap back on his thick, dark hair, the set of his mouth suggesting he was provoked. "You *will* go with us to the Whitcombs' tomorrow. I have no desire to go myself, but they are our neighbors, and they have made a friendly gesture."

Why should he be irritated with her? She picked up the basket. "Aye, sir, you are the master, and I but the bondservant."

His brow furrowed, and he looked like he might respond, but he only walked away.

❧ ❧

Heather spent the rest of the afternoon cleaning and scrubbing the cottage. It was the only way to work out her tension and anger at being forced to go to the Whitcombs'. Throughout the afternoon, chills and her burned skin plagued her. The butter she rubbed on her face, neck, and arms offered little relief. He was right. She should have remembered her bonnet.

Mary's superior attitude was equally chafing. What a relief when the children finally went to bed. She was enjoying a cup of tea when a sound at the door made her jump. The master had returned.

"We may be getting rain before too long." He poured water from the pitcher. "Is there any supper left?"

"Aye. I kept it warm for you."

Without another word, she placed a bowl of stew on the table.

The glance that passed between them was anything but warm.

"Perhaps I need to explain about the Whitcombs."

"There is no need, Mr. Stewart. Tell me when we are to be ready." She held her head erect but avoided facing him.

"I will work until about noon. We can head over there as soon as I clean up."

"Fine. Good night." With that, she left him sitting at the table.

The next morning, she and the children were scurrying around trying to get the necessary chores done before it was time to leave for the Whitcombs'. Matthew had gone out earlier than usual that morning, even missing breakfast. He said he wanted to work as long as possible.

Now she was having an impossible time corralling the children to dress for the day's outing. Mary was obstinate, and Heather's patience with the child was dwindling.

She noticed the tub containing the flour was tipped over. "Mark, you just got your bath. What have you done?" Any flour not on the floor was on the boy.

She wiped him off with a damp rag and began to clean the floor. "Mary, please put your apron on and stop teasing Mark. We must finish the pie before your father returns and is ready to go."

Mary's glare was chilling. "*You* finish the pie."

She flinched at the rebuff and wiped the perspiration from her tender, sunburned forehead. Biting her lip, she completed the pie and cleaned the kitchen. Not willing to confront Mary's impertinence, she threw the rag on the table, walked into the bedroom, closed the door, and sat on the edge of the bed. How had everything deteriorated in the course of a day? Mark's chaotic behavior that morning was understandable. He was excited about seeing other children. But how was she to cope with Mary's haughty attitude? She fell back on the bed and gazed out the window. It was no help their father was absent. *Oh, that invitation.*

Exhausted from the confrontation with Mary, she rolled onto her side on the edge of the bed, and tears filled her eyes. Last night was miserable, with little sleep from the sunburn and all the friction in the household. After tossing and turning for hours, when sleep finally came, the nightmares returned. Anything but rested in the morning, she found herself dreading the day ahead. She wanted no part of the Stewarts, much less the Whitcombs. Instead, she craved to be alone, free from their surly attitudes, pressing demands, and glaring eyes. But she had a job to do. She needed to get ready and make sure the wee ones were also, as Mr. Stewart would want to go soon.

Whether she liked it or not, it would have to be the mended green dress, for it was suitable for paying calls and in slightly better condition than the calico one. She slipped the dress on, fastened it, tied back her clean hair in a braided bun, and put the white linen cap over it. She took the silver plate down from the hutch in the main room and examined her reflection. She shook her head in dismay and laughed. Aye, there was plenty of color back in her cheeks, even if they were still a bit thin. After placing the plate back on the shelf, she found more butter to rub on her sore, reddened skin.

Glancing out the window, she spied Matthew approaching the cottage.

When he entered, they were all sitting quietly at the table. "Good, you are all ready to go." He went to the loft for a clean shirt.

Heather sat with her hands folded in her lap. Why should she fret about going to a neighbor's home? Something had gotten Matthew out of sorts, but it should not affect her. She rose from the table, put on her bonnet, and picked up the basket with the pie.

It was about a fifteen-minute walk to the Whitcombs' home. As they neared the place, Matthew's brow furrowed. "I think you will like George. He is a decent fellow."

She waited for him to make additional comments, but he remained silent, his jaw tense, no doubt still cross with her. She hoped the time with the neighbors would pass quickly.

The Whitcombs' home was not unlike their cottage, a frame and clapboard dwelling, with a chimney of brick.

Mr. Whitcomb met them at the door. "Good day, Stewarts." He ushered them all inside.

From the moment she entered, she was struck by all the activity in the house. Children ran in and out of various rooms. The Whitcombs' home was larger than the Stewart cottage and not well kept. Clutter was everywhere.

Matthew greeted a plainly dressed woman about his own age.

"Good day, Hannah. It is good of you to have us over." His friendly words came across affected.

Mrs. Whitcomb, in turn, nodded and eyed Heather with a dubious expression.

"Hannah, this is Heather." Matthew cleared his throat. "My wife." He sounded as if expecting a rebuttal.

"I see." Hannah nodded, her manner reserved.

George Whitcomb filled the awkward silence with a grin. "Yes, we met yesterday." He chuckled. "Over a few feathers."

Heather managed a smile, wishing she were in the company of the chickens today. "I brought a pie."

Hannah took it. "Thank you. It smells mighty fine. Elizabeth, God rest her soul, was a wonderful cook."

Heather stared at the woman. Had anyone else caught her graceless words? Apparently not.

The Whitcomb children ran through the house before disappearing outside, the Stewart children in tow.

After a few tense, silent moments, Matthew came away from the window, where he had been observing the children play. "I think we might be in for a storm, George. Those clouds are moving this way."

"We need the rain. I hope it will be a nice, gentle one, as I have planted seed and do not need it washed away." George lit his pipe and walked with Matthew back to the window.

"What are your plans, George? I will need to hire on earlier this year." He seemed at ease with his friend.

Heather lost track of the men's conversation when Hannah drew her into the kitchen and into their own discourse.

"George tells me you are from Scotland."

"Aye."

"We were so surprised to hear Matthew had married, but I suppose he had to in order to bring his children home."

Heather stood speechless, certain the woman had more to say.

"I knew he would marry someday, of course. But we were certain he would marry someone from these parts, or perhaps Alexandria. A woman, well, like Elizabeth."

Hannah put the goose on the platter and surrounded it with potatoes.

Heather shuddered. *Does the woman not realize her words are insensitive and might be hurtful?*

"Elizabeth was such a lady, city bred. I never figured why she chose to live out here on the farm. Her people were from Boston, of means and position. They must have been brokenhearted that she chose to leave Boston and move into these conditions when she could have lived more comfortably." Hannah leaned in her direction, eyes widening. "I heard tell they blame Matthew for her and the babe's death."

Heather's neck stiffened and a lump formed in her throat as she turned and walked over to where the kitchen joined the main room. The woman was obtuse. Was this why Matthew was reluctant to bring her here today? Had the men caught Hannah's words? Perhaps not. They were outside now. Relieved, she once again turned to the woman preparing their meal.

"Is there something I might do to help, Mrs. Whitcomb? Shall I call the children?"

"Pride. That is Matthew Stewart's problem. He would have had much more if he had been willing to accept help or a position from Elizabeth's people. They were offering it too, I heard." Hannah shook a spoon at her, splattering drippings on the table. "If my George or I had kin like that, well, we would have left here and gone to the city without ever a glance back."

The woman was a gossip and completely devoid of tact, not to mention disrespectful of Matthew. How could she respond to Hannah yet avoid a confrontation that would provoke an embarrassing scene for all of them?

"Perhaps the Stewarts were happy on their farm, Mrs. Whitcomb. Do you think we should call everyone for dinner now? It smells delicious and seems to be ready to eat."

"You fill the tankards while I call everyone." When she returned, Hannah continued her tale. "I hear the Moores, Elizabeth's parents, wanted the children when she died. But no, Matthew did not want them so far away. So he goes and leaves them with those folks in Alexandria, not even family. It was his pride again, not letting the grandparents have them. Those two would have been so much better off in Boston."

As the men and children appeared, the comments in the kitchen continued. "With his pride, it must have taken a heap of swallowing for Matthew to marry up with an indentured servant."

Hot tears filled her eyes, more from anger than hurt. After all, what was this woman to her? Her hands on her hips, she faced Hannah. "Our marriage is of no concern to you."

Hannah responded with a blank stare.

If only the woman would stop. She sat down and tried to quell the tightness in her chest. It did not appear the men had heard Hannah's insensitive diatribe. Matthew was distracted by the children, and George was laughing.

The families gathered around the table, and George Whitcomb offered the blessing. "Well, ladies, have you been getting acquainted? What have you been chattering about?"

She prayed Hannah would not answer his question. How many

of Hannah's remarks, if any, had Matthew heard?

As they ate, Heather hoped no one noticed that she only picked at her food. Matthew was distracted and often glanced at the window. It was not long before he walked to it and scanned the sky.

"George, those are ominous clouds. I want to get everyone home before this storm hits."

They hurried through the remainder of the meal and parted at the door. The walk home was silent. A day that had begun so poorly had only grown worse with the visit to the Whitcombs.

Matthew stopped upon reaching their property. "I am going to get Honey and the other animals settled. Take the children inside." He walked toward the pasture.

Large drops of rain began falling shortly after Heather and the children entered the cabin.

Mary was agitated. "Why did we have to leave so soon? We were hardly there any time at all."

It had seemed an eternity to Heather. She checked to make sure the windows were closed.

Mary continued to whine until Matthew returned from the barn.

The fussy child wore her patience thin. When Mary asked again why they had to return home so soon, she said, "We had to get home before the storm, Mary, but we can have the Whitcomb children over here for a visit soon, dear."

Matthew laughed as he closed the shutters. "Should we invite the children, or would you also like to have Hannah over to keep you company?"

"I fear we do not have much in common, Mr. Stewart." Did he know how badly the visit had gone? No doubt he was well acquainted with Hannah's indelicate remarks. He was difficult to read. Too often, she was unable to tell from his behavior and comments precisely what he wanted from this arrangement—a wife or a servant, as the Whitcomb woman had suggested.

"You will find friends among some of the other planters' wives.

There will be opportunities to meet them soon."

She caught his eye. "That is an encouraging prospect."

The remainder of the day was spent inside, away from the pelting rain. On occasion, Matthew ventured outside to discern if there had been any damage from the downpour. As the day progressed, the inside of the cottage grew more and more sultry. Reading to the children helped for a while, but the sweltering atmosphere was too distracting for anyone's concentration.

The warm rain subsided that night about the time the children settled into bed. Since the air was becoming slightly cooler, Matthew opened the shutters and windows to let in the refreshing breeze. It provided welcome relief.

"I fear this is not the end of it tonight." He glanced toward the windows. "The chickens and other animals are still edgy, and that is as good a gauge as any." He sat across from her at the table, his dark, expressive eyes focused on her. "I am sorry if Hannah said anything to upset you. She sometimes says things that can pique a person." He reached across the table, placing his hand on hers. His eyes searched hers. "Are you troubled?"

Slowly, she turned her hand over, returning his clasp. "I am well." She smiled. There was nothing to be gained sharing Hannah's unkind comments. His other hand reached over and caressed the top of her hand still in his. Could he hear her heart pounding? She could.

"You have been such a help here, Heather. It has made—"

The sound of footsteps interrupted the moment. "Papa, I am hungry." Mark had not been in bed long. He pulled at his father's arm and scrambled up into his lap, ending their personal exchange.

"I can get you a bite to eat." She rose and returned Matthew's smile before she walked to the sideboard to retrieve some of the biscuits. "If Mary is still awake, ask her if she wants something to eat also."

Mary, still sulking, declined any food. Within a half hour, Matthew took Mark back to their pallet for the night, leaving

Heather to seek the shelter of her room. Once inside, Heather leaned her back against the door. What was that all about at the table? Why, when they were together, did she grow short of breath and act so self-conscious? How confusing. She got out of her stays and clothes—what a relief. She poured water into the bowl to wash. The oppressive heat and the difficult day had left her exhausted. Splashing her face and neck with the tepid water brought only momentary relief. Would she ever get used to this heat and these people? She was too tired to think about the day anymore. It would all be easier tomorrow, after a good night's sleep.

CHAPTER 10

Heather woke up, startled by the sound of the rain blowing into her room. She got up and ran to the window to close it. It was stuck and would not budge. She looked down at her shift, now drenched. The crack of thunder sent a shiver up her spine as she fought with the window. Light filled the room, and strong, powerful hands drew her away from it.

The sound of the howling wind and rain was deafening. "I cannot close it!"

Matthew reached out and pulled in each of the shutters, fastening them carefully before securing the rest of the window. The only light in the room was from the lantern he had set on the chest of drawers.

"I got the other windows battened down before I went to sleep. Sorry, Heather. I should have closed yours before retiring."

She shook the water from her arms and pushed the wet hair from her face. For what seemed a long time, they stood still and silent, watching each other. Her heartbeat was rapid, and the throbbing in her ears was distracting. Her hands—she needed to do something with her hands, to fight the overwhelming desire to reach up and touch his face. *Be sensible, Heather. Guard your heart. Do not risk whatever security this life is offering you.*

"The children?" She was soaked to the skin and had to be an absolute sight, standing there in nothing but her wet shift. She clutched her arms across her chest and scanned the room for her shawl, but it was nowhere visible.

Matthew wiped drops of water away from his hair and face. The skin on his bare arms and shoulders glistened in the dim light.

"They are sleeping. When I checked on them, I saw no movement." His eyes, shining, held hers spellbound.

Was it minutes, or only seconds, before she glanced away? "Thank you for fixing the window. I should have closed it, but the fresh air was so welcome, warm as it was." She began to shake, and finally found the shawl resting on the chest. She slipped it around her shoulders. "I had difficulty sleeping."

"So did I." His voice was a hoarse whisper.

She stepped aside. "Well, good night, Mr. Stewart."

He hesitated. Turning to retrieve the lantern, he brushed against her arm.

She gasped. She saw his lips, smiling slightly, and drawing ever so near.

He brought his hand to her cheek, brushing a tendril of wet hair back off her face. Time stood still as their eyes locked on each other's. He leaned down and briefly met her trembling lips with his own. The sensation was exhilarating as he held her, caressing her face.

A second kiss, more intense, yet natural. It was pure bliss until she remembered. *What am I doing? How could I forget so soon that—*

"Where is Mary, Papa?"

Startled, Matthew released her and knelt down to the sleepy boy.

"What do you mean? Is Mary not in bed with you?"

"No."

Matthew turned and left the room. She followed with Mark in tow as Matthew searched the cottage. The anguish etched on his face was heartbreaking.

"Mary? Mary? She is not here. The door is unbolted. I will search outside. You stay with Mark." His voice cracked. He grabbed his shirt and slid his arms into the sleeves as he went out the door into the rain.

With her arm around Mark, she walked him back to the pallet and sat with him. Tension seized every nerve. *Dear God, please let him find her.* She turned to Mark. "Was Mary in bed when you fell asleep?"

Janet S. Grunst

"Yes, but when I woke up she was gone. The thunder scared me." Fear filled the bairn's face.

She cradled him in her arms. They both needed comfort.

It is my fault. She bit her lip. The child was frustrated when they left the Whitcombs'. Her mother's absence and Heather's presence truly tormented the girl. Right when Matthew appeared to accept—she stiffened. Had Mary seen them and felt betrayed somehow? The guilt that germinated in the kiss now flourished like a weed. Mary could not have gone very far—but where could she be?

Matthew returned a short time later, even more drenched. "I cannot find her anywhere. I searched the barn, hen house, cellar, and all around outside. Why would she do this? Where would she go?"

His furrowed brow and worried face brought fresh tears to her eyes. "Mark said she was still in bed when he fell asleep, so it had to be sometime after we retired. You mentioned they were both asleep when you closed my window. Did she, well, see us?"

Matthew shook his head. "It was dark. I did not actually see her, now that I think of it. She was all covered up. I saw what I presumed were the two of them sleeping." He stooped and hugged Mark, who had crawled away from Heather to attach himself to his father's leg. "You go to bed now, son. I shall find Mary, and everything will be fine."

As the small child trudged back to his pallet, Matthew's eyes searched hers, his face filled with regret. "It was my mistake."

A shiver traveled up her spine. *What does he mean by that?* "I think Mary has been very troubled about her mother's death."

"Yes, I am aware. We shall have to put these problems to rest once and for all. I will take Honey and search. She cannot have gone far. I will go to the Whitcombs' first—she may have gone back there."

"Is there anything I can do?" She got up, wrapped the shawl tighter around her shoulders, and followed him to the door.

"Pray." At the door, he turned to face her. "This has been a mistake. It was selfish of me to bring them back here. They probably would have been happier at the Duncans'—or in Boston."

She watched the door close behind him, and a new sadness engulfed her. His comment about it being a mistake—did he mean her being here was a mistake or that it was wrong to bring his children home? His words wounded her, but why? *It is not wrong. Families belong together. Does he regret making me a part of this family?* She walked to the window, hoping to see some sign of Mary. Realizing there would be little chance of getting any more sleep tonight, she went to her room and dressed.

Within a few minutes, she wandered back to the main room to sit and wait, occasionally glancing out the window at the rain.

Had she offended Mary and driven her off? She had tried so hard to be the girl's friend. What was she doing wrong? *Heavenly Father, please protect Mary, wherever she is, and give her the desire to come home and be at peace with her family.* Memories of what had happened earlier in the bedroom confused her, but now confusion was coupled with guilt. Why did she feel the way she did in Matthew's arms and find pleasure in his kisses when her love had been given to another? Surely it was Robert McDowell who had her heart, though she would never see him again. Despite how it ended, there was still that dull, throbbing ache inside her whenever she thought of him. She searched her mind, trying to remember his face, what his smile was like. As the months passed, it had grown more difficult. Robert was becoming little more than a memory, and one that she had promised herself to put behind her. It was challenging enough to deal with the present.

Her thoughts returned to Matthew and his kisses. Did he regret their brief shared intimacy? Would he address it with her? How should she respond? She had suddenly grown quite warm, so she reached for the *Gazette* resting on the table and began fanning herself. Would he kiss her again?

CHAPTER 11

Matthew, filled with frustration, strode to the barn. *Where has Mary gone, and what possessed her to leave? God, please guide me to find her and help her with whatever is causing her such distress.* The thought of going to the Whitcomb home, with all the potential consequences of informing them of Mary's disappearance, made him shudder. Hannah's snooping and gossiping ways had been a thorn in his side for years. But it was the most logical place to look. If only it were not the middle of the night.

He saddled Honey and headed up the path that led to the Whitcombs'. As he rode, Heather came to mind. *What just happened in the bedroom?* He had entered the room to close the window and keep the storm out. He may have provided a remedy to one storm and started another. There was no anticipating what came over him when he saw Heather there trembling. *I am attracted to her, but am I ready? Is she?* It was foolish to contemplate that now. He needed to find Mary. He shook his head. *She did return my kiss.* He smiled in the dark.

The rain had slowed some by the time he reached the Whitcomb home. The light coming from the front room this time of night gave him hope.

The front door opened. George came outside and waved to him to enter. "I thought I heard something out here. Mary is inside, Matthew. She is with Hannah. With it being so late, and the weather so bad, well, after she and Hannah had talked awhile, we figured it would be better to let her get some sleep and bring her home in the morning. The way she said she snuck out, we figured you might not even know she was gone."

"Thank you, George." Matthew dismounted and followed George inside. Mary was wrapped in a quilt on the settee. He sat down beside her.

After listening to Mary detail, with some pride, the chronology of her escape, he put his hand on her shoulder. As thankful as he was to find her safe, irritation filled him.

"Running away was a thoughtless and dangerous thing to do, Mary. We were concerned, wondering where you were and what happened to you."

She peered up at him through brown lashes. Looking into her sad eyes, it was difficult to determine whether she was repentant or not. But this certainly was not the place to discuss the situation. That would have to wait until later.

"George, Hannah, what can I say but thank you for caring for her. I am indebted to you for your kindness."

Hannah raised her eyebrows and opened her mouth as if she had something to say.

George put his hand up. "No trouble, Matthew. These young ones get some strange notions, and sometimes they act on them before thinking them through. I hope you both can get some sleep. The storm appears to have eased up now."

Matthew took Mary by the hand and walked outside to where Honey was tied. He placed her in front of him on the horse, waved good-bye to George and Hannah, and turned toward home. "We need to talk about this, young lady."

"May we do it later?"

She sounded contrite, and he hoped it was genuine.

❧ ❧

Heather gazed out the window of her room when the sharp sound of the door opening startled her. She ran out to see Matthew carrying a drowsy, soaked Mary.

"Praise be to God, you found her. Is she hurt?"

"No. She is cold, wet, and tired. Hopefully, she will not take a chill after roaming through the countryside in this weather." His voice sounded weary and a bit out of breath, but much calmer than it did earlier when they first realized she was gone.

"Take her into the bedroom. I will get her out of her wet clothes. Hopefully Mark will sleep a while longer."

"Yes, a good plan." He sounded distant as he gently lowered the yawning child to the soft quilt on the large bed. He took a deep breath, put his damp cap back on, and walked to the door. "I shall see to Honey and be back shortly. At least the rain acts as if it is passing now."

Heather slipped Mary's wet clothes off and replaced them with a dry shift. She reached over and caressed Mary's thick brown hair. *Father, only You can help this child get beyond her despair and disappointment.* She tucked the child in, then walked to the door and closed it behind her so Mary would sleep undisturbed.

She found Matthew at the kitchen table. His unshaven face and the dark circles under his eyes were a visible reminder of the weariness and stress of the recent hours.

She sat across from him. "Where did you find her?"

"At the Whitcombs'." His fatigue and frustration were evident in the way he leaned on the table.

"You should try to get some sleep. I am here if either of them awakens." Her questions could wait.

No words came as he studied her, evidently considering the suggestion. He rose. "Yes, I think I will, but only for a short while. I still have a full day's work ahead." He climbed the ladder to the loft as if he were carrying a tremendous weight.

The children slept, and she dozed for a short while in the chair by the hearth. When she awoke, she checked on Mary, fearing a fever might develop. The child was fast asleep.

Heather returned to the kitchen and began to prepare breakfast. When Matthew reappeared, she was able to learn of Mary's escapade in private.

"I followed a hunch that she went back to the Whitcombs'. Sure enough, when I got there, Hannah and George were awake and not terribly surprised to see me. As soon as I saw she was safe, my worry turned to exasperation. I wanted to swat her."

She poured him some tea and offered him a bowl of porridge and a plate of ham.

"I talked to her a bit. She must learn she cannot run off like that."

"Did she mention why she left?"

"No, not yet."

"When did she leave?"

"Shortly after we put them down, as soon as Mark fell asleep. She slipped out when we opened the windows because the storm had let up." He took a few bites of his meal. "Fortunately, she arrived at Hannah and George's before the worst of the storm."

She watched him, silently digesting all he was saying and relieved that Mary had not witnessed their kiss in the bedroom. "I am surprised Mr. Whitcomb did not bring her back. Surely they must have realized how frightened and upset we would be when we found out she was missing."

Matthew shook his head and reached for some more ham. "George said that by the time Hannah and Mary finished talking, it was raining too hard, and he did not want to bring her out in it, particularly if we had not discovered her absence. He planned to bring her back first thing this morning."

She knew she had raised her brows when he mentioned Mary and Hannah talking. Mrs. Whitcomb was probably delighted to listen to Mary's woes.

Matthew finished his tea and shook his head. "I am sure Hannah gleaned an earful."

"Aye, that is no doubt true." She began toying with the food on her own plate. "I will try again to assure Mary that I have no intention of taking her mother's place and that I only want to be her friend."

It was a simple, yet straightforward statement, but it brought them eye-to-eye again for a long moment.

"I hope she will stop considering you a threat to her mother's memory and that you can be friends." He got up from the table and walked to the door. "When she wakes up, please send her out to see me in the barn. I feel responsible for what happened last night and must make certain that it never happens again. She must be very confused and hurt to run off like that."

"Aye, hurt and confusion can motivate a person to run away from their difficulties, though avoiding them does not solve them."

His look suggested he understood her heart.

She watched the door close behind him. *Nay, trials have a way of traveling with you until they are dealt with one way or another.* She stacked the dishes and wiped the tabletop. *So, how do I pass on such wisdom to a child, not quite ten, when, at near thirty, I have not learned how to deal with my own problems?*

In the days that followed, there was a civil but tense atmosphere in their household. Mary's earlier impudence was replaced by a silent and sullen compliance. Heather and Matthew retreated to their previous impersonal relationship, neither referring to their shared intimacy, but the experience continued to creep into her mind. Something had been stirred in her, and it was adding to her distress. Withdrawing, she managed to get through each day's tasks without engaging the people with whom she lived. She knew her distracted state did not go unnoticed by any of them.

When she reached out to Mary, she was rebuffed. How was she to break through the barrier the child had built? Mary's independent spirit and self-centered attitude reminded her so much of Eileen. Yet there were also times when Mary would ask questions and seemed open to making peace with her.

An unspoken truce had flowed back into the household within a fortnight after the dinner at the Whitcombs'. One morning, Heather was on her knees cleaning the floor when a shiver traveled up her spine. She got up and went to the bedroom where the children were playing a game.

"What are you doing?" She surveyed the room, walked to the window, and glanced outside.

"Acting out the story you read to us yesterday." Mary held up a small crate. "I am Noah, and Mark is one of my sons. He is bringing all the animals, two by two, into our ark." The two children giggled as they arranged small rag bundles on the bed.

"Oh, I see." She treasured the grin on Mary's face. "Tell me when you and the animals want a bite to eat, and see that they wipe their hooves well before climbing on the quilt—I mean the ark."

She returned to the main room and resumed cleaning the floor. She was almost finished, and she wanted time to freshen herself before dinner. It had turned pleasantly cool the past few days, so all the windows were open, and the occasional breeze was refreshing. She was pleased with all she had accomplished that morning. The wash was draped on the privet hedge, and the windows were clean. She got up and stirred the simmering kettle of beans and glanced at the window. *Is someone there?* A chill ran through her again. Was she being watched? She surveyed all the windows. The hair on her arms and the back of her neck were standing on end. "Mr. Stewart, are you there?" No answer.

She resumed scrubbing, keeping her head down for the most part, but occasionally her eyes shifted upward to the silver plate on the hutch. There it was—the reflection of a movement outside. They were not alone.

When she glanced at the window, she saw a retreating shadow, a person. She got up from her kneeling position. Her heart pounded and the anxiety intensified as she reached the door.

"Who is there?" Her voice quivered.

Not a sound.

She tentatively opened the door. It was startling to see a tall, somber man standing there, leaning against the porch railing. Composing herself, she held the door only slightly ajar.

"Sir, may I help you?"

He stood still, eyed her up and down, and glanced past her as if he were searching for someone or something.

"Who are you? What do you want?" If only Matthew were present.

"Is Mr. Stewart here?" His grin revealed poor and missing teeth. "Whitcomb, up the path, sent me."

"He is over in that field." She pointed the way and tried to avoid his dark, brooding eyes. Relief and a twinge of guilt followed as she directed him to Matthew.

Without a word, the strange and foul-smelling man turned and walked off in the direction she indicated.

She watched the retreating figure for a while from the window before she moved the furniture back into place. She still needed to get the ham sliced and bread baked.

Within the hour, the children came out of the bedroom, bored with their game and hungry. Matthew came through the door as she was readying the table for the meal.

"Heather, have we enough to feed an extra mouth?" He lowered the water gourd from his mouth.

Dread filled her. "Aye, sir." She bit her lip when she saw the sinister man fill the doorway.

"This is Travis Thorpe. I have taken him on to help around here for the rest of the planting and harvest."

A foreboding filled her as she nodded in the stranger's direction.

"Well, man, join us for dinner. After that, you can go to the barn. You will find plenty of room there to bunk."

Why was Matthew not put off by such an unpleasant individual? She shuddered and avoided eye contact with Thorpe, wanting to ignore his menacing demeanor and acrid odor. At least he would be staying in the barn. Surely he would not always take his meals with them. She joined the others at the table.

The meal was unusually silent. The children did little more than stare at the repulsive intruder.

"Good vittles, ma'am." Thorpe's grin made her stomach knot up.

When the man departed, Heather cleared the dishes away, only to cry out in alarm when a noise startled her.

"My, but you are jumpy today." Matthew had a puzzled expression on his face.

"That man." She peered around Matthew to make sure they were alone and kept her voice low. "He is, well, very odd. Did you see the way he ate? And he smells terrible. Must he come in the house?"

At first, Matthew seemed annoyed. Then an emerging smile turned to a laugh. "Heather, you sound like Mary. I came back for a towel and a quilt so the man can wash and make a bed for himself." His eyes twinkled. "Perhaps I should offer him some violet soap."

Shamefaced and silent, she gathered the requested items from the chest-on-chest and handed them to him. She certainly was never as disgusting as that Thorpe fellow.

He chuckled again as he took them. "It would seem that I have a propensity to take in weary strangers badly in need of feeding and bathing."

Not amused by the comparison, she retreated to the bedroom and closed the door behind her. She was still uneasy about the stranger. *Am I being uncharitable?* One of them was wrong about that man, and she hoped, for all their sakes, that it was her.

She gazed out the window to the leaves on the maple tree swaying in the breeze, and after a few minutes began to relax. Still offended by Matthew's comment, she did see some of the irony in the situation. There was no comparison with the Thorpe fellow, for he was a free man, able to leave when he wanted, while she was a bondservant.

As time went by, Travis Thorpe did little to change her initial impression of him. Aye, he was a bit cleaner—at least he did not smell quite as bad as before—but he still had an undeniable aura of malevolence about him. For the most part, he remained outside of the house, but on occasion, Matthew would invite him to join the family for a meal. When Matthew wasn't observing, the man leered at her in a way that made her skin crawl.

One afternoon when Heather was preparing their meal, she set the kettle of stew on the table and went to the sideboard to gather the plates. Glancing out the window, she spotted Travis resting the pitchfork beside the barn door before entering. In one fluid motion, she grasped one of the plates, dished up some of the stew, and grabbed a biscuit before briskly walking outside with it in the direction of the barn. *This should avoid having him join us.*

It was dark inside without the lantern lit or the windows on the opposite side of the barn open. She turned at the sound of straw being crushed near one of the stalls.

"Mr. Thorpe." She called out to him when she spotted him opening a sack in a corner. "I suspected you might be ready for your dinner, so I brought it out here for you."

He glanced up. "Why, Mrs. Stewart, that is very good of you to trouble yourself by bringing me my food." A leer formed on his face as he walked toward her.

She hesitated. "No trouble at all, Mr. Thorpe." She shuddered, turned, and placed the dish and biscuit on a crate nearby. When she turned to leave, she jumped. Thorpe had moved around the barn, and he was now blocking the entrance. The dim light in the barn made his figure against the lit doorway appear dark and menacing.

How was she to get by him? Panic seized her, but she still had her voice. "Kindly move and let me pass." She hoped she sounded in control and unafraid. She was neither.

Thorpe moved toward her.

Run or stand her ground? Why let this surly, brutish man intimidate her?

"For you, ma'am, anything." He moved aside, but not so much that it kept him from brushing up against her as she left. Disgusted, she jerked her arm away from his touch.

Her chin up and shoulders back, she walked out of the barn and back toward the house with as much dignity as her shaking knees and labored breathing allowed. She was both repulsed by the encounter and relieved to reach the safety of the cottage. All in all, this service was a small price to pay to avoid his presence at their table.

The sound of Mary and Mark squabbling poured out the window as she approached the cottage. Inside, she spent several minutes trying to get Mary to stop teasing and fighting with Mark. "Mary, if you cannot stop taunting your brother, you need to go sit on your pallet alone for a few minutes."

Mary turned to her. "You are not my mother, and you cannot tell me what to do."

The young girl's smug attitude was infuriating. "Go to your pallet and stay there. I am not going to tolerate your insolent ways any longer. Do you understand?"

Mary stood her ground for a moment. With her arms crossed against her chest, she turned and went to her bed. "I am going because I want to, not because you told me to."

"Wonderful." She returned to kneading the dough for the bread she was making and tried to quell her frustration. "It is remarkable. Mary is Eileen all over again."

"Who is Eileen?" Matthew asked as he entered the cottage. "What has gotten you so upset?"

"I did not hear you come in. It is Mary. She has been tormenting Mark and was disrespectful to me, so I sent her to ponder her attitude." She glanced at him. Had she overstepped her bounds?

"And Eileen is—"

"My sister. Eileen was much younger, and I was charged to raise her. She was very headstrong and did not respect my authority." She gazed into his eyes, hoping he would not question her further.

"Do not fret. Mary is long overdue in being chastened for her behavior." He walked to the table where the iron pot was sitting and lifted the lid. "Mmm, smells good, but I need to wash before supper."

He turned to Mark, now at his leg. "Would you like to go down to the pond with me to wash up?"

"Oh, yes, Papa."

Heather sat at the table, trying to regain her composure. The encounters with Thorpe and Mary had left her nerves on edge. Matthew and Mark would be back soon, and she did not need questions she did not want to answer. She put the plates of stew on the table. They returned, teasing and laughing, obviously in high spirits. During all the commotion, Mary came to the table, careful to avoid her gaze, but joining in on the others' fun.

After Matthew offered the blessing, he nodded at her. "Shall I ask Mr. Thorpe to join us?"

"Nay." She was a bit too quick, causing the other three at the table to stare in surprise. "I mean—I—I took him his meal." She sat down, shaking. Unable to eat, she moved her food around in her bowl, not joining in the cheerful banter the others shared.

Matthew appeared to be stifling a smile. "Did I mention that I invited Mr. Thorpe to join us for Sunday services tomorrow?"

Her eyes flashed, and her stomach clenched. "You did?"

"Yes, but he suggested that he would rather not." Matthew's look hinted he was waiting for her response.

"Hmm. Well, we certainly would not want to impose on him."

Matthew took some bread and passed the plate to her. "Perhaps he will join us another time."

Heather just stared at him.

When the meal was over and the dishes cleaned, she excused herself and went to bed. The night was warm. Any other night, she would have enjoyed the fresh air from the open window, but it faced the barn, and tonight she chose to keep it closed.

CHAPTER 12

A few days later, having finished preserving some blackberries, Heather wiped the perspiration from her brow and removed her apron. "Mary, would you please get a jug of water? When I finish packing the basket, we can take dinner to your father and Mr. Thorpe. Mark, you can carry the blanket. They are sowing wheat in the west field."

Mary shrugged her shoulders, picked up the jug, and took it outside to fill.

Even with the longer summer days, and the added help of Travis Thorpe, Matthew spent little time with the children. She and the children took dinner to the men wherever he and Thorpe were working.

Her lips pursed. She was intent to ignore Travis Thorpe's coarse manners during their meal. Why, in spite of her deliberate attempts to avoid him, did he take such an inordinate delight in engaging her in conversation? Matthew acted as if there was nothing unusual about him—at least, he never commented on Travis' behavior to her.

When they reached the field and spotted the men at work, Mark ran off to announce their arrival. She and Mary spread the blanket and set out the food.

The men approached, each going for the tankards. She set out loaves of bread, meat, and cheese and sat down near Mary.

Matthew planted himself across from them, next to Mark, and reached for a few slices of bread. "This smells good. I have worked up an appetite as well as a thirst." He took some cheese and a few slices of the ham. "Were you able to finish your preserving?"

"Aye."

Travis took a large serving of bread and ham. He lowered himself beside her.

She shifted away from him and barely heard Matthew's blessing. Why was Thorpe so obtuse to proper behavior? She uncovered a wooden bowl. "We have some berries the children left for you." She got up and sat down beside Matthew. Placing her hand on her husband's arm, she smiled. "Here, Matthew, have some." She glanced at Thorpe. Perhaps she could dispel any notion Thorpe might have of the impersonal nature of their marriage. Matthew was private and reserved. He was not likely to have shared much with this crude character.

Not many minutes later, Matthew got up and stretched. "Thorpe, we need to get back to work."

Heather stood and faced the children. "We need to return to the cottage. Remember, Mary, we were going to do some sewing." She folded up the blanket and handed it to Mark.

As they made their way home, Mary stopped every few feet and picked some wildflowers growing along the path. "I do not really know how to sew."

"I can teach you. I think you will like it, and I suspect you will do very well."

Once home, Heather picked up a dress of Mary's. "You are growing so fast, I planned to let out the seams and take down the hem. This is such a nice piece of cotton that it would be a pity not to wear it as long as possible."

Mary picked up the edge of the gown. "But it is so plain."

"Well, we can embellish it a bit with some lace edging or embroidery. Would you like that?"

Mary shoved her chair closer and examined the garment on her lap. "Is it difficult to learn how to embroider?"

"No. Here, I can show you." She took a scrap of fabric and worked it with a needle and thread. "What do you think?"

Mary stared as she sewed the delicate little stitches into the piece of cotton. "That is beautiful. I wish I knew how to do that." Mary's eyes lit up as if she had just discovered a treasure.

"It is not difficult. Perhaps you would like me to teach you, though I must tell you, it has been a while since I have done much needlework. We can take it slow. Perhaps we might purchase some embroidery threads in a few days when we go into Alexandria."

"Oh, yes. I shall ask Papa tonight."

She grinned and patted Mary's arm, grateful for her genuine enthusiasm. Perhaps this new interest might help forge a friendship.

❧ ☙

The next morning, Heather and Mary were assembling the dinner to take a picnic to the far side of the pond, where Matthew was weeding the tobacco fields. Just last week, Matthew had explained that, while the Stewart farm did not produce a great quantity of tobacco, it was an essential cash crop. Once cured, it was sold for tobacco notes, a legal tender. With the notes, he purchased services and goods that were not produced on the farm.

Mark ran into the cottage, splashing water from the pail he carried. "I cannot wait until we go see the Duncans."

Mary took the pail and handed her brother a rag. "I am just as eager as you Mark, but we do not go until the day after tomorrow. Now settle down and wipe up your mess."

Heather shook her head as she watched the two youngsters. She looked forward to the planned trip into Alexandria also, yet with some reservations. How would Maggie, Adam, and others receive her? It would be splendid to forgo chores and enjoy the diversion of a visit to the city, and pure joy to spend an entire day far from Travis Thorpe.

"I know you are excited to see the Duncans, children, but there is much to do in preparation. Your father is busy, so he plans to work sunrise to dusk for these next two days. After I pack this basket, we can go meet him for our picnic."

Heather watched them chasing each other around the small cottage. "Will you be able to sit still long enough at the pond to make taking the fishing pole along worthwhile? It might be nice to have some fresh fish for supper."

Mark bolted from the room. "Yes, yes. I want to go fishing."

At the pond, they located a shady area where they spread the cloth, emptied the basket, and set out the food. Soon Matthew joined them and settled on a grassy spot beside the cloth. Heather leaned back against the trunk of the oak tree and watched the children digging for worms on the muddy bank to bait their line.

She nodded her head in their direction. "I wonder if they will catch anything."

Matthew took a wet rag from the basket. He wiped his face and hands, set the cloth down, and waved to the children. "Do you clean fish, Heather?" The skepticism in his voice was unmistakable.

"Aye, I have cleaned many a fish. The Tay, near my home, had salmon, and we enjoyed them often." His eyes met hers, and a warm sensation came over her. Their banter was fun. She grabbed the rag and threw it at him, hitting the side of his arm. What had prompted her to do that? No doubt the coming trip to town had made her lighthearted too.

A smile formed on his lips. "I meant no offense, woman. Living in the country must be a big change for you—not at all like city or village life."

"I took no offense." She laughed. "Cities and villages each have their charms and challenges." She removed her sunbonnet and fanned herself. The afternoon sun was not a threat under the shade of the tree.

He pointed to a slight incline lined with trees. "The fishing is better beyond that hill over there, at the river—the Potomack. George was over there yesterday and took home a whole line of bullheads and catfish."

Her eyes met his. "I did not realize that we were still near the Potomack River."

"Oh yes. It is a major river, extending far northwest of here. On the other side of the river is the colony of Maryland."

"Are there cities like Alexandria along both sides of the river anywhere near here?"

He gazed off in the direction of the river. "No, but the river is an increasing source of commerce as well as travel. There is a ferry not far from here." A gentle smile formed on his lips, and the look in his eyes suggested his thoughts were far from the shady spot under the tree.

"Elizabeth missed the company and activity of city life. We used to talk about adding on to the house—I mean considerably adding on." He had that distant gaze again. "We planned to open an inn—an ordinary, for travelers crossing the river or traveling the main east-west route that connects Alexandria with the settlements to the west."

"Do you still have hopes to open an inn someday?" What an intriguing insight into their marriage. She had bitten into a piece of the tender chicken when she spotted Travis Thorpe approaching them.

"No, those plans died with Elizabeth."

As Thorpe wandered nearer, Matthew eyed him also. "Ho, Thorpe, come over for some chicken and cider."

The man wore the same clothes he always wore. It was no wonder he smelled so bad. In truth, she had not offered to wash his clothes. They probably would have to be boiled. Who knew what might be living in them?

Travis pushed his fist into the basket and grabbed two pieces of chicken. "It smells good."

She flinched and glanced away. Hiding her feelings was not a gift she possessed.

Matthew's eyes met hers before he turned toward Thorpe. "I want you to work in the cornfield and take care of the animals when we go to Alexandria. When we return, you take the next day off for yourself."

The man only grunted at Matthew's request.

A loud squeal came from the pond. Heather dropped the warm bread she was unwrapping. Matthew and she both stood before they saw that the outburst was only Mary's excitement over a fish she was waving around for everyone to see.

"I am going to catch enough for all of us," she called.

Matthew looked relieved. "You do that. But be careful not to fall in."

They sat back down just as Thorpe helped himself to a handful of the savory bread.

She seethed. "Mary, come over here and take some of the food for yourself and Mark."

Matthew glanced at her and coughed into his hand. "I think it is time we went back to work, Thorpe."

Expressionless, Thorpe surveyed her. His gaze lingered a bit too long before he nodded at Matthew and rose.

She held her breath as Thorpe took off in the direction he had come, wiping his mouth on his sleeve.

There was more commotion at the pond. Evidently, another fish had made its way to Mary's hook and now onto the grassy bank. Matthew went to where the children fished and praised their success. Kneeling, she cleaned up the remains of the picnic and repacked the basket.

Heather felt a sudden painful stab on the back of her neck. She screamed and swatted at her neck as a bee flew off. She grasped the painful spot and felt it swelling. The children stood staring in curiosity as Matthew dashed back to her.

"What happened?"

"A bee just stung me." Breathless, she rubbed the nape of her neck.

"Let me see." Matthew lowered himself and rested his left hand on her shoulder. He probed the sensitive area. "Be still. I will pull the stinger out. Have you ever been bothered by bee stings before?"

"Nay." His nearness and touch agitated her as much as the

sting, yet she remained still as his fingers pressed on her skin. His warm breath on her neck and the gentle assertiveness of his hands was not unpleasant. Did he hear or sense the rapid beating of her heart?

"I have it. See?" He moved his hand around in front of her face. Meanwhile, his other hand rested on her shoulder, where it had dropped when he dislodged the stinger.

She eyed the small stinger. It was so small, almost impossible to see, yet it hurt so much. She gazed into his large brown eyes, now so close to her own. Her gaze lingered on his lips, now curling up. She turned her head. Was he aware of the unsettling effect he had on her?

"Thank you. I feel quite foolish about all the fuss."

"No need. A bee sting can be serious. I will pack some mud on it to keep down the swelling."

He returned with mud on his fingertips and knelt down again behind her. "Can you do something with your kerchief? I am afraid the clay will stain it."

She loosened the white linen kerchief tied modestly around her neck. His engaging nature and kindness broke down her intentional reserve.

The day had grown warmer—or was it her?

He rubbed some of the cool sticky substance onto her sore neck.

Mark ran up the hill to investigate. "Does it hurt?"

She wiped the perspiration from her brow. "Not really, laddie. A tiny bee sting has caused all this fuss."

Matthew pointed to a field nearby. "I shall be working right over there. Stay here and rest awhile."

"I am fine, truly I am."

Matthew rested his clean hand on her shoulder. "Relax a few minutes. It will give Mary more time to fish."

Mark returned to the pond.

She leaned back against the oak, watching the children

impatiently wait for the next fish to bite. It was impossible to ignore the turmoil going on within her. *What is the use of pondering what a genuine marriage would be like with Matthew?* She glanced his way. He was occupying more and more of her thoughts. If they had both been unattached and met under different circumstances, would they have been drawn to one another? It was pointless to even wonder that. Neither of them was truly free.

Biting her lip, a tear rolled down her cheek. She was beginning to forget Robert's face as well as his voice. She had loved the man without doubts or resistance. Trusting and opening her heart to him had left her vulnerable. Now, confusion filled her. Nay, she would not open her heart that way again. Better to stay distant, and remain safe.

Why had she been so foolish? Painful memories continued to surface. Would they ever subside? She would never forget when Robert McDowell entered her world and changed the course of her life forever. Had it been eighteen months since Robert came into Douglas Dry Goods in search of her brother? The charming barrister from Edinburgh had come to Perth looking for Ross because they had some business dealings. Heather flushed remembering how taken with this sophisticated gentleman she had grown over the months of his sporadic visits. She had long since given up hope for marriage and having children of her own. Her responsibility was to care for her father and assist in the shop. When Robert declared his love for her, she believed her life was taking a turn for the better. How wrong she had been.

CHAPTER 13

When the day of their trip to Alexandria finally arrived, Matthew brought the wagon to the front of the house shortly after dawn. They loaded baskets of farm produce to take to market. The plan was to use the proceeds to make necessary purchases from the local merchants. It was everyone's intent also to fully enjoy the day with the Duncans.

He checked the harness again and made sure that Honey's bag of oats was in the wagon. It would be so good to see Adam and Maggie again, and they would see that his family was faring well with Heather. He chuckled. The becoming lady he was bringing back to town today was strikingly different from the frail one he had married. There was no question that Heather was a novice at country life. Still, she had proved herself a willing worker and had been good for the children, even if Mary had not realized it yet.

Heather stepped off the porch with the basket Maggie had given her only three months earlier.

"Mr. Stewart, where would you like this in the wagon?"

"Here. I will take that." He took the basket. "I think that is everything. Are Mark and Mary ready to go?"

"Aye, I shall get them." She went around the side of the cottage and called the youngsters.

Thorpe was standing near the wagon. It was early for him to start working, but getting the horse and wagon ready for the trip woke him up.

The children got into the wagon. Heather had gone back inside to retrieve something she had forgotten. When she approached the wagon, Thorpe helped her up to her seat beside Matthew.

"Everyone ready?"

"Yes, Papa."

"Good." He glanced to his side. Why did Heather look so annoyed? She seemed pleased not ten minutes before. *Women!*

"I expect we shall be home around dark, Thorpe."

"Fine, I have plenty to do to keep me busy."

The first hour of their trip passed quickly. The children were in the back of the wagon chattering and playing guessing games. He and Heather rode in near silence up front.

He loved this time of day, and it promised to be a beauty. He glanced her way. Should he even try to find out what was troubling her?

"You are studying our route, Heather, as though you were worried about getting lost." He chuckled.

"I am enjoying the beauty of it all—the sounds of the birds and geese mixed with the chirping of insects, and the variety of vegetation. The trees, the dense underbrush teeming with life, and the cleared rolling hills make the scenery come alive. It is so very different from home—I mean Scotland."

He caught her glancing at him. *She is winsome when she drops her reserve.*

"It is very craggy in Scotland. Oh, there is grandeur about the moors, but there is serenity here."

He laughed. "It is refreshing to see it through your eyes. I have lived here so long that I fail to appreciate it enough. Too often I see only all the toil involved in making the farm prosperous. I am glad that Virginia pleases you."

"I do like it."

I am grateful she likes the place, but what about her feelings for the family? For me?

❦

Increasingly, when Heather thought about the quiet man whose home she shared, a fervent sense of pleasure filled her. Today, as at other times, she caught herself observing him. Other than the smile lines around his eyes, his skin had darkened from so many hours in the sun. His tall frame had also done some filling out since her arrival. Was she at least partially responsible? Matthew obviously had not eaten well, living alone. He was an attractive chap, but it was his admirable character that most impressed her. She turned her head away. Hopefully, he had not noticed her watching him or discerned her interest.

It was good to be heading to Alexandria. What a wonderful excursion for all of them, and what a relief to spend a day far from that Thorpe fellow. Even he could not upset her today, though he certainly succeeded in disgusting her before they left home. She cringed, remembering how familiar he had been when he lifted her into the wagon.

Nay, today she would be free of that unseemly fellow.

Matthew reached over and briefly placed his hand on hers. "I am going to stop in a while to water Honey and give us a chance to stretch."

"Aye, when we stop, I shall go sit in back and read to the wee ones for a bit. It might help them to pass the time faster."

A short while later, they came upon a small stream. Matthew drew the reigns, stepped down from the wagon, and unhooked Honey. He led the horse down to the stream and waited while she drank her fill. Within a few minutes, they were back on the road.

Mary moved a bag to make room. "Are you going to read to us again from the Bible?"

"Aye, I planned to. Shall we start from where we left off yesterday?"

"We were in the sixth chapter of St. Luke." Mary had a self-satisfied grin on her face.

The children quieted down and appeared attentive when she began reading.

"*But I say unto you which hear, Love your enemies, and do good to them which hate you. Bless them that curse you, and pray for them that despitefully use you . . ."*

Her stomach tightened, and a lump formed in her throat as she read.

They all sat in silence when she had finished the verses.

Matthew's voice startled her. "These are the precepts that we are entreated to live by, children. The very ingredients of righteousness. We cannot choose how people treat us, but we can choose how we respond, even when we think we are being badly treated."

She choked, trying to quell her emotions. His words were convicting. *Have I honestly lived by these precepts, Lord?* There was a barrier keeping her from peace with God. That joy she sought was elusive. Why had everything turned out so badly? She closed her eyes and wiped away a tear. *Tell me what you want from me, Lord.*

"Why are you crying, Heather?" The concern was evident in Mary's voice.

"'Tis nothing, Mary. 'Tis nothing."

❧ ❧

Something was troubling the woman. Perhaps a change in perspective would help. Besides, he preferred having her in front beside him.

"It must be getting rather cramped back there. You want to move up here, Heather?" He looked over his shoulder.

"Aye, I think I will." She got up and reached for his hand.

Perhaps sitting up here would shake her melancholy mood. He held out his arm and helped her come forward. They sat there in silence for a few minutes, keeping their eyes fixed on the road.

"Is something troubling you?"

"Nay. All is well."

Soon, Mark and Mary's cheerful banter provided a distraction and made the remainder of the journey go faster. Their chatter also masked the awkward silence between Heather and him.

When they reached the Duncans' home, the children did not remain in the wagon long enough for him to come around and help them down. Jean and Cameron were the first through the door to greet the new arrivals, followed by Maggie and Donald.

Maggie, beaming, ran and gave him a quick squeeze. "Matthew, it has been too long." She then turned her attention to Heather and the children. "Mary, come here for a hug. You too, Mark. I cannot begin to tell you how I have missed the two of you."

Pure joy showed on each of their faces as the three embraced.

Maggie nodded at Heather. "You look to be doing well. It appears that country life agrees with you. It is nice to see you again, Heather."

"Thank you, Mrs. Duncan. Anyone would look better than I did that first day here." They shared a laugh. "I was a pitiful sight."

As they walked into the house, Maggie turned to Donald. "Run down and tell your father that the Stewarts are here, would you, son?"

"Aye, ma'am." The lanky boy shot down the stone walk.

The children vanished along with the young Duncans, leaving the adults in the front room of the house.

"Adam had some work to do for the mayor this morning but planned to be back well before dinner. I must say, Matthew, you are faring a far sight better than you were on your last visit into town." Maggie smiled up at him with a twinkle in her eye.

"And you, Maggie dear, appear a bit altered. When do we get to see the new babe?"

"Wee William should be up at any time now."

"Maggie, I have a full wagon to take to market before stopping at Brady's for provisions. I decided to come by here first to inform you we had arrived and to turn the young ones loose."

"I am glad that you did. So be about your business and be back in time for dinner." Maggie smiled.

Matthew returned with the basket they had packed for the Duncans while Heather stood, appearing self-conscious.

He hoped that Heather would want to accompany him, but he knew he should give her that choice. "Heather." He lowered his tone as he handed her the basket. "You may stay here with Maggie or go into town with me, whatever suits you."

❧ ❧

Heather considered his remark. She was eager to see more of Alexandria but thought she should stay and help Maggie. It was hardly fair to leave Maggie alone to manage all the children while also trying to prepare a meal. She felt she should make an effort to be friendly and helpful.

Before she was able to decline going along with him, though, Maggie spoke up. "Matthew, what is wrong with you? Of course she wants to go into town. You have had her out in the country for three months. Heather and I shall have a chance to visit later, during and after dinner. Now go, you two."

Bless her. What a thoughtful and amiable woman. She wished that the Duncans lived as close as the Whitcombs. It would have been nice to have another woman around to socialize with, and it did not appear that Hannah Whitcomb would fill that need.

"Mrs. Duncan …"

"Please call me Maggie."

"Mrs. … Maggie, I would so like to see something of the city, but it is not right to leave you to care for all the wee ones while also preparing a meal. Would you please allow me to clean the dinner dishes afterward while you rest? Oh, and we have brought back your basket with some produce from the farm you might be able to use."

"Thank you, for both gifts. Now, go and enjoy yourself."

By the time they reached the wharf, she was in high spirits. "Oh my, look at all those ships in the harbor, Mr. St—Matthew."

Her excitement increased as she unconsciously rested her hand on his sleeve. She quickly withdrew it, but not before she caught his grin. How embarrassing. She was growing fonder of Matthew each day, but she dared not open her heart to be hurt again. Besides, she knew better than to confuse his friendly nature for a more serious attachment. In the days following Mary's evening excursion, he had never brought up their brief romantic interlude. And he certainly had not kissed her again. He had given her no hint of his feelings for her. Was she weakening and growing too attached to him? *Guard your heart, Heather.*

When she did return his gaze, she glanced beyond him. Sober memories filled her as she spotted the ships in the harbor.

They drew to a stop not far from Brady's. She caught Matthew studying her.

"What is the matter, Heather? One would think you had seen a ghost."

"Not a ghost, just the ships. It is a reminder of where I have been and what I am. Not long ago, I was out there in the harbor, looking in at this village."

"A great deal has changed since then." He stepped down from the wagon.

As he helped her from the wagon, he peered again at the ships. "Your life has changed in many ways since you left the *Providence.*"

After they unloaded the wagon at the farmers' market, he smiled and nodded at her. "I have a list here, Heather, of the things to be picked up at Brady's. Would you go there, give it to Mr. Brady, and see if there is anything else we need? If you are interested, there is a shop up the street that has fabrics and items for the ladies."

She hesitated.

"I have some notes." He reached out and passed them to her. "You said that you wanted some threads for Mary, and you might need some cloth for garments, for yourself or Mary. You decide. Say we meet at Brady's in about an hour."

She accepted the currency and returned the smile. He had extended her such liberty, and the sense of independence it brought was exhilarating. Minutes later, in the dry goods shop, she chose some loosely woven canvas for Mary's sampler, along with some needles and embroidery threads. After fingering some attractive brocades and damasks, she found some osnaburg and blue linen. It would do nicely for shirts for Matthew and Mark as well as dresses for Mary and herself.

"May I assist you, ma'am?" The clerk approached her, interrupting her perusing.

"Aye, sir." She gave him the specifics of what she wanted. "I shall be back in a bit to purchase them."

All in all, she had a delightful time selecting the few extras at the cobbler's and the dry goods shop.

Later, when she caught up with Matthew, he did not act at all concerned when she told him what they had cost. He had successfully sold all they brought from the farm, so it was no time before they were ready to start back to the Duncans'.

"I think Mary will enjoy the new primer, and she is excited about making a sampler." The smile on his tanned face warmed her heart as he helped her down from the wagon.

Adam had returned in the Stewarts' absence and was eager to introduce his friends to his tiny new son. The four caught up on all that had occurred in the months since their last visit. After a time, Maggie and Heather excused themselves to complete the preparations for their dinner.

"Were you able to find everything you needed in town?" Maggie handed her a platter of sliced ham. "I realized after you left, I never mentioned where you might locate anything."

"Mr. Stewart indicated where the shops were so I was able to pick up some fabric." Heather smiled and took the platter to the table.

Maggie's expression was quizzical. "So, is everything going well at the farm? I imagine that you are quite busy."

"Aye, we are, particularly Mr. Stewart, but he has taken on a hand until after the harvesting time." Her brow furrowed at the reference to Travis Thorpe.

"And the children? They appear to be doing well."

"Well, the truth is, they miss your family a great deal. They were very happy being with your wee ones. With their father occupied most of the time, I am their sole companion."

Maggie's glance was full of empathy as she placed the boiled carrots in a dish.

Heather took the dish to the table. "I fear this has been a bit hard on Mary."

"Hmm, aye, I can see where she might have a problem." Maggie nodded as she wiped her chapped hands on her apron. "Have you met your neighbors yet? I am sure their children would be companions for Mary and Mark."

"Aye, at church services I met the Turners and some other neighbors who live farther away. Oh, and I met the Whitcombs."

She did not miss how Maggie's eyebrows lifted when she mentioned the Whitcombs. "Hmm. Better call everyone to dinner."

The conversation during the meal was amiable. She felt a bit left out but not by anyone's actions or words. It was her own introspection and her changeable emotions throughout the day—excitement, sadness, shyness, independence, and now confusion. What was ailing her? Was she being overly sensitive of her precarious position in this family? Would she ever get beyond this sense of defeat, this emptiness, this restlessness, this isolation?

Maggie touched her arm, interrupting her introspection. "Would you care for a piece of pie?"

"Nay. I am not very hungry. I will clean the dishes." She got up and collected the soiled dishes, grateful to escape the group. As she scraped the plates, she listened to their conversation.

Matthew reached for his steaming tankard of coffee. "We saw quite a few ships at the wharf while we were in town. Makes one wonder what the state of our trade is with Britain these days, now that the Townsend Act has been repealed."

"We still have duty on the importation of tea. That is why we are drinking more coffee these days." Adam poured some of the hot brew for himself. "Did Maggie tell you the widow MacKenzie married old Harry Walker only a month ago?"

"No, Adam. But I have always tried to avoid that particular subject. How is old Harry? Still doing poorly?"

"Well, when I learned he was marrying Hattie, I was certain the gout had spread to his head, but I saw him last week at Reed's smithy, and he was as fit as can be, not even limping as bad as usual." Adam laughed. "Says Hattie treats him like a king. But the Walkers are not as comical as Reed himself since he married that lass he bought from the ship."

Matthew's eyes met Heather's before he glanced at his friend. "How so?"

"Do you remember the lively little wench Thomas Reed bought? Well, I have never seen a more blatant example of—"

"Adam Duncan, stop your gossiping." Maggie tapped him on the arm.

"That is hard to believe of Reed." Matthew sounded surprised. "But if she is in any danger, Adam, you should notify the proper authorities."

"The lass is in no danger, Matt. It is poor Thomas I am worried about. Why, that tiny female has a ring through that big ox's nose. He is so besotted with her that he has become her slave. He follows her around like a puppy dog, with her shouting orders at him on the street and even in his shop. It is all so amusing."

Heather continued drying the dishes, but she worked quietly, so she would not miss a word. She wiped the dampness from her hands. Was Millie in duress? She almost dropped the clean dish when Adam roared with laughter.

She glanced at Matthew and caught him studying her. She turned her back, wanting not to appear at all interested in what they were discussing. Millie may have behaved a bit strangely at times, but after all, they had shared a similar fate.

Matthew and Maggie apparently enjoyed Adam's story, for they laughed right along with him. Were her own situation or mood different, she might also have seen the humor in the reversal of the Reeds' relationship. But now, she only craved fresh air and a chance to subdue her restlessness. She would go outside, check on the children, and take a short walk.

The children were playing together in an empty lot next to the house. She made her way along the stone path in front of the dwelling and reflected on her inner distress. Today had truly been a wonderful day, so why was it so difficult to enjoy it? She continued down the street and up the other side. *Lord, I have been so wrapped up in myself. I am sorry. When I focus on You, I see the beauty in the world, the way You have protected me, and I have peace. But when I focus inward … I grow sad. Please help me get beyond this, Father. Show me the way.*

The children were disappointed when it came time for the Stewarts to return home. Mary was only quieted after Maggie assured her that very soon they would make a trip out to the country. When the children were in the wagon, Maggie brought out a large package and drew close to Heather standing by the front door.

"I asked Matthew if you might be able to find a use for these, and he allowed that you would. Feel free to enjoy them."

"Free? I am anything but free."

Matthew walked by, his brow furrowed as he glanced her way.

Heather took the bundle. "Thank you for being so kind to me. You have a delightful family, including the beautiful babe."

"I want to help, in any way that I can." Maggie gave her arm a squeeze. The openness and sincerity of the woman touched her fragile emotions. Tears came, and she trembled. With an arm around her for support, Maggie walked her to the wagon, where Matthew helped her onto her seat. Farewells given, the Stewarts were on their way.

Matthew was eager to get started home; it had been an enjoyable time but also a long day. The trip out of town was quiet except for the cheerful chatter of the children in back. They were headed west and into the sinking sun.

When all was quiet, he glanced over his shoulder. The children were asleep—just what he had hoped for, so he could question Heather. He had imagined she would appreciate a trip to Alexandria, a day to get away from mundane chores and enjoy being around people.

He glanced to his side. She was twisting a tendril of pale golden hair that had escaped her cap, a tendency of hers when she was contemplative. Her lips were closed and turned down. A pity. Her smiles were so engaging. Something was ailing her. "I thought it was a nice day. Did something happen or was something said to trouble you, Heather? You seemed, well, uncomfortable."

"It was a very pleasant day, Mr. Stewart. If I seemed ill at ease, if I disappointed you, I am sorry. The Duncans are very nice people." She glanced away.

"You have not disappointed me in any way." Her mood certainly seemed capricious today. Was she on the verge of tears again? "Do you want to talk about what is distressing you?" How was he to approach her so she would tell him why she was so unhappy? Hers was too pretty a face to be so glum.

"Heather?"

"Nay. Nay, sir, I … cannot."

"Perhaps another time." He would make it his goal to break through her shell. "It appears that you were successful on your errands today. Did you find all you were looking for?" *That will surely perk up her spirits. What woman does not like to shop?*

"I did. I found fabric for clothes and some notions so that I can help Mary with some sewing skills. Thank you again for allowing me to shop."

"No need to thank me. It just was the most natural and reasonable thing to do."

The remainder of the time on their trip home passed quickly, especially when Mary and Mark awakened. He listened to the children's conversation as they approached the lane that led to the cottage. "We are almost home. Perhaps we could have a light supper once everything is unloaded."

Heather nodded. "I will put something together."

"Thank you. I hope Thorpe's day went well."

He glanced in Heather's direction again. She appeared deep in thought. She sat so straight. What had happened to this lovely woman that made her erect such a wall? It was obvious that below her reserved exterior, she was in turmoil. *Patience, man.* It would take time to figure this all out.

CHAPTER 14

Why was it so difficult to sleep? Was it the confusing dreams that made her pitch and turn in bed? Their faces were so angry and full of accusations. The disillusionment on her father's face was unbearable. She rolled and clutched her pillow. Someone was threatening her, but it was impossible to make out who. The sound of a child crying woke her.

"Mark!" Heather climbed out of bed and reached for the cotton shawl. She dashed out of the room, her feet bare and her hair hanging in loose waves around her shoulders. Matthew sat on the children's pallet, leaning over the crying boy. Mary was curled up in a chair, sleepy and looking annoyed by the disturbance.

"What is wrong with Mark?"

"He has a fever and lost his supper." Matthew sounded worried as he gently wiped his son's face with a damp cloth.

Her eyes traveled back and forth between the two children and their father. It appeared they all had experienced a rough night.

"Mary, you go sleep in my bed. I will dress and watch over Mark."

Without any argument, the little girl allowed herself to be guided to the bedroom and into the large comfortable bed, where she quickly drifted off to sleep.

Heather dressed and returned to Matthew and Mark. "You must be tired, Mr. Stewart. Try to get some sleep. I can watch Mark and bathe him down."

He sighed, rubbing his hand over a full day's growth of beard. "Perhaps I will sleep for a while, but if he continues to get sick, or if the fever gets worse, wake me, and I will go for the doctor."

She reached out and touched his hand. "It may have been something he ate that disagreed with him, or perhaps the excitement of the day." She hoped to convince herself as well as him. "I promise to wake you if there is any change. Please do not worry. He is a strong laddie."

"I should not wait too long to get the doctor if he worsens." He sounded exhausted as he climbed the wooden ladder to the loft and his bed.

She continued to sponge off the restless and whimpering child. Mark had been a bit flushed when they led the children into the house after the trip. Travis had helped Matthew unload the wagon while Mary sliced some bread and poured cider. Why had she not noticed that Mark was unusually quiet when she set out the bread, fruit, and cheese? Aye, she should have realized that he was more than tired when he ate only a few bites and sat so quiet at the table.

She studied the lad, now resting so still, cheeks too pink. Fear filled her as her thoughts turned to Katie and Emily. *Please, Lord, let his sleep bring the fever down. Save him and heal him.* For the next hour, she kept a vigil, continually changing the damp cloths. But the child grew fitful and perspired more. The clock on the table showed it was not even three o'clock. It would be hours until daylight.

She hated to disturb Matthew, but she had made a promise to wake him. Thunder rumbled in the distance. She climbed the ladder to see into the loft. It was a shame to wake Matthew, but she nudged his arm.

Dazed at first from his sound sleep, his eyes met hers.

"Mark's fever feels higher."

He grabbed his shirt and followed her down the ladder.

He placed his hand on Mark's brow. "He is hot. It may mean that the fever will break, but we cannot take a chance. I will go for Doctor Edwards. I should be back within an hour or two. Thank you for seeing to him." He rested his hand lightly on her shoulder.

"Be careful, sir. It sounds like another storm is coming."

She moved the chair over next to the pallet and continued putting the cool damp cloths on the boy's brow.

"Thirsty." Mark's voice was no more than a whisper.

She gave him small sips of water, fearing he would not keep it down. There was not much more to do for him. He was not lucid enough for her to read to or even tell him a story, as her mother had done with her when she was small. She would sit and wait.

She leaned back in the chair, thinking of another time, another place, and another one she took care of. From the time her father was first stricken, until his death over seven years later, she had assumed total charge of his care. Aye, she had grown weary of being his nurse, thinking that would be all life had in store for her. Who would marry her when so much of her life was consumed with taking care of her father? Waves of guilt engulfed her. He was her father, and she truly loved him. It was not his fault he was unable to care for himself. Would he not have taken care of her if she had fallen ill? Ashamed of her selfishness, she resolved to try harder to give of herself with a cheerful heart.

For the first four years, Father was still able to take care of most of his physical needs. It was his lapse in memory that would cause problems, or his incessant chatter, or demands that would drive her to the point of losing patience. Then came that day when Angus Douglas suffered his most severe attack. This time, the paralysis did not all disappear, and his speech became practically nonexistent. Over time, he made only minor improvements.

Sitting in the chair beside Mark's pallet, she put her head back and closed her eyes. She remembered the hurt on her father's face when he accused her of bringing shame on the family. If only he had lived long enough to learn the truth.

Heather opened her eyes with a start when Mark called out to her. He was lying very still on the pallet but looked much improved. She changed the damp cloth on his head and noticed that he was much cooler now. The fever had finally broken. "Thank you, Lord." She pulled the thin blanket up and covered him. "You are going to be fine now, Mark." She got up and stretched, still watching the child as he fell back asleep. The tension gradually left her weary body. She needed some fresh air, and Mark was well enough for her to step outside for a few minutes. Dawn would soon be here.

She sat on the stoop, enjoying the tranquility of the early morning. It was still dark, too early for the birds and animals to herald in the dawn, but the cool breeze was refreshing against her damp dress, face, and hair. The heat and anxiety of the last few hours had left her spent, but now a peace filled her heart.

She walked to the well to refill the water pitcher and took a drink from the gourd.

"The boy doin' any better? Mr. Stewart said he was ailin' when he took off for the doctor."

She gasped, dropped the gourd, and turned. Travis Thorpe was standing directly behind her. "You startled me, Mr. Thorpe. I had no idea you would be up yet. Aye, Mark is much better. Now, if you would excuse me, I had better take this in—"

"I am sure his papa will be relieved to hear that when he gets back." Travis stepped in front of her.

A growing sense of alarm robbed her of the peace she had finally found after the long night. She stood back and glared at the large man, dressed only in breeches, blocking her path.

"I expect him back any minute, as he did not have far to go." She hoped he did not discern the uneasiness in her voice.

"He may be gone longer than you think, little lady." He was leering at her again as he stepped closer.

"Why?" Had something happened to Matthew? Had he done something to Matthew?

As she backed away, her concern for Matthew's whereabouts and safety was overshadowed by fear for her own. She was backing in the direction of the barn, with fewer options for easy escape. She attempted to dart to his right. Not fast enough. Travis reached out and grabbed her arm.

"Leave me alone!" She began beating wildly at him and kicking all the while. But his grip on her grew stronger. Her efforts to free herself only appeared to incite him more. As he picked her up and carried her toward the barn, the bitter taste of fear rose in her throat. Her head hit the frame of the barn door, which stunned her. Oh, the throbbing. What was he saying?

Inside, the barn was dark, and the smell of the hay and animals was almost obscured by his odor. He dropped her down onto the hay.

"Let me go!"

"Now, little lady, do not make me hurt you. You should be a little sweeter to me. I see the way you sneer at me, always trying to avoid me. You think you are better'n me, but I know the truth about you. Your services are bought and paid for, just like mine."

She tried swallowing the bile rising in her throat. He reeked of ale and sweat. *How do I get my footing and escape this madman?*

"Here, a little something to drink will loosen you up and make you friendlier." He handed her a jug.

She forced a smile to her lips and a shaky hand out to reach the jug. It was the only weapon available. "Aye, perhaps that would help."

His breathing became deeper and more uneven.

With all her strength, she took the jug and threw it toward his face, launching herself in the direction of the open door. He grabbed her around the middle, knocking the wind from her. By the time she got her breath back, she was down on the pile of hay again.

"You should not have done that. Now be still, or I will have to get rough with you." He reached for the jug. He dropped down beside her and drank from it, one large hand holding tightly onto her wrists.

"Here, you have some."

"Nay. I do not want it."

"Do not fight me." He became more enraged and grabbed her

hair, forcing some of the burning liquid down her throat.

She choked as she reached out and grabbed Travis' face, scratching him.

He made a guttural sound, threw the bottle against the wall, and dropped onto her squirming body. She flinched as his mouth came down on hers. One hand played with her hair while the other was at her throat.

"Please let me go." She gasped for air when he finally took his mouth off hers.

He frowned as he wiped a tear from her cheek. "I do not want to hurt you, really. You should talk nice to me."

"You are frightening me." Tears flowed into her tangled hair. *Please, Lord God, help me escape.*

He continued wiping the tears from her face. His caresses, though more gentle, did nothing to subdue her fears.

A different tactic. "Trav—Travis, stop forcing me so, I promise I shall be kinder to you. Please give me another chance."

"Are you trying to run away again?" His voice and dark eyes softened as he peered into her tear-filled ones.

"If you would let go of me, I shall sit here and talk to you awhile. You said that was what you wanted."

A moment of his silent scrutiny passed before he got up, one hand still wrapped around her arm. She slowly sat up, and with her free hand tried brushing some of the hay from her hair. In their combat, her kerchief had loosened, exposing more of her neckline than usual, and the sleeve of the calico dress had separated at the shoulder seam.

Travis moved close beside her, still holding on to her. "We can run off right now, just the two of us. I have friends south of here where we can hide awhile." His face lit up with excitement as he spoke. "We can go to North Carolina, Cape Fear. There are many of your kind there, and some that owes me. You would be free, little lady." He rubbed his thumb down her neck and across her collarbone.

Horrified by his suggestion, she merely stared, eyes wide, saying nothing. *What am I to do, Lord?*

"I would take good care of you. You may be a servant, but I spotted right off that you were a lady. How does going south sound to you?"

"Too dangerous." Her mind searched for a way to escape. "We should plan this out a bit better … wait for a time when the master will be gone longer." *If only I can gain his confidence and stall him.*

"No. We ought to make a break for it now. Even when he comes back, he would not leave the younguns, especially a sick one. This is our best time."

Gathering her courage, she rose to a kneeling position but almost fell over from the dizziness that suddenly engulfed her.

"Let me go back to the cottage and get a few things—some food to take along. I will come right back. Then we can go."

Her consent excited him. This time, when he held her close, kissing her lips and face, she dared not resist. *He must trust me to let me go to the cottage alone.* She drew her arms up to put around his shoulders. It was like lifting cast iron. Her body, her mind, and her soul wanted to fight his every caress, but this was her only hope. Once inside the cabin, she would bolt the door and go for the gun.

"Travis, Travis, not here, not now. We must hurry before Matthew returns. It is getting light out."

He grunted as his foul-smelling mouth traveled down her neck. Now, she was able to see beyond him—directly into Matthew Stewart's eyes and silent rage.

CHAPTER 15

Matthew nodded at Doctor Edwards as the two men got down off their horses. "Go on in the cottage. I will be there as soon as I take Honey to the barn." He stopped near the barn door as he heard the sound of Heather's voice. Why was she in the barn? What did she just say? She was begging Thorpe to let her go back to the cottage to get a few things? Matthew stood inside the door of the barn, stunned. She had promised to go away with Thorpe.

His stomach tightened, and his whole body tensed as he walked deeper into the barn. Unbelievably, they were on the hay in a passionate embrace.

"Matthew."

Travis turned, facing him with a challenging glare.

"Thank God, you are—"

"Get in the house, Heather. I shall speak with you later." It took effort to maintain some self-control.

Heather got up and rushed past him without another word.

"Get your things, Thorpe, and get out of here now." His fists were itching to hit the man, but he resisted the urge. Thorpe's smug expression only angered him more.

Travis Thorpe dusted the hay from his pants and walked over to his pallet to gather his few belongings.

Matthew followed him out of the barn and watched him head down the drive. "And make sure you never come back!"

Thorpe was one problem taken care of. Now he would have to deal with Heather. But how? Was she that unhappy here, desperate enough to go off with someone she found so crude?

Mark. He needed to get inside and see how Mark was. He tied

Honey to a rail.

In the house, Doctor Edwards sat with Mark. The child was taking some water and, except for his color, he was very much improved. Mary had returned to the pallet and was fast asleep beside her brother.

"The fever is gone." Heather was breathing heavily as she sat on the edge of the pallet, caressing Mark's cheek. "Shall I give him something to eat?"

Doctor Edwards nodded. "Nothing too heavy. Some broth would be good. If he keeps that down, give him some porridge."

"Aye, Doctor. I shall see to him."

Matthew put his hand on the older man's shoulder. "Well, Thomas, it seems I disturbed you for nothing. It appears the little fellow is on the mend. May we offer you some breakfast?"

"No, thank you. I am delighted to see the boy does not really need me. I think I shall head back. The Bradfield girl has taken a turn for the worse, so I wanted to check on her today. Stop by and see us, old friend." Doctor Edwards extended his hand toward Heather. "Nice seeing you, ma'am. I hope the boy is fully recovered soon, and no one else takes ill."

"Thank you, Thomas." Matthew extended his hand.

"I hope the next time we see you, Matthew, will be at the Taylors' barn raising." The doctor walked down the steps and hooked his bag on the saddle before getting on himself.

When Matthew came back into the house, he went right to Mark. "If you are better now, son, I shall get started on the day's chores. Have a little broth, but I want you to get some rest, understand?"

"Yes, Papa." He yawned.

Without even a glance in Heather's direction, Matthew left the cottage. He needed time alone to determine what to do next about her.

He had not even reached the barn when the sound of her running and calling out made him slowly turn to face her.

"Mr. Stewart, Matthew."

She still had pieces of hay on her skirt and in her hair.

"I wanted to thank you, Matthew." Her quivering voice was full of emotion.

"So now it is Matthew, is it?" *She has a way of charming you. Watch out.* "I hardly need to be thanked for being a fool. Loyalty was not a prerequisite in a wife, but I had not counted on betrayal." He turned and unhitched Honey and headed deeper into the barn. She was still following him. *Do not sin in your anger, man.*

He turned to face her. She was furious, not in the least contrite.

"He attacked me. Why are you angry at me? It was *my* life that was in peril."

"Peril? The only peril you were in was being caught." He strode back toward her and stood within a couple of feet of her.

Her mouth dropped open. "You have made a terrible mistake, Mr. Stewart. You saw … the man was forcing me! I was trying to get away from him."

"You were having a nice tussle in the hay, and enjoying it."

She stood there, mouth agape.

"I had no idea you were so free with your favors, but when they are that freely given, they are not worth much."

She reached up and slapped his face with a force that appeared to shock her as much as him.

For a long moment, they stood staring at each other. As tears welled up in her eyes, she turned and ran back to the cottage.

❧ ❧

When Heather reached her room, she was relieved that Mary had gone back to her pallet so she could be alone. *What a hateful remark. What is the matter with the man? How dare he think and say such things about me!* Once in her room, Heather threw herself on the bed, beating the quilt with her clenched fist, her face bathed in tears. She wept until there was nothing left in her, wept for all the injustices, a lifetime of grievances.

Much later, when she woke, she lifted her aching head and
glanced around the now familiar room. Her dress was torn and
adorned with bits of hay. All she wanted now was to remove any
remnants of the morning's memories. She needed to gather her
resources and see to the wee ones. With all the angry words and
irritation, she had completely forgotten the children. What must
they be thinking?

She walked to the door and peeked out, hoping not to be
observed. Silence. Mark was sleeping in his pallet, and Mary was
nowhere to be seen. Creeping farther into the main room, she
peered out the front window and saw Mary sitting on a blanket
beneath the large oak tree. Perhaps Matthew was still in the barn.

Back in her room, she began the job of making herself more
presentable. Her hair was frightfully tangled and full of hay. She
carefully took the muslin dress off so as not to tear it further. It was
too warm a day for the green wool. This would be a good day to
try the yellow lawn dress that Maggie had put in the package for
her. It was a bit short, yet fit quite well for a dress of Maggie's. The
length could be adjusted later. Right now, she needed something
to wear, and she appreciated Maggie's kindness in giving it to her.
When she had opened the package the previous night, she was
overwhelmed to find this dress, along with another buff-colored
one, a light cotton shawl, and a woolen cape.

She peered in the looking glass. "It is a lovely dress." When her
eyes traveled from the reflection of the yellow gown to her face,
she broke into tears. *Lord. I cannot bear this. How could he think me
so faithless?* She combed her hair, removing every remnant of hay
from it. *I have been searching for, chasing, something I may never find.
Where is that safe haven?* She swallowed hard. *I shall find it. I must
find it.*

A knock on the door startled her. "Aye? Come in."

Mary opened the door. She stopped suddenly, eyes wide.

"What is it, Mary? Are you well? You are not ill now, child?"

"I … Papa wants to know when dinner will be ready?"

"Oh my! I completely forgot about dinner. Tell him half an hour."

When Mary left, Heather tied a ribbon around her loose hair and placed her cap on her head. She would not let Matthew insult her like that again. She had tried to defend herself and had no reason to be ashamed. And servant or not, she did not have to take his vile remarks.

Matthew stopped abruptly when he entered the cottage. He eyed her and looked like he was stifling a comment before he sat at the table. Surely, he would not continue to insult her in front of the children.

Dinner was a strained affair. They ate in silence. Even the children had nothing to say, though their glances between the two of them and each other displayed their confusion. It was obvious they sensed the tension.

"Papa, where is Mr. Thorpe?" Mark drank some broth.

"He is gone—gone for good."

"Why did he go?" The curious child naturally had to ask.

"Well, Mark, Mr. Thorpe was attempting to take something that was not his. Now we cannot have that, can we?" He directed his gaze at Heather.

"What was he stealing, Papa? He was not going to steal Honey, was he?"

Heather relaxed her clenched lips. "Mark, would you like some porridge? I made some for you, as the doctor suggested. Do you think your stomach is strong enough for it?" A change of subject was what they needed.

The boy nodded and reached for a spoon.

"No, son. He was not going to steal Honey. But no matter what the value of the property, the principle is the same. It is wrong to steal. Thorpe is gone now. We shall have to get along without him."

Heather surveyed Matthew's face. The kindness she had once

seen there was gone. His dark eyes were now full of reproach and condemnation. There was so much she wanted to say to him, but not in the children's presence. It would not be fair to them. And sometimes it was better to say nothing. Instead, she rose and cleared the dishes away.

It was not until the children had gone to bed that night that she had an opportunity to be alone with him again. The desire to confront him with his crude and incorrect conclusion had grated on her throughout the day. She did not want a confrontation, but the hostility that had built up within her was unbearable.

When he went out to secure the barn and see to the animals, she would follow him and settle this misunderstanding far from young and curious ears.

She spotted him from the window as he left the smokehouse and headed in the direction of the barn. She left the cottage, dreading the confrontation but determined to find the courage she needed.

Matthew was seated on a crate, preoccupied, as she approached him in the barn. "Mr. Stewart, you have made a terrible mistake. I want to explain about what you *believe* you saw this morning."

He looked up from sharpening the sickle. His sad expression dispelled some of her anger. "I do not want or need the details. All I want from you is for you to take care of the children and mind the house. I had no idea you were so desperate for your freedom." His words were slow and deliberate.

She needed to guard her comments also. It would be easy to say something she would later regret. Her head began to throb. "You are mistaken. Please allow me to explain."

Matthew's eyes searched hers. "You did not have to run off with the likes of Thorpe to achieve it. You will have your freedom. Grant me some time. You owe me that." He shook his head as he studied her.

Why was he so uninterested in the truth of the matter? So be it. But the comment about restoring her freedom was so completely unexpected and unsettling that she stood silent, staring into eyes that seemed devoid of emotion. Retorts and explanations ran through her mind, things she wanted to say to him, but she was helpless to verbalize any of them. He had distanced himself to a place she was unable to reach and feared approaching. Her head ached, and she knew if she stayed her tears would flow. Drained, and with a heavy heart, she slowly walked back to the cottage, resolved to honor her commitment to care for the children. But she wondered what he meant by giving him time. Did he plan for her to leave soon?

Heather went into the cottage and leaned against the closed door. She looked around the small dwelling, a place she had begun to think of as home. When she reached the kitchen, she peered out the window in the direction of the barn. If only Travis Thorpe had never come to their farm. If only there were some way of changing the likely events to come.

The haven she sought was not here, but with God's grace she would still find it, especially if there was hope for freedom in her future.

CHAPTER 16

In the week that passed since Travis' departure, confusion and disappointment had periodically plagued Matthew. His memories of the scene and the words spoken between Thorpe and Heather in the barn stuck in his craw. His hope that she had grown to accept her place in the family was shattered. He had opened his heart and had grown to care for her, perhaps too much. How could he have been so wrong in believing she had a growing affection for the children—and for him?

Matthew left the cottage early each morning and spent most of the day on farm tasks. He and Heather remained civil toward each other and avoided confrontations of any kind. Were it not for the innocent cheerfulness of the children, the entire household would have remained in a glum state.

The last two days had been unusually warm, and today promised to be no different. As usual, Heather and the children brought him dinner. The children bantered, but his conversation with her was minimal. Heather sat under the oak tree and fanned herself with the *Gazette* she had brought with her. It was hard to figure her out. At times she looked sad, other times annoyed.

He scanned the sky—not a cloud in sight. *Lord, please bring some rain. And wisdom. I need wisdom to know what is best for everyone.*

Mary finished eating, scooted over to the rock where he sat, and parked herself in his lap. "Papa, you are not going to stay out here working late again tonight, are you?"

"I fear I need to, child. There is much to be done around here, and it is only me now. If only it would rain. With the weather so dry, I am afraid that we are going to lose some of the crops."

Heather passed him the bowl of berries they had brought. "We have been watering the garden and doing the laundry with water from the pond. What else can we do to help?"

"Nothing. We are all bathing in the pond now. I just pray that the situation changes and soon." He glanced her way. They had said hurtful things to each other, or was it just he who was accusatory? She looked downcast. Did she have any second thoughts or regrets? What happened in the barn exposed her desperation. She had come to Virginia to serve an indenture, and he had pressured her into marriage. After their earlier confrontation, he had told her he needed time to remedy the situation. Why was he so reluctant to act on it?

Heather's glances his way were detached and brief. "Children, I think we should head back and let your father get back to work."

He had to admit to himself that he cared for her and did not want to lose her. But if he truly cherished her, he had to let her go. It was up to him to follow through on his promise to grant her the freedom she so wanted.

❦

Heather wrapped up the remnants of their meal. She and the children bid Matthew good-bye and headed back toward the cottage.

Mary plodded up the hill, carrying the half-empty jug of cider they had taken for their dinner. "It is so hot." The perspiration was running down her cheeks. "May we go down to the pond this afternoon?"

It was difficult to act like nothing was wrong, but Heather was determined to not take her frustration with Matthew out on the children. "Aye, I think that would be a good idea. Also, Mary, we need to do some sewing. You can work on your sampler while I work on our dresses."

Mark's face broke out into a smile. "I will bring the fishing pole so we can catch fish."

"That sounds fine with me, laddie. It would be a nice change for supper. We should also take the basket this time and pick some more berries."

Their afternoon at the pond, splashing, fishing, and berry picking, energized them all and was a balm to her wounded spirit. Heather pondered her uncertain future as the three of them walked back up the hill toward the cottage. Where would she go if she were free? What would she do? Leaving the children would not be easy. Over these months, they had established a tender place in her heart. Mary had become more agreeable and less moody this past week, an unexpected gift. She had feared Mary might be more temperamental after seeing their old friends in Alexandria.

Mark was struggling with his load.

Heather shook her head. "Are you sure that you do not want me to carry the catch? Your basket must be getting mighty heavy."

"No, I want to." He panted, carrying his scaly treasures.

"Well, set them down on the porch." She handed Mary the basket of berries. "I need to gut and clean these fish before I can get to the sewing. If you want to work on your sampler, you may want to bring it to the porch in case you need any help."

Mary nodded and went inside to retrieve her work.

"Mark, please go see if we need to get more water for the troughs." She reached down and kissed Mark's dark curls, enjoying the closeness their relationship afforded.

He smiled and bounded off.

When the fish were prepared, she and Mary went inside and sat at the table with their sewing projects.

"This stitch, Heather, it does not seem right. I cannot remember where I am supposed to put the needle."

She set aside the blue dress she was sewing for Mary and studied the stitches. "It is fine, dear. You just left one stitch out. The chain stitches are beautiful. It takes time to learn and be more confident about your work, but with practice, you will embroider beautifully.

It took me a long time to make my first sampler. I remember how jealous I was when Eileen did hers so quickly."

Mary's face brimmed with curiosity. "How old was Eileen when she made her first sampler?"

She picked up the dress and continued sewing at the seam. "Let me see … I suppose that she was about six. It was shortly before our mother died."

Mary's eyes were inquisitive, and her head tilted toward her. "You said that she was pretty. What was she like?"

"Aye, Eileen was bonny, with long blonde curls. She loved to laugh and have a good time." Lowering the blue dress to her lap, she leaned back against the wooden slats of the oak chair, while memories of Eileen came flooding back.

"Does she have any children?" Mary glanced up from her sampler, waiting for her to continue.

"Nay. I do not believe she has any wee ones." Sadness filled her for a moment. "Say, you told me that you wanted to make a cobbler with the berries. If so, you had best be washing them."

"Yes, ma'am. But will you tell me more about Eileen?" Mary put her embroidery aside and got up to see to the berries.

"Aye, we shall talk more about Eileen later." Heather picked up her sewing again, but her mind remained on Eileen, an ocean apart, a lifetime away. Neither of them had lived up to Mother's hopes. They were sisters but never friends. They were so different in nature, and they resented each other. Perhaps, as women, they would have learned to be less judgmental, instead of always wanting to change each other. It was easy to be jealous of her sister's carefree spirit. She had been unforgiving when Eileen made her tasks more cumbersome. Now she had so many regrets.

Mary returned to the table when she had finished washing the berries. "Heather, tell me more about Eileen. Where is Eileen now? Does she live in Scotland in a fine house?"

Mark returned and hovered around the table too.

"I have no idea, Mary. She was married to a seaman, and for a while lived in St. Andrews, in Scotland. They were married when she was but fifteen, quite young."

Mary frowned. "Mark, no more berries for you. These are meant for the cobbler." She walked back to the worktable and pulled the bowl out of his reach. "Many girls marry at that age here. That is not young."

"It may not sound young to you, but I do not think Eileen was ready to settle down and take on the responsibilities of being a wife. And it was painful the way she went, without our father's blessing."

"Does she sail with her husband to many fine places?" Mary sounded intrigued.

Heather set her sewing aside to help prepare the cobbler. "Nay. I believe she sees very little of him. I do not believe Eileen has had an easy life." She prepared the batter for the cobbler.

Mary focused on the berry mixture she poured into the baking dish, but her interest seemed to be all about Eileen. "Was your father very angry? Did he forgive her?"

"He was angry, and I am not sure about his forgiving her. You see, it was right after she ran off that he became ill. We did not see much of her, only a visit now and then."

"I wish I had a little sister."

"Well, I think you are fortunate to have this wee fellow, but I am afraid that he is going to turn into a berry himself if he does not stop nibbling them."

Once the cobbler was baking on the hearth, they returned to the porch, but the children were too full of energy to sit still for any quiet activity, so they set about a game of hide-and-seek.

Heather watched from where she sat and continued working on Mary's new dress, while her mind kept returning to Eileen. Perhaps if Mother had lived, Eileen's life would have taken a different path. Her sister never abided with restrictions placed on her while she was home, or even after she left. Perhaps if the baby she carried had lived, or if she had been able to have more children, her restless spirit would have been quelled.

Eileen, I am so sorry for all the times I failed you. I should have been more understanding, loved you more and resented you less. I was wrong. Wherever you are, I hope you can forgive your imperfect sister and find peace and happiness.

CHAPTER 17

The following Monday, everyone at the Stewart household was up earlier than usual. It had been decided the day before, at their church service, that Tuesday would be the day for the Taylor barn raising.

"Mary? Mary? Mark? Where are you?" Heather took the last of the laundry off the privet hedge. The children appeared around the corner of the house. "Oh, there you are. Listen, once these clothes are in the house, we can go down to the pond for a bit. You must bathe today so we can get an early start tomorrow for the Taylors' barn raising."

"Do we really need a bath?" Mary put her hands on her hips. "I am not dirty."

"You certainly do need a bath, and you need to wash your hair also. We shall be seeing many of the neighbors, so you want to look your best."

The squawking of several chickens in the yard distracted her. Mark was laughing and chasing one of the smaller ones.

Mary would not give up. "Sounds to me as though we shall get dirty all over again if we are building a barn."

She chuckled. "Your father tells me it is the men and older boys who will build the barn. The women, girls, and young children shall have far lighter tasks. We shall help by getting the food set up and served and making sure the men have plenty to drink. I have never been to a barn raising so I may be wrong, but I believe it is a social time as much as a time to work. You might want to bring your sampler to work on, as your father said the women do handwork while they visit. But you may be too busy with the other children."

"Well, if I must." Mary followed her back to the cottage. "Are you going to take a bath?"

"Certainly, but not until later, when I have gotten more of the baking done." She walked over to the hearth and took a peek at some of the cornbread baking in a skillet and beans simmering in a large iron pot.

"Is there anything I can make to take along?" Mary reached for the bowl of fruit on the table.

"That would be a fine thing if you would like to help. A couple of pies would be nice."

Once the needed kitchen duties were completed, they walked down to the pond so the children could wash. It was a refreshing break, and it took as much effort to get the children out of the water as it had taken to talk them into it.

Back at the house, Mary sat on the bench drying her hair. "Will the Whitcombs be at the Taylors' tomorrow?"

Mark pulled up his stockings. "I hope so. I want to play with Teddy."

"Your father said they would probably be there." Heather bit her lip as she helped Mark put on his breeches. She dreaded encountering Hannah's sharp tongue and tendency to gossip. She tied Mary's stays around her shift. "We have the baking to finish and the garden to tend to yet this afternoon. There are beans and squash ready to pick."

"I will pick the beans." Mark smoothed back his hair, tying it into a club.

"Aye, but this time, only the biggest ones, Mark."

The rest of the day sped by. Matthew had taken food out to the field for his midday meal, so Heather and the children had more time to finish all that needed to be done to prepare for the barn raising. When he returned to the cabin early in the evening, the children were already anticipating the following day's activities.

Matthew bent over the table sniffing at the beans. "That smells wonderful. You have had a busy day here, I see."

The warm, exciting sensation that filled Heather when he brushed by was immediately replaced by remorse. *He cares nothing for me. Like the rest of us, he is enthused about tomorrow's festivities.* She wondered when he would give her more details about the release from her indenture.

"It is for tomorrow. Would you like some now for supper?"

"Yes, and some of the cornbread please." He walked over to the table where Mary was perusing the primer, while Heather dished up his meal. "How are you, young lady? What kind of day did you have?"

"A nice day, Papa, except we had to have baths. I helped Heather make berry cobblers and worked in the garden. I am going to wear my new blue frock tomorrow and have a fine time."

Caught up in the child's exuberance, Matthew smiled and pulled at a strand of hair hanging down from her cap.

"I will remember that tomorrow, as I am splitting logs, or trying to lift and mortar them into place in the hot sun, and think about what a fine time I am having."

"Oh, Papa." Mary giggled.

"It shall be a pleasant day." He smiled. "With everyone joining in, the barn will go up in no time. We all help each other out when there is a need, and besides that, this is a time for neighbors to gather and spend time together. I suspect the biggest challenge will be dragging you and Mark away when the day is done."

Her work completed, Heather got up from the table and headed toward her room. "I am going out for a while. I shall be back before it is time to put the children to bed—before dark."

"Where did you plan to take your walk?"

"To the pond." *Does he think I would run away?*

"I will finish up in the barn while you do that. We shall see you later."

"Aye."

She left the cottage, carrying soap and her clean clothes wrapped in a cotton cloth. She passed by the barn and saw the three totally absorbed in caring for the animals.

The lack of privacy made her anxious about bathing in the pond. She quickly waded in up to her neck. The cool water felt good against her warm skin. The barn raising tomorrow might be a good day for all of them. The children would enjoy it, and perhaps she would find friends like Amelia Turner among the other women present. She lathered her hair and dunked under the water. Rinsing her head a final time, she began checking off a list in her head of all she wanted to do to get ready for the next day. It was growing dark—time to dry off and get dressed. A sound in the nearby bushes startled her.

"How is the water? Inviting?" Matthew's teasing tone was unmistakable.

The chill of the pond was nothing compared to the one that traveled up her spine upon hearing his amused voice. Turning her head quickly in his direction, she was thankful it was dusk and that she was still in the water up to her shoulders. He knew she planned to come here to bathe. What mischief was in his head?

"Were you searching for me?" She could play his game.

❧ ❧

Matthew fought the impulse to grin. "Yes, I was. You sounded unsettled when you said you were going for a walk. I wanted to make sure you were safe." It was a relief to be merry, after the tension that had prevailed between them for so many days. "Honestly, I was not expecting to encounter a water nymph this evening."

"Mr.—Matthew, did you think I was trying to escape? I believe you promised me my freedom."

Heather's comment was a painful reminder of her romantic interlude with Thorpe. His intention to cancel her indenture was a thorn in his flesh. He needed to let her go but hated the thought of losing her. "Your point is well made, Heather. Would patience be one of your virtues?"

"I was not aware you thought I had any virtues."

That stung. He sat down not far from her pile of clothes. "You are not without certain charms." He leaned back against the trunk of a nearby tree and focused on the path. He avoided looking at her. His intent was not to embarrass her. "Your virtues ... let me see. You have done a fine job caring for the children and teaching them. The laundry and the house are kept clean. Mary is warming up to you, as difficult as it might be for her to admit it. Hmm, what else? You do not hesitate to take on new challenges, like seeing to the chickens, both alive and deceased, and tending the garden. You have been a willing worker and a good cook. So, as you see, Heather, I am acquainted with some of your attributes."

She was still up to her chin in the water when she caught him glancing her way. "Well, Mr. Stewart, as much as I would like to remain here and listen to you recite my praises, I am getting a wee bit cold, so I would be much obliged if we continued this conversation back at the cottage."

"We can do that. Allow me to assist you." He wished their repartee had not come to an end. He picked up the cotton wrap she had brought to dry herself. He stood and held it up as a screen.

"Nay. That is not what I had in mind. Be on your way, and I will follow soon. Should you be leaving the wee ones alone this long at night?"

"Ah, true. Yes, I will go back now." He got up and walked a few steps, but not before turning his head and grinning at her. "Do not dally. You will want to watch out for snakes. They get more active this time of night since it is when they hunt. And they are more difficult to see."

"Oh, my!"

He laughed and headed back toward the cottage. If only their relationship could be as lighthearted as it was tonight. He still needed to find a way to secure Heather's freedom, but his inclination was to stall. He was in no hurry to see her go.

※ ※

Snakes? Gingerly, Heather stepped from the cold water, then quickly dried herself and dressed. She flinched at every sound. He seemed to take a great deal of pleasure in vexing her. Hmm, snakes. Her eyes darted about, scanning the ground around her all the while. She wasted no time gathering her things, and then headed home with a brisk stride.

Matthew Stewart applied the charm when it suited him. He made it quite plain that he enjoyed their verbal sparring immensely. Well, if he was in a mood to tease her, it was an improvement over the days of being reserved with each other.

Once the children were in bed, she would retire. She'd let him humor himself all he wanted—by himself. With the cotton cloth now wrapped around her wet hair, she cautiously walked back the rest of the way to the cottage. She wanted no encounters with snakes.

※ ※

The next morning, everyone prepared for the outing with great excitement. Mary was delighted to be wearing her new dress. Heather decided she would also wear something new, the other gown that Maggie had given to her. Heather left her room, carrying the straw hat for Mary.

"I trimmed your hat with this blue ribbon. It is about the same shade as your dress."

Mary studied her with an odd expression on her face.

"What is the matter, child? Do you not like it?"

Mary's eyes appeared glazed when she answered. "Nothing … Nothing is the matter. I do like it. Thank you. Please tie it on for me."

"Certainly. And I must say, you are lovely in your new frock, Mary."

By nine, the wagon was loaded with the remaining tools and provisions. Matthew lifted the children into the back of the wagon before assisting Heather. Once seated, his glance at her was perplexing. Had she not dressed correctly for a picnic and barn raising? She straightened the skirt of her petticoat and retied her straw hat. There was no understanding the enigmatic expression on his face.

The children chattered the entire time it took to ride to the Taylors' in the late-summer sunshine. Many of the neighbors had already arrived when they pulled up in their wagon. Once stopped, Heather helped Matthew unload it. Mark toted the cornbread, and Mary carried one of the jugs of cider. When the food was deposited on a nearby table, the children stood back shyly, surveying the crowd. They were obviously searching for familiar faces.

As the Stewarts approached the gathering of neighbors, George Whitcomb and a man with very red hair came over to greet them.

"Matthew, 'tis good to see you." The red-haired man grabbed Matthew's arm and slapped his back in a genial greeting.

"You also, Samuel, and it is good to see you, George." Matthew turned toward the younger man. "Samuel, it must please you to see such a turnout. We should be able to complete it today."

"Yes, and we are blessed to have the weather cooperate." The tall redhead glanced at her.

With his arm resting lightly on her back, Matthew drew her into the circle. "I do not believe you have met my wife, Heather, and you have not seen my children, Mary and Mark, in a long while."

Samuel nodded to her. "Caroline and I are so grateful that you all joined us here today. Oh, here she is now." He walked over to the woman approaching. "Caroline, this is Matthew's wife, Heather, and you remember Mary and Mark."

"Of course I do. It is a pleasure meeting you, Heather. We were told Matthew had remarried. They said you were lovely, and I can see it was no exaggeration."

Embarrassed by the compliment, she curtsied.

The young woman's hair reminded her of black satin, and her complexion was creamy with a slight smattering of freckles. Her clear blue eyes gave the woman a striking appearance.

"Thank you for including us. We shall do what we can to help."

Caroline took her arm and guided her toward a group of women. "Shall we go join the other women and leave the men to their work? Come, children."

Heather studied the woman next to her, younger than she by several years. She wished she had Caroline's self-assurance and grace.

"Now, do not worry about Mark and Mary. They shall mix in." Caroline's confidence and sweet demeanor were inviting. "It will take no time for them to make friends."

Heather smiled. "Have you any children?"

"Yes, we have one child, a baby boy."

Heather watched Mary and Mark happily scamper off with the Whitcomb children. She was not concerned about the children's ability to fit into the group, but about herself being accepted by the other women. Observing them, she was certain that she had made the right choice in selecting the buff-colored frock to wear. Once she had lowered the hem, it fit perfectly.

Amelia Turner came up to her. "We are glad you came, Heather, and will have a chance to meet more of your neighbors."

"Thank you. I look forward to it."

Caroline introduced her to the women seated nearby on benches and logs. There were Betsy Edwards, the doctor's wife she had met at church, and Hannah Whitcomb. Sally, Amelia, and Margaret were the other ladies. Babies sat on their mothers' laps or lay on blankets set out on a grassy area beside them.

She excused herself to set the basket on the table brought outside for the day's activities. Ignoring the whispering among the women, she braced herself, turned, and walked back toward the group with as much confidence as she could muster.

"Heather, how nice it is to see you again." Hannah Whitcomb was seated on a bench near the other ladies. "And how is everything in the Stewart household?"

"We are very well, Mrs. Whitcomb. I must thank you again for the dinner and the hospitality you extended to us."

"It was our pleasure, and so nice to see the children again after so long." Hannah motioned for her to sit beside her. "How fortunate Mary did not take ill after that terribly stormy night. She was so upset. We heard that Mark was ill and gave you a scare a while back. Is everyone well now?"

"Aye, everyone is fine now. It is kind of you to inquire." It had taken Hannah no time to bring up Mary's escapade. And she knew about Mark. How much more did Hannah know of the goings-on in their home?

She turned to Betsy Edwards on her other side. "It is nice to see you again, Mrs. Edwards. We were so grateful when your husband came and checked on Mark. We were worried about the wee lad's temperature. But I fear we troubled the doctor needlessly since he was already on the mend."

"No need to apologize. We are quite used to seeing people at all hours." Her smile was warm and inviting. "Tell me, dear, what do you think of Virginia?"

"Oh, it is beautiful and very different from Scotland. The climate here is warmer."

"Summers are warm, but the fall is delightful. I hope you will be happy here."

"Thank you, Mrs. Edwards." She smiled and relaxed a little.

Amelia Turner pointed to where Mark and Mary had joined a group of children. "I see your youngsters are already joined in with my children and the others playing blind man's bluff." Amelia flashed her engaging smile.

Caroline Taylor waved to the women. "Ladies, if any of you need to heat your food, the fire is ready now."

Two tripods had been erected on either side of the large open pit. An iron rod with several hanging hooks suspended the pots over a low flame. Heather took their large iron pot full of beans and hung it from one of the many hooks. It would not take long for them to heat up. There were many savory dishes, as well as a fair number of bowls and plates of baked goods.

She walked by where the children were playing before going to see the barn, which was taking shape.

❧ ☙

The men had formed organized teams and were busy constructing the barn walls on the ground, getting all the pieces in place. Jugs of cider sat on a table next to a water barrel for the men to quench their thirst.

Matthew spotted Heather standing nearby and walked over to her. She looked comely today in the buff-colored frock, and so much healthier than when she arrived in April. He reached down for the water gourd and took a long drink. "How are you doing with the rest of the women? Getting acquainted?"

"Aye, they are very nice. Caroline Taylor has made me at ease in the group. I chatted with Amelia Turner and Betsy Edwards again. And the children wasted no time in finding friends." Her smile warmed his heart.

"The Turners are fine friends, and Caroline and Samuel are good people. Caroline had a baby not long ago." He took a kerchief out and wiped the sweat from his brow and neck. He caught her smiling up at him. It was encouraging to see her mix well with the other ladies. Perhaps that would make her feel more like she belonged here.

"You are making good progress on the barn. Does everyone have a specific job?"

"Yes. A great deal of planning and preparation is done before the men even start construction on timber-framed buildings. The more experienced men draw up the plans and calculate what is needed. The men gravitate toward certain skills they have honed over the years. Samuel and Aaron, over there, are masters at joinery and doweling work." He filled the gourd and took another drink.

"I see even the older boys are put to use."

"They fetch parts and tools, all while learning from the men. They will be doing this one day so they need to learn. Wait till you see us raise the walls."

"That must be fascinating to behold. What a blessing it is cool today, and there is a breeze." Her eyes remained on the growing structure as they talked.

He refilled the gourd, drank again, and gazed skyward. "If only we would get some rain. Every planter around will suffer if this dry spell continues."

She smiled. "Perhaps the rain is waiting for the roof of Mr. Taylor's barn to be on."

"Good thought." He longed for moments like this with easy banter, but the men needed his assistance. "I had better get back to work. Enjoy your time with the ladies." He smiled and headed back toward the barn, then turned and watched her return to the ladies' gathering spot. It was not surprising that the other women welcomed her. Heather had a winsome way about her.

❧

Heather glanced back and watched him walk away. Matthew Stewart was occupying more and more of her thoughts. She could no longer deny that she had feelings for him. Was he unaware of his appealing looks and manner? Perhaps that was part of his charm. He had a pleasant and kind nature. Her shoulders stiffened. How could he have been so quick to misjudge her and think she would leave with Travis Thorpe? And what was his intention in dissolving her indenture? *I must not dwell on it.* Not here. Not now.

The women were arranging the table for the meal when she rejoined them. They were an easy group to enjoy.

Caroline placed a platter of sliced meats on the table. "Heather, please help me gather the children."

Once the wee ones were served and seated on blankets under the trees, Caroline called to the men. The older children had been strategically placed far enough away so as not to disturb the adults, yet close enough to keep an eye on them. When everyone had filled their plates, they separated into two groups. The women gathered back on their benches and logs, near the babies, in the shade of two large oak trees. The men sat under a nearby maple, clearly enjoying whatever it was they were talking about. Their laughter grew loud on occasion.

Heather took a seat next to Caroline.

Hannah sat beside her. "George tells me that your hired man is gone. I thought Matthew planned on keeping him through the final harvest. Change of plans?" Hannah continued eating the entire time she was quizzing her, rubbing some cornbread in a circular motion in the puddle of gravy on her plate.

"The man—" Heather cleared her throat. She glanced around the group and noticed all eyes on her. "He, Mr. Thorpe, proved to be untrustworthy, so he was dismissed." Hopefully, that would end the questioning.

"Dismissed?" Hannah chuckled, shaking her head.

Heather's eyes traveled around the group. Would one of the women change the subject? Perhaps she would strike up a conversation with—

"Whatever for?"

She gulped. The heat rose to her face. "It is a private matter."

"Hmph!" Hannah studied her for a long time before continuing. "So tell us, Heather, what brought you to Virginia?" The woman was determined to draw her into conversation. "Do you still have family in Scotland?"

Heather sat for a moment in silence. "We were shopkeepers … my family owned a dry goods business in Perth." She hesitated and noticed interest in the women's faces. "My parents are both deceased."

Perhaps the simple explanation would suffice. She smiled at Caroline.

"But you did not say how it was you came to Virginia—as an indentured? I mean it is odd that—"

"Mrs. Whitcomb." She turned toward the older woman. "I choose to live in the present and not dwell on the past. Right now, I would like to enjoy this lovely day and the blessing of spending it with everyone here." Had she been too abrupt? Hopefully, the other women had not noticed her shaking.

Undaunted, Hannah rested her hand on Heather's knee. "How auspicious for you to be pur—I mean, to have the opportunity to begin your life over again with a home, husband, children, and even the deceased wife's wardrobe. You have done quite well."

Stunned by the remark, her eyes were fixed on her plate. Heat rose to her face. *I am wearing Elizabeth's clothes? Maggie said he approved giving them to me.* A lump formed in her throat. The woman was a menace. She needed to get away from her.

Caroline gently placed her hand on Heather's arm. "Heather, would you help me get some more cider from the cellar?"

You are good, Lord. Still silent, she got up and followed Caroline in the direction of the small frame dwelling, grateful to escape the group of women with some small portion of her dignity intact. Her mind raced. Why had Matthew not said anything to her about the gown? Maggie should have told her it was Elizabeth's. It was no wonder that Mary was so taken aback seeing her this morning. She must have remembered the dress. Details of the morning continued to crowd her mind until she reached the cellar.

"Please do not let what Hannah says upset you, Heather. She is a difficult one to get along with and often manages to say the wrong thing or find someone to torment. We all have learned to tolerate her insensitive ways. There is nothing wrong with your wearing Elizabeth's clothes." Caroline paused, slightly out of breath, and handed Heather another jug. "I think it was a kind and generous gesture on Matthew's part. It is a good sign. It means he is recovering from the grief of the past year." She picked up two more jugs, turned, and smiled. "Now we can take three of these to the men and save one for us."

Once the cider was delivered to the men, they made their way back to the other women. As they walked, Caroline reached out, giving Heather's hand a squeeze. "I was very fond of Elizabeth. We all were. She was a lovely, special friend, whom we all miss. But that does not mean that we cannot welcome you and hope to be your friends also. As for Hannah, do not fret about her odd comments. Elizabeth lived much closer to her and had to contend with her much more often than we did, and it was not easy for her either."

So Hannah was unkind to Elizabeth as well. Perhaps Hannah was just an unhappy woman who lived to harass anyone in her sphere of influence. Poor Elizabeth.

The heaviness in her heart lifted as she recognized a new kinship with Matthew's late wife. "Thank you for your kindness, Caroline—for recognizing how uncomfortable I was, and for rescuing me."

Caroline hugged her, and they both laughed.

CHAPTER 18

It was dusk by the time the Stewarts arrived back at the cottage, after an active day in the late August sunshine. Even though the ride was short, the children managed to drift off to sleep. Heather and Matthew each carried a child into the house without waking them.

She whispered as they laid the children on the pallet. "You look weary. I can get them settled into bed. You go see to the animals. Do you need any help when I am finished?"

"No, not out there. I am exhausted. Would you check in the hutch and see if you can find any of the salve? I suspect I will be sore tomorrow. I am off to the pond to wash when I finish in the barn." He shivered, imagining her hands covering his tired muscles in salve. Would she? Or would she hand him the bottle and excuse herself for bed? If only … "If onlys" did not happen. Not in this life. All she wanted was her freedom, not a widower and two unruly children.

He climbed to the loft to find some clean clothes, while she finished bringing in the day's remnants from the wagon.

When he came back down to the kitchen, she stood by the table, looking beautiful in Elizabeth's clothes. Maggie was wise to suggest they would meet her needs. She handed him the bottle of salve. "Are you hungry?" she asked quietly.

Hungry? Yes, but not for food. He shook those inclinations from his head. He briefly glanced at the bottle in his hand before catching her eye. Her head was tilted waiting for him to respond. "No, thank you, Heather. I am thirsty, though. I will go fill the jug with water before I go."

She walked over to the children's pallet and gently pulled off the sleeping boy's shoes. She glanced over her shoulder at him with a teasing look. "You be careful at the pond. One needs to keep an eye out for snakes, particularly at night."

With the lantern in hand, he walked to the pond. A dip in the cold water was exactly what he needed, and not just to get clean. Was there any way to alter the direction their relationship was headed—to her departure? There had to be a way to reach her. He was not ready to give up. Not yet.

❧ ☙

Everyone was very busy the next couple of weeks. Matthew, like many of the other local farmers, gathered wheat to take to the mill, as well as the tobacco and corn crops to take into town. The weather was so dry that all the farmers were anxious to get this harvest behind them. Matthew was grateful for the yield, given the drought that had plagued most of the summer. In another month, the land would be plowed again for the planting of barley and rye.

Late one morning, Heather had just finished weeding the garden bed in front of the cottage. She got up slowly and stretched to relieve her sore muscles, then walked to where the children had been playing on the side of the barn. Where were they? She searched in every direction.

"Mary, are you in here?" She stepped through the doorway into the hot, dark barn. There was the rustle of hay, and Mary appeared.

"What are you doing in here, lass? Did you not say that you would watch over Mark while I worked in the garden?"

"Yes, ma'am. But I got tired of watching him. I decided to get some hay and make a bed for my doll. I am going to stuff it in this old sack." She had a sheepish expression on her face as she held up the small canvas sack.

Heather bit her lip, fearing she would say something she would later regret. She dashed out of the barn and finally spotted Mark on the other side of the cottage, playing with a large squash in the vegetable garden. Mary stood watching from the barn door.

How could she convey to Mary the seriousness of the situation without alienating her? She reached out to the young girl and took her hand, aching at the sight of her guilty face. "Mary, Mark is still a wee laddie and needs to have someone watching out for him. I asked you to help by minding him so that I could get some work done. I depend on you, Mary, because you have proven to be reliable, and because I believe you will call me if you need help. In the future, you must tell me if you cannot watch him. Now, will you please go get Mark so we can carry some water up from the pond? The garden is so dry."

"May we wade in it for a while, please?"

"Aye, but only for a bit. Your father said he would be home for dinner, and we must get that started."

"I am sorry that I stopped watching Mark without telling you."

She smiled down at Mary's contrite face and gave the child a hug. "Thank you, dear. All is well." Perhaps there was hope. Mary certainly was more cooperative and agreeable these days.

❧ ❧

Later, when dinner was over, Matthew got up and put on his hat. "I am going to the Whitcombs'."

Mary reached for her father's hand. "Papa, may we go also?"

"No. Not this time, poppet. It will only be some of the men getting together to plan the new church. Now, with the harvest over for another season, we need to start rebuilding it." Matthew searched for some papers in the drawer of the hutch. "When we were at the barn raising, the men decided to rebuild the church after the harvest. We have imposed on the generosity of the Turner and the Edwards families long enough to open their homes for our church services."

Heather cleared the dishes from the table. "I expect the pastor is ready for the church to be rebuilt also."

"Our itinerant clergyman visits infrequently, as he has various congregations under his care. As you saw, when he is not in attendance at church, the men take turns reading from the Scriptures. After the harvest and the fall crops are planted, the church construction will begin."

Matthew was almost ready to leave when the sound of a horse approaching at a gallop caught their attention. He hurried outside, and she and the children followed behind him to see what the commotion was all about. "I wonder why George is in such a hurry."

George Whitcomb was nearly out of breath from the ride. "Matt, there is a fire at the Taylors' farm. Others are on the way there. I wanted to tell you." He turned his mount and departed the way he had come.

Matthew ran for the barn with Heather following.

"What can I do to help?"

"Nothing, yet. Please pray everyone is safe. And look after the children. They will be worried."

"Oh, aye, I shall."

"Thank God, there is a creek near their place." He saddled Honey and walked her out of the barn.

Mark stood with Mary in front of the cottage. She ran to his side. "Papa, be careful."

"I will, poppet. You mind Heather." He headed into the dust stirred up by George's horse.

Still stunned from George's news, Heather and the children walked back into the cottage. Distracted, she began clearing the dishes from the table, but stopped and called the children to her.

Mark was obviously confused, while Mary looked worried.

"Your father and other neighbors are going to help put out the fire at the Taylors' house. I think we should pray for all of them." They all knelt.

"Almighty God, please be with Caroline, Samuel, and their son.

Protect them and give them strength to persevere this day. Please grant that the fire is put out quickly and that no injuries befall them … or those offering assistance. We ask these things in the name of our Lord Jesus Christ. Amen."

Mark tugged at her skirt. "When will Papa be back?"

"Do not fret. He will be back as soon as he feels he has done everything he can for the Taylors."

Restless, she made multiple trips to the window, wondering what was happening at the Taylor farm. Smoke was visible in the sky when she wandered to the porch.

When she came back inside, Mary came and stood beside her, also staring out the window. "We shall have to wait, children." She placed her arm around Mary. "Please, Lord, let it rain."

The afternoon stretched on forever. Heather's ears were always half listening for the sound of hoof beats, but none came. Instead of kneading the bread dough, she found herself pounding it. *This is foolish. Everything shall be well. Believe that.* With the bread set aside to rise, she took on the floors, scrubbing with a vengeance. Finally, exhausted, she went out to the front porch to sit and wait. The children followed her.

Mark went to the yard, where he appeared to be playing with a beetle.

Mary sat on the step. "I am frightened. I wish Papa would come home."

"So do I." Heather got up from the chair and sat on the step, putting an arm around the child. She scanned the sky. "Try not to fear. I am sure your father is just doing all he can to help. It looks like we will get rain."

It was not long before the rain did come. It was a gentle rain, the best kind. They all moved to the porch chairs, out of the rain. Heather sat enjoying the sound it made falling on the ground and foliage. What an answer to prayer. She was just getting up to go inside, to prepare the children's supper, when she saw two riders approaching. Walking to the edge of the porch, she squinted.

Uneasiness filled her as she watched them slowly approach. Something was wrong.

"Children, take your things and go inside. I shall be there in a minute." She glanced at Mary, who also watched the approaching horses. "Go on now, please." Matthew was approaching on Honey—who was the other rider? It was too hard to distinguish them in the rain, but it appeared to be a woman. Her stomach tightened, and fear rose in her throat. *Nay. Nay. Surely there must be a good reason.* She was off the steps and taking long strides to reach the two as they approached the house. In a moment, she was searching Caroline Taylor's pale face—a face in shock.

Matthew also appeared ashen and somber as he approached her. "There has been a terrible accident, Heather. We shall speak of this later. Caroline is going to stay with us. Please help me get her settled."

Without a word, they helped her off the horse, and Heather guided her into the dry cottage.

Matthew followed. Inside, he poured Caroline a cup of cider while Heather put her cotton shawl around the woman's soaked and shaking shoulders. She wrapped her arms around Caroline and held her in a long hug.

"Caroline, drink this." Matthew handed her the pewter cup.

He whispered softly in Heather's ear. "Please find her something dry to wear and help her into bed?" His face was nearly as gray as the wet shirt he was wearing.

She nodded and guided the distraught woman to the bedroom. There she undressed Caroline, who remained dazed and speechless. She helped her into her own clean shift and gently led her to the large bed.

The young woman's dazed expression broke her heart. She helped her lie down, and then pulled the covers up around Caroline's stricken face. She gently stroked her hair. "There, now you try to sleep. We can talk after you have had a chance to rest."

Heather closed the door of the bedroom. In the kitchen,

Matthew had gotten the children seated for a small meal.

Mary touched her father's hand. "Why is Mrs. Taylor here, Papa?"

His face was sooty and somber, his clothes wet and filthy. "We will talk about it later, children."

Heather dampened a cloth and began to reach out and wipe his face, but stopped and handed it to him. "You had best be changing into something dry too. Caroline is in bed. I hope she will be able to sleep." She glanced at the children, who were finishing their supper. "Once we get them settled for the night, please might we have a few minutes, Matthew?"

"Yes." His shoulders sagged as he made his way to the loft. "Bring us some tea to the porch."

When the children were finally quiet on their pallet, she joined Matthew outside. He had cleaned himself by the water barrel and was now in dry clothes, leaning against a beam that supported the porch roof and gazing off into the distance.

She set the tea beside the lantern on the small table and settled into the chair, wrapping the shawl tightly around her. Anxiety filled her as she waited to learn the details of the fire.

"There was nothing to do except make sure the fire did not spread any further. It happened so fast." He shook his head and rubbed his bloodshot eyes. "Apparently, Samuel was in the new barn when Caroline ... I think she was setting out the wash ... anyway, she noticed smoke and flames coming from the house. She started screaming, and Sam ran into the house to get the baby. A beam must have fallen on him. Aaron Turner was on his way over to the Whitcombs' by way of the Taylors'. He spotted the smoke, and it is a good thing he did. I think Caroline might have tried going into the house after Sam and the baby."

"Samuel and Seth ... both gone?" She gasped.

He nodded.

Her chest tightened, and a bad taste rose to her mouth. How? Had it only been a fortnight since they were all enjoying each other's company at the Taylors'?

"How awful. That poor woman. Oh, Matthew, I am so glad you brought her back here. Losing her husband and wee bairn that way—I cannot imagine." She shook in anguish, tears rolling down her cheeks. "Has she any people of her own around here?"

He finished his tea and set the tankard down. "It occurs to me that Samuel once said her family lives in Maryland, near Baltimore, I believe. We can ask her. She has the farm, and the barn and the animals are left, but she may not want to go back." He put his hands to his face before running his fingers through his hair, obviously weary from the calamitous day. "Samuel was a fine man and a good friend. He will be missed by all of us, and now we must take care of Caroline for him."

She studied him, touched by his distress over the death of a friend and his concern for Caroline. What could she say to help Caroline or Matthew? After a few silent minutes, his gaze rested on her.

"The men are going to gather at George's tomorrow morning. We will plan on what to do to assist Caroline. Sam and Seth are with the doctor and Betsy Edwards to be prepared for their burial service. The plan is to bury them tomorrow afternoon."

Slowly Heather rose from the chair and walked back toward the door to go inside. Stopping, she tentatively reached out, gently touching his arm. "I am so sorry about Samuel and the bairn. Will you tell the children?"

His eyes, filled with sadness and regret, raised to hers. "Yes, tomorrow."

"I shall go in and check on Caroline now. Good night." With a heavy heart, she went inside.

❦

The service and burial for Samuel and Seth took place as planned at the Taylors' farm. A dinner followed, with all the neighbors bringing food to share. But how different an atmosphere it was than the one at the barn raising, just a couple of weeks before. What had been joy and merriment was now sadness and loss.

In the days following the tragedy, friends dropped by the Stewarts' farm to offer Caroline their condolences. Matthew and Heather made every effort to comfort her. When Caroline finally started talking about what happened, her acceptance of the situation and the healing process had begun.

Two mornings after the fire, Heather spotted Amelia Turner approaching the cottage. She brought some clothing and other items shared from neighbors to meet Caroline's needs.

No one was surprised when Caroline said she wanted to go to her family in Maryland. Matthew saw that her letter to them was posted. Meanwhile, she was made very much at home with the Stewarts.

"You have all been so good to me, Heather. I so wish that you would let me sleep in the loft, though. I regret putting Matthew out of your room. Though I must admit, having you there beside me when the nightmares come has been such a comfort. How generous Matthew has been."

"Do not fret about it, Caroline. We would not want it any other way." *Nothing dishonest about that.*

"I do miss them so, Heather." Once again the tears came. "Why is it you must lose someone before realizing how vital and precious they are—how much you love them?" The anguish on Caroline's face nearly brought her to tears. "I shall never get over the loss of Seth. That baby was part of me. Even though I did not have him very long, he had such a grip on my heart. But Heather, I never realized that Samuel also was so much a part of me—how much I loved him. He was always there, as long as I can remember. I was but a girl when we became acquainted. Every year, Samuel would visit his cousins in Baltimore. That is how I met him. What is worse, I never told him how much I loved him. Not really."

She put her arms around Caroline and hugged her. "I cannot

believe that Samuel was unaware. While you may not have shared the depth of your affection for him, I am sure you demonstrated your love in many different ways. Aye, and you gave him the wee bairn."

Their hands were clasped together. The desperate look in Caroline's eyes was heart wrenching. "I hope you are right."

❧ ❧

With Caroline's decision to return to Maryland, the neighbors rallied to help her dispose of her farm. Three of the neighbors that bordered on the Taylor farm offered a fair price for those parcels that abutted their properties. The fourth parcel, several acres that remained, was purchased for the site of the community's new church. The men decided it was a far more desirable location, with the creek nearby and the barn already standing. With modifications to the barn and some finishing touches, it would be reconfigured for a church. It would make a more than adequate schoolhouse when a more permanent sanctuary was built. Samuel and Seth, both buried on a grassy slope nearby, would be the first in the new cemetery. Everyone benefited from the transaction, and Caroline would return to her parents' home with some funds in hand, where, hopefully, she would make a new start.

❧ ❧

"The wagon is here, and I think we had better go." Matthew stood on the cottage porch. "Caroline, are you sure you are up to this? Everyone will understand if you choose not to come."

"Thank you, Matthew, but this is important to me. I need to see the place this one last time, and I need to thank everyone for all they have done. When my father comes for me, I shall be better able to walk away from it all. And I would like to share in the first

Sabbath in our … in your new church."

"Caroline, it shall always be 'our' church. The Taylors shall always be a part of it." Matthew put his arm around the small, delicate woman as he led her from the cottage. "Come. Heather and the children are waiting in the wagon."

The men had worked diligently to refashion the barn into a chapel. More windows were cut, and an altar and benches built.

Despite their joy in sharing their first Sabbath morning in their new church, the community did not forget Samuel and little Seth Taylor. When the morning's readings were over, and the chapel had been dedicated, Matthew asked for a moment of silence to remember Samuel and Seth. He offered a prayer for Caroline.

"Almighty God, we ask your blessings on Caroline as she leaves us. Watch over her, and through the power of Your Spirit, help her to find peace, comfort, and joy. May she discover friends in her new home who will support and encourage her. And grant that she never forgets the friends she has here. We ask this in the name of our Lord and Savior, Jesus Christ. Amen."

Everyone brought food for the social that followed the service. Several of the men carried benches from the church outside to provide seating.

Matthew tugged at Heather's elbow and nodded in the direction of Hannah Whitcomb, who was approaching them. "I think Betsy Edwards and Amelia Turner might like to join Caroline and us here for dinner. Hopefully, we might avoid any of Hannah's unanticipated and possibly inappropriate remarks," he said in her ear.

Heather glanced from him to Hannah. "Aye, you are right. I shall ask them." He watched as Heather walked briskly to where Amelia and Betsy were standing speaking with Caroline. She had been remarkable these past few weeks, welcoming Caroline into their home and caring for her with such love. Heather was stunning, standing there in one of Elizabeth's frocks. He took a deep breath. Their marriage made it possible to have the children home. But it was more than that. She had brought joy back into his life. He looked forward to seeing her at midday and every evening. If only things had worked out differently between the two of them. *Lord, I believed this marriage was an answer for all of us. If it is Your plan that Heather stay, please show me what to do, and speak to her heart.*

While the festivities were somewhat subdued, it was a chance for people to reaffirm their need for a place for worship and acknowledge that they did, in fact, depend greatly on God and each other in times of need.

Three days later, Caroline Taylor's father arrived by carriage. They said their good-byes early the following morning, amidst tears.

"I cannot thank you enough for all the love and support you have both given me these last few weeks. Heather, I am sorry for all the restless nights. Now you shall be able to get some sleep. Thank you, Matthew, for all the encouragement and for putting up with a weepy woman."

Caroline's father placed his daughter's bags in the carriage. "Matthew, our home is always open to you and yours." He handed Matthew a piece of paper. "I have written down where we are in Baltimore. We have a big house so you will not put us out. And again, thank you for all the care you have given my daughter. I am sorry that I was unable to arrive here any sooner."

"Our pleasure, sir. It was time well spent, and we were happy to open our home to Caroline. We will miss her." The men shook hands, and Caroline's father joined his daughter in the carriage.

The Stewarts all waved at the departing carriage, and the children walked back into the house. Matthew turned to Heather. Looking into her clear blue eyes distracted him from what he wanted to say. It would be so easy to take her in his arms. No. This was not the right time or place. "Thank you, Heather, for all you did for Caroline. When you lose your mate and child, it tears you … well, thank you for being so good to her."

"I shall miss her. She was good company. I pray that she will recover, and one day find another to fill her heart." Heather turned to go inside.

Matthew followed her. "That is a good prayer. Caroline would make someone a fine wife." Heather stopped and wheeled around to face him, and he came to an abrupt stop to avoid ramming into her. She had the oddest expression on her face—as if he had told her the answer to a riddle. Women—would he ever understand them?

CHAPTER 19

Later that same week, the Duncans made their long-awaited visit, bringing joy and laughter back into the Stewart household. It was late morning when the sound of a wagon coming up the path caught Heather's attention. She came around the side of the cottage where she had been spreading laundry. The children were watching the tadpoles they had found at the pond and now had in a bucket.

"Mary, please go tell your father the Duncans are here. He is over in the south field." Brushing a few wild strands of hair off her face, Heather made her way to the front of the cottage. It would be so good to see Maggie again.

As the Duncans and their children poured out of the wagon, she took off her apron, smiled, and waved. "What a wonderful surprise. It is so good to see you all. May I get you something cool to drink? We have water, cider, or some tea. You must be thirsty after the trip."

"Some water or cider would be wonderful." Maggie carried William and followed Heather to the porch. "Jean, please place the packages inside on the table." She turned to Heather. "I brought a few things for dinner and the family. You must try the sweet bread. The trip out here was so pleasant, but the leaves are turning so early this year. I suppose because it has been dry."

Adam joined them on the porch. "How has the harvest been, Heather? Everyone has been hard hit by this drought."

"Mr. Stewart had been most concerned about it. He says the crop was somewhat smaller this year, but we should have plenty to eat, and we are putting up a lot for the winter months."

Maggie had a puzzled frown on her face when Adam whispered, "Mr. Stewart?"

Heather shuddered. They did not realize she heard his remark.

Adam returned to the wagon and began unhitching the horse. "It has been hard on everyone. There has not been as much produce coming into town. You appear to be adjusting well to living out here on the farm." He tied the horse to a rail near the water trough, and they walked into the cottage.

Heather set a pitcher of water on the table. "I am learning new tasks all the time. It is more isolated than I am accustomed to, but it suits me fine. I am becoming acquainted with the neighbors. And now that we have a church to attend, I will meet more families."

Adam's eyebrows were raised in amazement. "The church has been rebuilt?"

Heather recounted the story of the barn raising and the subsequent fire as Maggie and Adam listened. As she talked, she poured water and cider for everyone.

The children had stayed outside, as Mark wanted to show them the bucket with the tadpoles. Heather went to the front door and waved for them to come inside.

Matthew and Mary came in as Heather finished telling Adam and Maggie about Caroline and her father's departure. Smoothing out his wavy hair, Matthew greeted his old friends.

"Matthew Stewart, your skin is as dark as molasses," Maggie chided him. "Are you in need of a shirt?"

"No. Sometimes it is cooler to work without one. This way makes a bit less wash for my wife, too."

Heather's face grew warm when he referred to her as his wife. She was hardly a wife—more like a housekeeper. Gazing at him chatting with his old friends, sadness seeped in. What would it have been like to genuinely be a part of this family? There was an unmistakable barrier between them. Had she erected it or had he? She tucked her emotions away and began to arrange dishes for the meal.

Maggie joined her, a welcome interruption to her troubled sentiments. "Is there anything I can do to help you with dinner?"

"Nay, Maggie. Talk with me while I baste the meat and finish shelling these peas." A brief sadness filled her as she gazed at the baby in Maggie's arms. Gently, she rubbed a finger against the baby's soft cheek as his mother sat and began to rock the child. Her heart ached when she remembered Caroline and the loss of her baby son.

"Wee William has truly grown in … these six weeks, I guess it has been. Such a bonny laddie. You must be delighted."

"Oh, aye, we are all lovin' the wee lad. But I should not think it would be too long before you have a bairn of your own."

"Nay, t'would take a mira—" She reddened, caught her breath, and turned away, picking up the pea pod she had dropped, but not before noticing the questioning expression on Maggie's face. "Maggie, I have been meaning to thank you for the lovely dresses, cloak, and shawl."

Maggie got up and went over to a basket by the hearth. "I am so glad you like them. I had a cape and did not need another. And as you can see, the dresses are more than a mite snug for me. You are slender enough for them."

She followed Maggie over to where she was settling William in his basket. "Maggie?"

"Aye?"

"I did not realize the clothes had been Elizabeth's. I think it gave Mary a start to see them on me. And I am surprised that Mr. Stewart did not mind my having them. I mean, I would think it would pain him to see me wearing his wife's clothes."

Maggie straightened and shook her head. "I am sorry, Heather. I suppose I should have said something, but I was certain Matthew would. And I had not considered that Mary would remember the dresses. Matthew is a practical as well as a generous man. He recognized that you needed clothes. And honestly, Heather, he was certain it would have been Elizabeth's wish that you have them.

After all, dear, you are raising her children. I am certain that she is smiling down on the job you are doing with them."

"I suppose that if I am to live with a ghost, I should praise God that it is a saintly one that resides here." She gave a nervous laugh as she sat down and went back to shelling her peas.

Maggie came over to the table beside her and started cutting the bread. "Here, taste this." She handed her a piece of the bread.

"Mmm, that is delicious. You must tell me how you make it."

"I will." Maggie put the knife down and faced her. "Heather, are you sure it is the ghost of Elizabeth Stewart that is troubling you? Or might there be some ghosts of your own?"

Heather was grateful to be rescued from any more of Maggie's probing questions when Adam and Matthew's voices grew louder. The two men were embroiled in a political discussion, which continued until dinner was ready.

"I shall go and call the children to clean up." She wiped her hands on her apron as Maggie finished setting the table.

"I am off to put on a clean shirt for dinner," Matthew called as he made his way to the loft.

She turned to Maggie. She wanted to ask her how to make that sweet bread.

Maggie watched Matthew climb the ladder to the loft. She exchanged a befuddled grimace with Adam.

"It is not our affair, Maggie." Adam quietly warned.

"It does not appear to be theirs either. His clothes are in the loft." Maggie shook her head.

Heather overheard the exchange and blushed. So now the Duncans knew the truth of their marriage, too. She turned and left to find the children.

Despite the awkward moments, the afternoon passed pleasantly, and everyone was still in lively spirits when it came time for the Duncans to leave.

As they walked to the wagon, she squeezed Maggie's hand. "Please come again soon. I do not remember when I have had such a grand day."

Maggie embraced her and smiled. "I wish you realized what a blessing you are to this family, Heather."

Adam bid farewell to them as his family climbed into the wagon and headed off. "We shall come again before the weather turns. You take care."

Later that evening, after the children had been put to bed and Matthew had gone out to the barn, she went outside and sat on the chair. She resisted the pattern she had established of slipping off to her room as soon as the children went to sleep and her work was done. Twilight was beautiful, and she wanted to enjoy it, with the breeze light and cool against her face. She pulled the cap and pins from her hair, freeing it to float around her shoulders. It was refreshing to be outside on such a pleasant evening, listening to the night sounds. Aye, it had been a nice day with so much laughter—welcome sounds in the house after weeks of sharing Caroline's sorrow. She had already begun to miss the young widow and wondered what would become of Caroline. She had no doubt that she would marry again, and God willing, to someone who would give her another bairn. Caroline was too kind and lovely a person to be alone for long.

"May I join you?"

Matthew's words startled her. "Aye, of course." She straightened and sat very still and upright. "I was enjoying the evening air and reflecting on what a delightful day it has been."

"Yes. It has been a fine day and a long time since the Duncans visited. It was good to have them here again."

For a few moments, neither of them spoke. The silence was tranquil, not awkward, as it had been at other times.

"Mr. Stewart, I never thanked you for the clothes. I mean, allowing me to wear her ... your wife's clothes."

"Hmm." He leaned against the doorframe. "The dresses are becoming on you." His gaze rested on her. "You are a lovely woman, Heather."

She was intensely grateful that the darkness hid what she was sure was a crimson face. "I have no doubt that your wife was a beauty, seeing her children and hearing of her many fine qualities. You must miss her terribly." She closed her eyes in dismay. *Oh, for mercy's sake, what a mindless comment. I should go inside before I say anything else so foolish.* The man was entitled to his privacy.

"Yes, she was beautiful and good. Elizabeth was a generous, kind, and loving wife, and a joy to be around."

Heather was torn. She wanted to stay and hear more of what Matthew wanted to reveal, and yet hearing such personal reflections made her uncomfortable. She gradually moved to the edge of her seat, preparing to leave, but stopped. He was in a mood to talk.

"Yes, I miss Elizabeth. I miss what we had together—the sharing, the joy, the laughter, and even the misunderstandings. We were very close." His jaw tightened as he crossed his arms. "I was not always as considerate as I should have been, but she loved me, and I never doubted that. I wanted to work this farm and, against her parents' wishes, she chose to come out here and work it with me. I loved her and let her come out here and struggle and die without providing her with the care she needed." He shook his head and strode off the porch in the direction of the barn.

Stunned by his frank revelations, she sat and stared after him. Mary had said he believed he bore responsibility in Elizabeth's death, but she suspected it had merely been an immediate reaction to their terrible loss. She watched him enter the barn, then rose from the chair to go back into the cottage. There was nothing she could do to help him. *I should go inside and let him work through it by himself, whatever he is experiencing.* However, upon reaching the door of the cottage, she turned and gazed once more in the direction of the barn—in his direction. She slowly but deliberately picked up the lantern and walked toward the barn.

CHAPTER 20

From the corner of his eye, Matthew saw Heather approach the barn, holding the lantern high to see her way. For a long moment, she stood in the doorway. She might still turn and go back to the cottage. The woman had a way of remaining at a distance.

Heather entered the dark barn but appeared unsure of whether to stay or leave.

Well, man, are you going to stand here by the horses and ignore her? He relaxed his grip on the pitchfork. "Thank you, Heather. I came out here in such a hurry I did not think to bring a light." He lit his own lantern from hers, then turned, picked up the pitchfork, and began spreading the hay. She was shuffling behind him. He needed to keep enough space between them that he wouldn't drop the pitchfork and take her in his arms. What would she do if he did?

"It was thoughtless of me to bring up—"

"No." He shook his head but kept his back to her. "I needed to say what I did. I have kept everything inside too long. I think it helped to put it into words." He glanced at her over his shoulder. Did she read his true intentions?

"Aye. Putting our recollections into words can bring clarity. I meant to say that I wish it all had been so very different."

He turned and faced her. His arms rested on the handle of the pitchfork; his eyes searched hers. Why had she come out to the barn? Only because she was grateful for the clothes and sorry that she had brought up Elizabeth? Heather was so approachable at times, but something would happen, or he would say the wrong thing. Then she would draw that curtain of reserve around herself. Was she unaware of the effect she had on him? He longed to hold her in his arms. Still, he was sure that was not what she wanted. What did she mean that she wished it all had been so very different? Why was he at such a loss to know how to reach her—to draw her out of her shell?

❧ ☙

There was an intensity and power, yet warmth, in his expression. It made her heart race and her skin feel aflame. For a moment, she was helpless and unable to move. As her breath returned, she tried to swallow, relieving the dryness in her throat.

"I—ah—good night, Mr. Stewart." She turned, and with trembling hands struggling to hold the lantern steady, she left the barn. When she reached the house, she took brisk steps to the porch. "Coward!" she said under her breath. The tranquility and solitude of the bedroom were what she needed.

Once in her room, she tried to calm down. Question after question raced through her mind as she undressed and washed her face. *Why did I bring up his wife? What is wrong with me?* She should never have addressed that subject. The pain was still so raw, his emotions still so near the surface. She understood loss, pain, and regret. It grieved her that he was so distressed.

Why am I so confused? I loved Robert. I must still love him. Surely I could not stop loving a man I loved with all my heart. Yet I can barely recall his face. Has it been so long that now I can see only Matthew's? She glanced out her window in the direction of the barn. What a tangle she was in. She wasn't sure what she was feeling, and she was married to a man who was still very much in love with his dead wife.

Drained, she collapsed onto the bed, laid her head back on the pillow, and gazed out the open window at the stars twinkling in the early autumn sky. Matthew was not the fool. What he loved was real. She, however, had been in love with a dream, a lost dream. As the tears ran down her cheeks and into her hair, she once again was haunted by the memory of Robert McDowell. How could she have been such a fool? How could things have turned out so wrong?

Whatever Robert McDowell's business was in Perth or with her brother, Heather had not fully understood. However, he had continued to return every five or six weeks through that winter and spring, spending many hours with her family. In the beginning, Ross and Robert were at odds with each other, but by the time summer arrived, they acted more like old friends, which pleased her.

When Robert finally declared his love, he told her he was preparing a life for them in Edinburgh. He described how things would be in glowing detail. She was overjoyed when he said he wanted her beside him. And after all the years of caring for others, she was thrilled to think she would have a home and family of her own. He asked her to give him time. But she grew impatient and wrote that letter, a letter that would have far-reaching consequences, and be the beginning of the end for their relationship.

❦

Matthew finished his work and sat on a barrel inside the barn. From there, he could make out the glimmer of light coming from Heather's window. He could not make her care for him—love him. That was not her plan in coming to Virginia. She had indentured herself for seven years with the intent of being free to start a new life here. That April day on the quay, he thought he had been thinking only of a way to bring his children home again. But if he was honest with himself, that was not the only thing that had been on his mind. He had been lonely and missed having someone to share life with, someone whose face would light up when he came through the door. Her smile when she and the children brought the midday meal and when he walked through the door each evening to find her busy making supper warmed his heart. She was sensitive and deft at figuring out how to deal with Mary's moods, and Mark was besotted with her. They would all miss her. *If you truly love her, you must do what is best for her.*

He got up and left the barn, closing the door behind him, and walked toward the well. His mind raced. Should he put aside what he wanted? There were others whose needs had to be addressed. And honoring her desire was becoming more important to him with each passing day. He took a drink and washed his face with a rag that was on the edge of the well. *I must let her go—but not without telling her how I feel.*

❦

Heather sat up in bed. The memories brought fresh tears, making sleep impossible. The past was behind her. She knew she must let it go. She had come across the sea to escape it. It was foolish to allow memories to follow and torment her, and there was no changing what had happened.

She got up and washed her tear-stained face once more. As she looked in the mirror, she heard a soft knock at her door. Could one of the children need something? She padded to the door. When she opened it, she was astounded. Matthew stood in the doorway, a silhouette against the dimly lit room beyond.

"Aye? Did you want me, sir?" She glanced to where she had set down the light cotton shawl. He sighed as he ran his hand through his hair.

"Heather, we need to talk. May I come in?"

She motioned him in, picked up the shawl, and wrapped it around her shoulders.

He closed the door, set his lantern on the table, and sat on the bed as if it were the most natural thing to do. "Out there, you said that you wished things had been different. Did you mean that you wish that events had been different for me … or you … or us?"

"Well now, I—" She took a deep breath. "I wished for your

sake that your wife and child had lived." It was awkward being alone with him, not fully clothed, in the small, partially lit room. "I wanted a different path for my life also. If our lives had followed the different paths we wanted there would be no … us."

"What brought you here to Virginia? You have never told me why you left Scotland, or even what your life there was like. Please tell me, Heather. There are no small children here to interrupt or overhear us. We are alone, and I want to understand Heather Douglas and what burdens she is carrying."

She stood quiet and trembling against the cabinet that stored her clothes and the linens. He certainly did not need to remind her that they were alone in the room. Of that, she was all too conscious. Even with the door closed, the lamplight and moonlight filled the room enough so that she clearly saw his face. He had every right to ask those things. But what would he think of her if he knew? Would he understand?

He patted the quilt beside him. "Come here. Sit down, please." His voice was gentle but authoritative.

She padded slowly to the side of the bed and sat near him, eyes averted to avoid his disarming and penetrating stare. "I, ah, I do not like talking about the past. I left Scotland, came here to get away from what happened before, to start my life over again. I am trying to do that—to forget. There is nothing you need be unsettled about." She rubbed her forehead. "I have committed no crimes. I have hurt no one. You have no cause to be concerned that I would harm your children." She shook as she spoke.

"It is not the children I am concerned about now."

She looked up at him. The sincerity in his eyes penetrated the barriers she had erected.

"Something, someone has hurt you." He moved closer, taking her in his arms in the same way he did Mary and Mark when one of them was upset or crying. "I did not mean to distress you so." He held her against his chest, stroking her hair. "If you truly hope to make a new start, Heather, you will need to examine and resolve whatever it is that is troubling you. Tell me what is causing you such pain. Trust me." His plea as he whispered into her hair sounded genuine.

His words cut through her defenses. His skin was warm against hers. The beating of her heart pounded in her ears. As his lips came down on hers, she was flooded with fear. The fear was not of him, for his kiss was gentle and giving, not urgent or forcing. It was her emotions that were at war within her. When her arms gradually crept up and encircled him, she returned his kiss and felt complete. Was this truly what they both wanted? But there were still two others between them—or was it only one? Nay, it was still Elizabeth in his heart. He had said as much himself. Or did he?

Matthew's kisses were growing more ardent, his voice more tender. "Heather, I want you beside me, always."

Those familiar words were like a punch to her gut. Doubt, confusion, and hurt filled her. He acted surprised as she pulled herself free of him. "Nay, this is not right."

Matthew let her go. Why had she pushed away from him? She had returned his kiss. "I do not understand, Heather. I would not hurt you. Trust me."

"Trust? Trust? I cannot. I do not even trust my own judgment, and so much stands between us."

Was she angry? No, she sounded more fearful, but why? "Is it all men you distrust, Heather, or just me?"

She stood and backed away. He knew that look, confused and frightened.

"You speak of trust, Matthew Stewart, but did you trust me when you saw me being mauled by Travis Thorpe? Nay. You suspected the worst of me. Do not talk to me of trust. Please go away—and leave me alone."

He sat a moment longer before getting up. "You confound me,

Heather. Is there nothing left to say, or hope for?"

She turned away from him. How had it come to this?

When he reached the door, he turned. "Heather, if I have hurt you, I am sorry."

He had gotten his answer. It was not what he had hoped for, but he would remedy the situation, and he would need to do it soon.

CHAPTER 21

The early morning sun was shining by the time Heather awoke. Once again, a restless night had caused her to sleep too late. It was hard to focus on objects in the room. She struggled out of bed and into her clothes, her head throbbing. Hours of tears and nervous pacing had taken a toll on her stomach also. When she opened the bedroom door, she saw Mary and Mark playing quietly by the hearth.

"Good morning, children." The smile she gave each of them belied her true feelings. She walked to the window and glanced all about. Where was Matthew? The children—she needed to see to them. "I am sorry to be so late getting up. Have you eaten yet?" Her shaky voice was sure to make them wonder about her well-being.

"Yes, Papa gave us our breakfast."

"Oh." She peered through the other window, wondering where he was.

When she finally sat down with a cup of tea, Mary approached her, carrying her doll. "Are we going to make the candles today?"

"Well, I think we should wait for a cooler day." She would also prefer one when she was more rested and without a headache.

"Your eyes are all red and puffy. Have you been crying? My eyes get puffy when I cry." Mary cocked her head in an inquisitive, innocent way.

"I did not sleep very well, and I am feeling poorly this morning."

"Well, what are we going to do today? Since it is so warm, may we go to the river today rather than the pond?"

"Aye, Mary, perhaps a bit later, after our lessons." Her voice lacked its usual enthusiasm. All she really wanted to do was crawl back into bed and be alone.

Later, despite her fatigue and headache, she acquiesced and accompanied the children to the river. It drained her of what little energy remained. Perhaps, now that the children were occupied playing on the riverbank, they would leave her in peace. She rubbed the knot that had formed in the back of her neck and paced back and forth while observing the children at play.

Why did Matthew come to her room? He said that talking and getting everything out into the open would help. It had not. Why was he so curious about her past? How would he regard her if he learned about it? She sat down under a tree and tried to relax as she gazed up at the cloudless sky. Was Matthew growing to truly care for her? Nay, that business with Thorpe demonstrated that he did not trust her. He was lonely, and he missed his wife and the love they had shared. She had no desire to be a substitute for an absent wife—not in that way.

I am so confused, Lord. Why do I find fault with him, when it is my own choices and those of others that have brought on my difficulties? She picked up a pebble and pitched it into the shallows. How could she still be in love with one man and want another? *Lord, I do not want to be hurt again. Please help me.*

Mary approached the tree she was leaning against. "Heather, come here. Mark has found a baby rabbit." Mary's eyes were wide, and she was very excited. "May we keep it? We can take it home, and we will care for it. It would not be any trouble. It will be our pet."

"Oh, Mary, I am not sure. It is a wild animal and should be with its own kind. It may have a mother who is searching for it."

"There were no other rabbits around it. Please? It might be lost and need us to take care of it."

Heather smiled. The girl had a remarkable talent for persuasion. Her temple throbbed. She was in no mood for arguments and had even less energy to deal with the child's disappointment that would likely follow if she refused the request. "Try to understand, lass. The rabbit would hate being a prisoner, not being able to live like other rabbits. If you truly care about the wee creature, set it free."

Mary was not going to give up easily. "But if I loved the rabbit, fed it, and gave it a home, it would want to stay with us. It would not be a prisoner. It would be the rabbit's choice to stay if it was happy."

The child reasoned like her father. Heather leaned her head against the tree. "Well, you do make a good point, lass. We shall have to see what the wee rabbit chooses, *after* we make sure it is permissible with your father."

❧ ❧

Matthew entered the cottage later as she ladled a thick soup into bowls. She rubbed the nape of her neck as she faced him for the first time since their parting last night. She suspected he, too, had not slept well, for there were dark circles under his eyes. Perhaps he was angry with her. She set the bowl down in front of him. Once more, the children's chatter masked their silence and tension.

"Papa, I found a little rabbit." Mark grinned as he took a seat beside his father. "We want to keep him."

"Oh yes, Papa, we will feed and take care of him, and he shall be no trouble at all." The plea in Mary's voice matched the one on her face as she sat down at the table.

Fatigue and sadness showed on Matthew's face as he watched his children. He looked at Heather. "What did you tell them about the rabbit?"

"I admit at first I did not think it wise for them to keep the wee animal confined, but Mary assured me that she would let it go if it chose to leave. I told them to ask you."

He watched her intently, and her heart began to race as she recalled the events of the previous evening.

His eyes continued to hold hers captive until heat rose to her face. She turned to Mary and saw the children glancing back and forth between them, obviously waiting and wondering about the future of their pet.

Mary smiled at her father. "I promise he will not be any trouble, Papa."

Finally, Matthew leaned back in his chair and his austere expression relaxed. "I agree with Heather. You may keep the pet as long as it causes no problems and wants to stay. But, I caution you both. Be wary of growing too fond of the little creature, for it may seek its freedom." He glanced her way.

She turned away from him. Was Matthew intentionally trying to hurt her? Her father's words when she turned down a suitor burned in her ears: "No man appreciates being rebuffed, Heather."

"Oh, thank you, Papa." Both children hugged their father and ran off to fetch their newfound friend from the barrel where they had left him.

Later that night, exhausted and grateful to get the children tucked into their bed, she was about to go into her room when Matthew stopped her. "I would like a few words with you, on the porch."

Reluctantly, she followed him out and sat in the oak chair, too tired for any more confrontations.

"Heather." He sat on the porch step and turned to face her. "In a few days, I shall be finished planting the barley and rye. After that, I am leaving for a few weeks. I have some business to take care of in Philadelphia."

"Oh, I see." She was stunned, completely unprepared for his declaration. "This is so—the children—shall miss you … miss you terribly."

"This is the right time for the trip. If I wait much longer, the weather might be bad. It will only be for a few weeks. I will purchase provisions while I am in Alexandria, and the Duncans will bring them when they come for a visit. George will check on you and be available if you need him."

"I see." She did not want to let her disappointment show.

"I will also pass through Baltimore and probably see Caroline and her father. If you wish me to take a letter or message, I will be happy to deliver it to her."

"Thank you." She tried to imagine the farm without him.

"Oh, and Heather." He got up to leave. "When I return, you shall have your freedom. A solicitor shall draw up the proper and necessary papers. It should not be difficult to secure an annulment, as we both can attest that the marriage never truly existed."

The words stung. As unexpected as his announcement was that he would be gone a few weeks, this came as a bigger blow. But why? Was this not what she wanted?

"What—what about the children? Who will care for them?"

"I am taking care of that. You need not concern yourself. You shall be a free woman, Heather. It is what we both desire."

CHAPTER 22

Over the next few days, Matthew was scarcely around the house. Now that the fall planting was completed, he set about repairing tools, loose shutters, and broken fences. Keeping busy was best, and physical activity helped to keep the frustration and disappointment at bay. There had been little opportunity, or inclination, for the two of them to talk. What was there to say? He had tried every way he knew to reach her, to no avail. Perhaps being apart would help give them some perspective and resolution.

He heard the rustling of hay. Someone had entered the barn. "I am over here at Honey's stall."

"Hi Papa, I was looking for you." Mary's plaintive voice touched his heart. Holding her doll, she climbed up on a bale of hay. "Are you still going in the morning?"

"Yes."

Mark was holding the rabbit when he joined her on the bale. "When will you be back?"

"I told you, it will only be a few weeks, as long as it takes to complete my business. Then I shall return."

"We will miss you, Papa." The sadness in Mary's voice was unmistakable.

Tears ran down Mark's cheeks.

"Believe me; I shall miss the two of you also. Now, go out and play with that rabbit of yours for a while. It is almost time for bed."

"His name is Randolph, Papa." Mary put her free hand on her hip but managed a smile before she and Mark departed.

When the children were finally in bed and quiet, he stood by the chair near the hearth and packed the items he had set aside for his journey. Heather stood just outside the bedroom door, folding laundry and occasionally glancing at him.

"I have decided to take Caroline's horse and leave Honey here with you. She would be a bit easier for you to handle. And again, George said he would stop by and see how you are faring. If there are any problems, do not hesitate to ask him for help."

"Aye, sir. Thank you." She stopped folding and took a deep breath. She walked toward him, her voice low. "I wanted to ask you. Do the children know anything about my leaving when you return?"

He stopped loading his sack and caught her eye a moment before he resumed packing. "I considered telling them, preparing them." He turned back to her. His eyes held hers. "I think you should be the one to tell them. And how much … or how little you say, I leave to your judgment. You cannot help but be aware that in these last several months, they have become very fond of you. I am sure you will be sensitive to their feelings and reactions." He glanced down at her but remained silent. What was she thinking? Did she have any regrets? "You said you had a letter ready for Caroline."

"Aye." She went to her room and returned with a folded piece of parchment. He stood by the table where he had put his knapsack. Her hand was shaking as she held it out to him. Taking this journey brought him no joy. It was not what he wanted, but it would secure the future she wanted.

"Well, we had best retire now. I have an early start in the morning." He gazed intently into her face. Heather's lips were parted as if she wanted to say something, and her eyes looked as sad as he felt. If only she would offer him any encouragement or reason to hope. She bit her lip, turned, and went into the room. Shaking his head, he headed to the ladder and loft.

❧ ❧

Two days later, Heather sighed, still downcast, when the children came to the table for breakfast. It was time to end this melancholy atmosphere. "We will spend a half hour on lessons, and then we need to make candles, so I am delegating the tasks."

Both heads looked up expectantly from their bowls of porridge.

"Mary, your job will be to straighten the candle wicks hanging over the candle rods. Mark, you can hold one end of the candle rod while I hold the other."

Mary pushed her bowl away. "When will we start our lessons?"

She moved the bowl back in front of the child. "As soon as you both finish your breakfast."

An hour later, their moods had improved dramatically.

Heather dipped six of the wicks into the large iron pot on the trivet on the hearth. "After we dip it straight down into the tallow, we carry the candle rod very carefully over to where Mary is standing and hang them to cool. Can you do that?"

"Yes, ma'am." Mark was completely focused on the job at hand.

"Good. We will have to dip the wicks several times, cooling them between each dipping so they will be the right size."

Mary counted all the wicks hanging from the candle rods. "There are so many, this will take most of the day."

"It will take a good portion of it, but if we finish early enough, perhaps we can go down to the river for a picnic. Would that please you?"

"Yes." Mary smiled and nodded at Mark.

As anticipated, it was late afternoon before the messy, but necessary, chore was completed. They gathered the picnic supplies and headed to the riverbank. Matthew had assigned her a difficult task, telling the children of her departure. Well, there was no hurry; she could put that job off a while. It made no sense bringing that up now while they were still trying to get used to their father's absence. She would pray about the best way and time to tell them. For now, her priority was to settle in her own mind what she would do with her eventual freedom. Where should she go? And what would she do?

As they approached the river, the children squealed with delight. This part of the Potomack was not very wide. The lack of rain had reduced the flow significantly. Random boulders along the edge appeared larger now. Both sides of the river were lined with trees and shrubs and an occasional sandy beach. She had been amazed when Matthew told her the river was hundreds of miles long.

The children brought small gourd boats to sail in the shallows of the river. They would use long branches to keep the vessels from sailing too far from the bank.

Lord, give me the wisdom to understand what Your will is for my life. Please guide my steps through the choices I face. Help me to trust You and act in accordance with Your will.

The children's laughter was a welcome distraction. "Not too close to the edge, Mark." She watched the small boy flirt continuously with falling into the river. The sandy beach extended to a rocky shoreline. Still, it would prove dangerous if they fell into the deeper water. "Let the gourds sail away and watch where they go. We can always make new boats."

Sitting beneath a nearby tree, the tension melted for the first time since Matthew left. It was peaceful to simply sit and enjoy what was left of the day. The children, cheerful once again, affected her mood greatly. How easily they recovered from disappointment. Two days ago, one would have believed the world was going to end when he left. But here they were as if nothing had changed. How she would have loved to share their gleeful spirit and not regret his absence so much. It was unsettling to admit that. Matthew was good company. She glanced to where Mary and Mark played and reached for a piece of the bread they had brought with them as a snack. Matthew was a caring and kind father, good-natured and not one to yell or become moody or irritable, and he did so much around the farm to keep it running well. Now, for a time, it would be her sole responsibility. What a frightening and exhausting notion.

She shifted under the tree, unable to attain the sought-for peace. She got up and began pacing. What was the matter with her? It was not the extra set of hands to help her with the work she missed. It was him.

That admission made her vulnerable, a sensation she loathed. It had been difficult to say good-bye the morning he left. She managed to hold back the tears until after the children had retired for the night. There was nothing to say to set things right.

Matthew had been unreasonable and unfair. It was unconscionable that he believed she would have conspired with Thorpe. He had misjudged her and had never even given her a chance to tell him what really happened. She picked up a stone and threw it at a nearby tree. She would be better off taking on the chores back at the cottage—too much time alone to think only caused her more anguish. A tear ran down her cheek. Had she intentionally kept Robert as a barrier to protect herself from being hurt again? Had Elizabeth also been a convenient shield she had erected to protect her heart?

"Come see the goslings." Mary's waving arms and excited voice interrupted her troubled reverie. "Come closer to the river."

She was more than grateful to escape some truths her heart was revealing.

A large goose was honking and pecking wildly at the children.

"Stand back and watch, children. The mother is unsure of you and wants to keep you away from her goslings."

As she reached Mary, the goose turned and lunged at her. Startled, Heather slipped, lost her balance, and fell backward into the river. After a couple of attempts to right herself, she finally was able to stand, soaked in water up to her chest.

The children stood by with their mouths hanging open. When they saw her break into laughter, they joined in her mirth.

Mary continued to giggle. "That was so funny. Are you hurt?"

"Nay, but I feel a bit foolish, especially after warning you two to be careful around the riverbank." She picked herself up and began wringing the water from her skirt. "What do you say we gather our things and bid goosey good day? I would like to dry off. The water has gotten considerably cooler."

The sound of brittle leaves beneath their feet was a reminder of the autumn season well underway. Heather glanced at the copse of apple trees. "We should pick some more apples later."

Mark's grin was infectious. "Some pie or dumplings would be fine."

When they arrived back to the cottage, they saw George Whitcomb standing in the yard. She groaned. Once again he had caught her at her worst. "Mr. Whitcomb, I hope you have not been waiting long. As you can no doubt guess, we have been down by the river." She continued to fan her skirt to keep it from sticking to her legs.

The children ran up to the porch to check on Randolph.

George laughed. "Heather Stewart, you do have an uncanny way of totally immersing yourself in your activities. I stopped by to see how the three of you are doing. I plan to fix that garden gate. Is there is anything else you need done?"

"Nay, we are doing fine, but I appreciate your help and thank you for stopping by."

"Well, Hannah and I would like you to join us for dinner tomorrow, if you can."

"May we?" Mary's voice was full of excitement.

Heather smiled at the two joy-filled faces. She could not deny them the chance to play with the young Whitcombs.

"That would be very nice, Mr. Whitcomb. Thank you. And please thank Mrs. Whitcomb."

"We shall expect you around two." George got back on his gray steed and rode off down the path.

Heather watched the horse and rider grow smaller as they headed off in the direction of their farm. Dread began to fill her. She was in no mood for Hannah's nosiness, but the children needed their companions. If only the woman would not gossip or pry for once. She mounted the steps to go inside. *Lord, please give me a patient and understanding heart.* She did not have it in her to withstand the woman's barbs. Back in the house, they put away the remnants of their meal.

"May we go to back to the river tomorrow to fish—after we come back from the Whitcombs'?" Mary petted Randolph, who was resting on her lap.

Mark smiled. "I want to go fishing."

"Perhaps, later, but only if we get our chores done."

After picking enough apples for a pie and completing the day's activities, the children were ready for bed. Her work done for the day, she settled herself in the chair next to the hearth with a steaming cup of tea. Her eyes fell on Randolph, sitting in his box, busy chomping on a carrot. The small rabbit had endeared himself so much in the past week that it was impossible to banish him to the barn.

"You really are a remarkable rabbit, Randolph, and unusually tidy. However, I am not sure you are going to convince Mr. Stewart that you should reside in the cottage." She took a slow sip of her tea, still reflecting on the furry creature. "Will you stay with us or seek your freedom? You are safe here and cared for. Would you give up this haven, Randolph, for the potential problems that lie beyond these walls and fields? It is a big, unknown world, full of danger and disappointment."

As she stared back to the flickering flame, and away from her tiny companion, she winced. Oh yes, the world was full of disappointment. She had only to think back nearly a year to remember. What had prompted her to send that letter to Robert? Ahh, yes—holding Ross and Anne's baby.

Wistful, Heather recalled how she had gazed down on her newest nephew, kissing his tiny head. "Oh, how I would love to have someone like you of my very own."

"Well, you better get that barrister fellow to marry you, lass, and soon, for you are no longer young." Her father's sharp words stung.

"We plan to, Father. Robert is very responsible and wants everything to be perfect for us when we marry."

"Is it a fine house and position you want, or a husband?" Her father was irritable but remarkably lucid that night.

Later that evening, she would write Robert and tell him. He needed to know that all she desired was to be his wife—that being by his side was what she truly cared about—not about starting their marriage with a fine house and furnishings.

Heather took a deep breath. Perhaps the whole episode of the letter was providential. After all, in the end, it uncovered the truth about Ross' guile and his dealings with Robert. It also divulged many previously unknown aspects of Robert's life and character, as well as her own naivety.

She came back to the present with a start. The fire was out and her tea cold.

It was over. She would never understand why Robert chose the path he took. Somehow, time, distance, and all she had gone through since made all the anger and bitterness meaningless. *I must forgive him, Lord. I thought I had, but the hurt has continued to cripple me. It was foolish to have been taken in by his charm. I know I am forgiven in Your eyes. It was not Ross who saved me from a wrong entanglement, Lord. It was You.*

Strangely, for the first time, she was not overwhelmed with depression when examining her past. Her heart had been broken. However, how much more pain she would have experienced had their relationship continued. Exhausted, she was ready to sleep. *What man meant for ill, You used for good. Thank You, Lord.*

CHAPTER 23

"Mary, Mark, it is time to say our good-byes and go home," Heather called to the group of children playing near the barn as she stepped out onto the Whitcombs' front porch.

"It was kind of you to have us over today. Thank you both." She smiled at the Whitcombs, grateful the time spent there had passed with very few awkward conversations with Hannah. "And George, thank you again for fixing the garden gate. It would have taken me so much longer, and I am sure I would not have done it nearly as well."

Hannah said goodbye and returned to the house. George walked beside Heather to the path leading home. "I have had more opportunities to perfect that skill. And I meant it, Heather, tell us if you need anything. Without Matt around, you may have jobs come up that are better left to a man, and with Thorpe gone, I am the closest one around."

"How true. I appreciate your offer." She smiled and turned toward Mary and Mark, who were already headed down the worn trail toward home.

George coughed. "Did I mention I saw that Thorpe fella when I was in Leesburg a few days ago?"

Her body grew tense at George's casual remark, grateful she was not facing him for fear he would note the distress on her face. "Do not go so far ahead of me, children," she called. "I shall be there in a minute."

She turned toward George, wanting to appear as calm as possible. Surely the Whitcombs were not aware of the details surrounding Thorpe's departure from their farm.

"No, you had not mentioned that. We had no idea that Mr. Thorpe was still in the area."

"Matthew did not say why he left your place, but I had the impression it was not under the best of circumstances. Thorpe was picking up some farm supplies for the place he is working at now."

"I see. So you had occasion to speak with him."

"Only to learn he hired on at a nearby farm for corn harvesting and was staying through hog killing time."

"You did not happen to mention anything about Matthew's absence, did you?"

"No. I cannot remember saying anything about that."

"Well, we will be off, George. Be sure to thank Hannah again for us."

Relieved, she turned and made her way to where the children were picking berries off some shrubs along the side of the path. Leesburg was around twenty miles from their farm, so it was unlikely that they would see any more of Travis Thorpe.

The air was pleasantly cool, and the brown leaves crackled beneath their feet as they walked home. Cutting through a field, the family quickly arrived home. The leaves' vibrant fall colors were breathtaking. She and the children made plans to go apple picking again the next day, after church.

"Mark, we need to get you inside for a wee rest if you want to go fishing later." She gently led the child up the steps before turning to Mary. "Would you check the squash and other vegetables to see if there are any ready for picking?"

Mary nodded and headed to the garden with a bucket.

Not many minutes later, while she was working in the barn, she heard Mary's voice shouting from the house. She ran to see what had upset the child.

Mary's angry, tear-stained face appeared almost crimson as she stared at Mark. "You broke my doll. Her head is broken."

Mark was huddled against their pallet. "Sorry, Mary," he wailed, large tears rolling down his face.

Heather put her arm around Mary. "What happened? I heard you hollering from the barn."

"He broke my doll's head to bits. It is ruined."

She examined the doll and studied each of the children.

"I am sorry. It fell from up there." Mark pointed to the loft.

His small, penitent face touched Heather's heart. "And what was the doll—or you—doing up there, Mark?"

"Dolly wanted to sleep in Papa's bed."

"Well, Mark, you should not have taken Mary's doll up there. I do not even like you climbing up there. You might have fallen and gotten hurt."

Mary's arms were crossed, holding the doll tight against her chest. "He broke my doll. I hate him."

Heather kneeled down in front of Mary and wiped a tear from her cheek. "Now wait a moment, lassie. You are angry, but we both know you do not hate Mark, and you certainly should not speak to him that way. He said he was sorry, Mary. It was an accident. You need to forgive him."

"No. I shall not forgive him. Not ever. Why are you taking his side? Mama gave her to me." Mary shook her head, all the while cradling the broken doll.

"I am not taking anyone's side." She reached out and took Mary's hand in hers. "I am sorry your doll is broken. You love your doll, particularly because your mother gave it to you, and you are sad, but nothing is to be gained by unkind words or staying angry at Mark."

Mary pulled her hand away. Her fury showed in her furrowed brows and clenched lips. Still holding the doll with one hand, she placed her other fist on her hip.

Mark approached his sister. "I am sorry. Please forgive me, Mary."

"No. I do not have to." She stood defiant, shaking her head and staring all the while at Heather.

Mark, sniffling, walked back to the pallet.

She was torn. Which child needed her most at the moment? She once again took Mary's hand. "When you do not forgive, Mary, you not only hurt Mark, but you hurt yourself. Resentment and anger can fester like a wound, and grow. It will injure you more in the end."

Stubbornness remained evident in the young girl's eyes and stance.

"Mary, how would you feel if you had an accident or did something wrong? What if you were genuinely sorry and wanted to be forgiven, and the person you wronged denied you the forgiveness you sought?"

The girl said nothing.

"Mark has done his part, Mary. He is genuinely penitent for what was an unfortunate accident. Now, as difficult as it may be, your responsibility is to forgive and not hold a grudge." She headed toward the pallet to comfort Mark. "Perhaps you need time to think about it for a bit."

When Mary walked out the door without a word, Heather turned to Mark. "Give her some time. She will come around. Now, please take a rest. And no climbing up to the loft anymore, understand?"

"Yes, ma'am."

When she stepped outside, she found Mary sitting on the porch chair, her chin resting on her hands. Mary turned her head, averting her eyes, evidently intent on not furthering the conversation.

"I need to finish up in the barn, Mary. If you want to talk about it, you are welcome to join me."

She spent the next hour in the barn completing her tasks, but she was burdened by the earlier exchange she and the children had shared. She was a fine one to be speaking to anyone about forgiveness. Pushing the conflicting thoughts from her mind, she returned to the cottage. Mark was playing with some toys on the pallet. Mary was sitting quietly at the table working on her embroidery.

She glanced at Mark. "It is a lovely afternoon. Do you want to take our supper down to the river and fish for a bit before it gets too dark?" She knew he would eagerly agree with her plan.

Mark jumped up. "Oh yes."

Mary kept her eyes on her work. "Perhaps." She seemed determined to hold on to her anger. They each set about their separate tasks in preparation. Mark went to dig some worms from the garden, Mary gathered the fishing poles, and Heather prepared a light meal and placed it in a basket. Before closing the door, she returned to collect a quilt to sit on.

The walk to the river was quiet but not wholly unpleasant. Each of them was in their own little world. Mark was content carrying a bucket of worms and dragging a stick through the leaves along the path, Mary carried the poles, and Heather had the quilt and picnic basket.

When they got to the riverbank, Heather helped Mark bait his hook. The children each found a spot to their liking to wait for the fish to bite. Once the quilt was spread beneath a tree, Heather made herself comfortable, grateful the wee ones appeared to be in a temporary truce. Mary, sitting nearby, glanced back at her. Mark was thoroughly absorbed in the fishing. What were those Scripture verses she knew so long ago?

"I have thought about our earlier conversation, Mary. If someone, a brother, sins against us, we can rebuke him, but if he repents, we must forgive him."

Was Mary even paying attention? She hoped to reach the child. *"We are to be kind and tenderhearted to one another, forgiving one another, even as God, for Christ's sake, hath forgiven you."*

Mary's eyes welled up with tears. "That is easy for you. You do not have to forgive a brother for being mean—for breaking something of yours."

Heather jerked back as if she had been slapped. A lump formed in her throat as she went to help Mark put another worm on his hook.

Staring at the river, tears came to her eyes. The choice to forgive was not totally dependent on the penitence of the offender. How swift she was to observe the lack of forgiveness in others, yet slow to note it within herself. Perhaps she needed to remove the "beam" from her own eye before she admonished anyone to remove the "mote" from theirs.

Was she sincerely willing to forgive Robert ... and Ross?

Later that night, she asked Mary to stay up with her after she tucked Mark into bed.

"Mary, earlier you suggested that forgiving a brother would be easy for me. Well—" She sought the right words, hoping her motives were honest and pure. "I know how hard it can be to forgive someone."

The young girl's amber eyes glistened in the dim light.

She had Mary's attention. "I have people in my life whom I held grudges against, including my own brother, for a wrong he committed against me. This whole episode with you and Mark has reminded me of my own need to extend forgiveness and grace to others. I have been wrong. As Christians, we have been forgiven by our Father for all our sins. I cannot hope to teach you to forgive Mark if I am incapable of pardoning others. So, I am confessing my own lack of forgiveness and my hypocrisy. I must forgive my brother, and others, for any and all offenses committed against me. I need to ask the Lord to take the bitterness from my heart." She smoothed the child's dark tresses.

"What did your brother do?"

Heather paused. How much should she tell the child? "My brother deceived me. He was selfish and unkind." The specific details did not matter, nor need mentioning. "What is important is that I did not—I have not forgiven him, and it has remained like a poison within me since before I left Scotland."

The girl's golden-brown eyes searched hers, waiting for something more.

"Mary, we are not responsible for others' choices, accidents, unkind words, or actions. But we are accountable for how we respond to them. If someone wrongs us, even if they do not repent or ask for forgiveness, we must forgive them. If we do not, we sin. When Mark made a mistake by accidentally breaking your doll, he did apologize and ask for forgiveness."

Mary bit her lip and glanced away.

"God is faithful, Mary. When we confess our sins and are truly repentant, He forgives us and cleanses us from all unrighteousness."

The young girl's face softened and a sliver of a smile appeared—a priceless treasure Heather would not soon forget.

They rose and headed toward the pallet. "Sweet dreams." She stroked the girl's cheek.

"Good night."

She walked back to the hearth and sat watching the dancing flames. She heard the children's voices over the crackling logs.

"I forgive you for breaking my doll."

"Thank you, Mary. I love you."

"I love you too."

Tears of joy filled her eyes. *I do not require Ross's—or Robert's—repentance to forgive them. I do it because You, Father, have forgiven me. Thank you. I am sorry it took so long.*

CHAPTER 24

Amelia and Aaron Turner beckoned to Heather and the children when they arrived at church, right before the service began. Heather smiled as she, Mary, and Mark took their seats on the bench beside the Turners. After the service, Amelia encouraged them to join the rest of the congregation at the potluck picnic.

Heather eyed the children, then Amelia. "I am not sure we should stay. We did not bring anything to share."

Amelia laughed. "We always have more food than we know what to do with, probably because we expect folks to stay who may not have planned on it."

"That is very generous."

After sharing dinner and fellowship with their neighbors, Amelia gathered the remnants of their meal and prepared to leave. "Would you and the children be free to join us for dinner tomorrow, Heather? Do you remember how to get to our farm?"

"Aye, thank you. I remember where it is, and I am sure the children will be delighted. May I bring a dessert?"

"There is not a one in our home who would say no to that. Come around two. Mary said that you are proficient at needlework, and I want your advice on a quilt I am attempting to repair."

Mary said that? Hmm. "By all means. I would be happy to offer any help. We will see you tomorrow."

The next day at the Turners' was filled with good food and laughter. After dinner, Amelia pulled a large quilt from a cupboard. She spread it out on the cleared table. "You can see there are stains and tears that are beyond repair. My mother made it, and I cannot bear to not use it anymore."

Heather studied the quilt. "I think this can be easily and quickly altered so that no one would ever suspect there had been a stain or tear. Do you have some extra material that we could use to piece a fabric design onto it?"

Amelia's face lit up. "I never thought of doing that. I do have fabric, and in colors that would complement it."

"Since the tear is so close to the center and not far from the stain, I suggest you create a design right in the center of the quilt. No one would ever know it had not been part of the original arrangement."

"That would be perfect, Heather. Thank you for suggesting it."

Almost two hours later, Heather looked up from their work when the children came inside. "Oh, my. It is getting dark. We had best be getting home."

"I hope we can get together again soon, Heather. And it is wonderful to see Matthew happy again. He was so lonely without Elizabeth and the children. You have truly been a blessing."

Heather was stunned. "It is having the children home that has helped him to recover."

"That is only a part of it, Heather. I see the way he looks at you."

Heather reached for her cape and basket, hoping the warm flush on her face was not evident. "Please come over with the children sometime soon."

On the ride home, while the children chattered, she could think of nothing but Amelia's parting remarks. She had not noticed any significance in the way Matthew looked at her. Might Amelia expand on her observations? That was tempting to think about. What irony to discover a friend when soon she would be leaving. Nay, it was too fine a day to dwell on that sad thought.

Two days later, Heather woke before sunrise to the sound of wind and rain. She wrapped a shawl around herself and walked to the window. She did not think the storm would prove damaging. Going back to bed made no sense, but it was far too early for the children to be up. She lit a lantern and heated water for tea. Once the water was hot, she poured it into the teapot. Placing the lantern on the side table, she picked up her Bible and sat in the chair, curling her legs under her. The weather had grown chilly.

In the quiet of the early dawn hours, she studied the room. In recent days, memories had surfaced, some painful, some sweet. But the past was no longer something she wanted to run away from. Rather, it was something to study and evaluate. Each problem, each heartache, was a bundle she would unwrap, examine, and dismantle, saving any fragments of value and discarding the rest. Her tears flowed onto the Bible, but they were cleansing a heart that was beginning to heal.

She shook her head. What a wall she had erected around her heart over the months since Ross and Robert's betrayal, all to shield herself from further hurt. Her unforgiving attitude had separated her from God. Sara was the first one who had tried to reach through that barrier. Maggie and Matthew had tried as well. Sara was right. God loved her. He understood, and extended mercy. He had been incredibly patient with her.

Matthew had been gone almost a fortnight, though it seemed much longer. However, each day she gained more confidence in her ability to maintain the farm. The remaining crops in the garden required little care compared to the real growing season. When she went to bed each night, she thanked God they had made it through another day with the farm, livestock, and family all sound. She hoped Matthew would be pleased at finding everything under control when he returned. She opened the Bible to the Gospel of John, where she last was reading. The fourteenth chapter had been encouraging. When she reached the twenty-seventh verse, a warm sensation filled her.

Peace I leave with you, my peace I give unto you: not as the world giveth, give I unto you. Let not your heart be troubled, neither let it be afraid.

Fear—that was something she was all too familiar with: fear of disappointing others, and fear that others would betray her. What was that verse in 1 John? She searched her mind.

There is no fear in love; but perfect love casteth out fear: because fear hath torment.

She needed to reflect on that. Seeing the dawn light come through the windows, she got up and went back to her room to dress for the day.

She was in the kitchen an hour later when sounds came from the children's pallet.

Mary approached the steaming kettle where she was working. "What is that? It smells so good."

"I am stewing some of the apples. It is the apples and spices you smell."

"Makes me hungry." Mary sat at the table, still very sleepy looking.

Heather dished up some porridge from another pot and put a spoonful of the steamy apple mixture on top. She took it over to the table and placed it in front of Mary.

"Thank you."

"Hmm. Is Mark still asleep?"

"Yes."

"I have some osnaburg left. I think we should use it to make a couple of new shirts, one for Mark and one for your father. Shall we work on it together today?"

"Yes, I suppose so."

After breakfast, she showed Mary how to set out older shirts onto the flat, heavy cloth to use as a pattern for the new shirts they would make.

She stopped when Mark appeared. "You must be ready for breakfast."

"I want whatever smells so good."

He sat at the table and devoured the porridge and apples she placed before him.

Mary examined the fabric. "I am ready to start."

"Wonderful. Now, we must allow extra for seams, and a bit more for Mark, as he is outgrowing this one." Once the fabric was cut, she took it and showed Mary where to stitch the seams.

While Mary worked with total concentration on Mark's shirt, Heather stitched Matthew's. It would be a welcome-home gift.

Heather studied her handiwork and smiled. Her father had always taken such pride in her sewing abilities. Had he not been so ill all those years, she would probably have done more dressmaking. It was Father's suggestion years earlier that she hire out as a dressmaker for the shop. Any plans to pursue that endeavor ended once her father took ill. Nay, her vocation became caring for him, and to a lesser degree, the shop. Since her grandfather first opened Douglas Dry Goods, it had maintained an excellent reputation for carrying a large variety of the finest fabrics and notions. Both gentry and common folk came, purchasing items from the finest velvets, woolens, and silks to common muslins, needles, and threads.

Mary put her sewing aside. "Perhaps I will go play with Mark and Randolph for a while. I promise to finish the shirt later."

"Fine, I can take my work to the porch, so please stay in front where I can see you." Heather gathered her work, went to the porch chair, and continued sewing.

Her thoughts returned to her father. Papa had changed so much over the years. He had once been the strong and powerful head of their family, but with her mother's death, his commanding presence declined, and he yielded more to Ross' selfish desires. As Papa's illness progressed, his reliance on those around him, especially Heather, grew. It was not long after Eileen ran off with her sailor that Papa had an attack that left him requiring constant care. The paralysis was short-lived, however, and over time, he regained his mobility, speech, and most of his memory. Eventually, he was able to get around and speak with only a slight slur, but he was forgetful and very dependent on her. And the shop demanded her attention as well.

First her mother's death and then her father's illness ensnared her. She had been resentful and unhappy. Did she have to travel an ocean away to see her life clearly and admit that she, too, had made mistakes? Too often she had felt trapped. In reality, she chose to care for her father out of love as much as duty. She could have left. She might have married. She chose to stay. But, instead of giving freely, she had acted the martyr. How much happier they all would have been had she been wiser.

The children screaming and running toward her brought her suddenly back to the present.

Mary pointed down the lane that approached the cottage. "Heather, look, a wagon!"

"It certainly is." She strained to make out who was heading their way. "I believe it might be … aye, it is the Duncans." Her excitement matched the children's. "They might have news of your father."

CHAPTER 25

The Duncans, full of smiles and waves, came to a stop in front of the cottage. Adam helped Maggie, who held the baby, down to the ground.

Heather embraced Maggie as the other children hopped down and raced all about with Mark and Mary. "I am so happy to see all of you."

"We have been anticipating it for days. This was the first time we could come. We thought all of you would be ready for some company."

Heather's heart pounded. "Aye, we are. Have you any news from Matthew?"

Maggie smiled. "Nay, but I do not imagine that he will be gone much longer."

"Let me offer you some refreshment. Please sit down. I will only be a moment." Heather went to the cellar for cider while Adam saw to their horses and unloaded the supplies.

After catching up with each other's activities, she and Maggie prepared their meal.

"Heather, I believe this is the happiest I have ever seen you. I hope it is not because Matthew is gone." Maggie laughed as she rolled out the crust for the apple pie.

"Nay, it is not that at all. I find it difficult to explain." She wanted to be honest. After all, Maggie had been the first to suggest her joining this family might be part of God's plan. And she had sincerely offered her friendship. "I have prayed so long for God to give me some answers, to resolve some things from my past." She was surprised at her candor, but she longed to talk with someone and found it freeing.

Maggie's face was the picture of compassion.

"I have begun to understand God's timing in answering prayer. He was waiting for me to acknowledge my own choices, my own failings, and my attitudes. My responses to circumstances and people were faulty. I needed to forgive others … and even myself."

Maggie squeezed her hand. "That is such an answer to prayer."

"What do you mean?"

"Adam and I have prayed that whatever was causing you such distress would somehow be sorted out." Maggie drew her to the chairs by the table, and they both sat, facing each other.

"I am still struggling, Maggie, so please continue to pray for me."

"Be assured, my friend, I will be. God is gracious. I am delighted your prayers are being answered. And I am touched that you confided in me."

"Thank you."

Maggie dusted the flour from her hands and gave her a hug that meant so much more than any words. "Now, shall we finish this pie?" They both smiled, returned to the worktable, and resumed their preparations.

Heather poured the apple mixture into the pie shell. She looked out the window and spotted Adam. "Oh, bless him. He is out there splitting more wood. There is plenty. He does not need to do that."

Maggie placed the pie into the oven by the hearth. "He wants to help."

"I really believe I have done reasonably well in Matthew's absence."

"Matthew, hmm." A smile appeared on Maggie's lips. "Aye, he will be very pleased to see how you have managed."

Heather turned to face her. "Are you aware that he has offered me my freedom?"

Maggie bit her lip. "Aye, he mentioned it on this last visit."

"Did he tell you that he was going to Baltimore to see Caroline

Taylor?"

The confused expression on Maggie's face was unmistakable but replaced shortly by a subtle smile. "I do believe he said something about stopping in Baltimore and, of course, calling on the widow and her father. He mentioned that you had all grown quite close while she was staying with you."

"Aye." She sighed as she cut out the biscuits. "We did grow very close. Tragedy can do that." She placed the biscuits on a rack on the hearth. "Caroline was very kind to me, a very sweet soul, and so lost without Samuel and Seth." She stood silent. "She is very beautiful."

"Matthew did not comment on that."

"Oh."

"How did the children take the news of your departure?"

"I … I have not told them yet." Heather walked to the window and stared at the children playing in the yard. Her head began to throb. "At first, I wanted them to get used to their father's absence. Now, I guess I have not figured out how to tell them."

Maggie walked over to her and placed an arm around her. "Heather, what are you seeking that you do not have right here?"

"It is not that simple. I am unsure of his feelings, and even my own. And my being bought, well, it is not a natural marriage."

"That much I had guessed."

"He still loves his wife, Maggie. He loves Elizabeth." Her heart was heavy. "How could I ever fill that place in his heart?"

"He *loved* Elizabeth. They had a fine marriage. But Matthew Stewart is alive, and where is he to give his love now? Excuse me for saying this, Heather, but I always figured that it was you who had someone you were carrying in your heart."

"There was someone, once. But no more."

Maggie took her hand. "Sometimes it helps to talk about it. You can trust me, Heather. I am your friend." They sat at the table.

Aye, she needed to share it with someone, and who was closer or would be more understanding than Maggie?

Heather took a deep breath. "I left my home under a cloud of scandal. Almost two years ago, I met a man, a visitor to our dry goods shop. He was a barrister from Edinburgh in town to conduct some business with my brother, Ross. His name was Robert McDowell. He was tall, well spoken, and amiable. In the many times that he returned to our village over the months, he was welcomed into our home and, well, we became quite fond of one another."

Maggie took her hand. "Did he propose marriage?"

"In a manner of speaking. My father was disabled and dependent on me, so Robert's plan was to send for both of us to join him in Edinburgh. Robert said he had family business that had to be settled and financial arrangements to be resolved before we could join him." She looked up, grateful the children and Adam were still outside and the baby slept for this time of private conversation with Maggie.

"Maggie, I grew impatient, so I wrote him a letter. Ross offered to post it for me. I only knew Robert's business location, but Ross had his home address and sent it there." She looked at her hands folded in her lap. Maggie was sure to see her flushed face if she looked up.

"Please continue, Heather. I think it is important that you share what is on your heart."

"I know you are right. It is just—well, around a fortnight later, when Ross and I were working in the shop, a beautiful and elegant woman I had never seen before entered. Her hair was dark amber, her features flawless, and her clothes were of the finest quality. She introduced herself as Barbara McDowell. I will never forget her words. 'I have come from Edinburgh, with my three children— our three children, Miss Douglas. I am Robert's wife.'" A warm sensation rose to her cheeks. "You cannot imagine how shocked I was, Maggie. I had no idea that Robert was married, or I would never have formed a relationship with him. Believe me."

"Of course I believe you, Heather." Maggie's brow was

furrowed, and her eyes glistened with tears.

Heather continued her story. "I was stunned when Barbara McDowell produced an envelope. It was the letter I had sent to Robert. She told me that she and Robert had been married for ten years. She was not rude at all. I think she could tell I was completely unaware of Robert's family situation." Heather wiped a tear from her cheek. "Mrs. McDowell asked me to refrain from sending any more letters to their home, as it would prove quite awkward were they to get into the wrong hands."

Maggie shook her head. "Heather, I am sorry you were so badly used."

"Mrs. McDowell said she regretted causing me distress, and she believed me innocent, but she thought I would want to know of his ... attachments."

Empathy filled Maggie's eyes as she listened to Heather's story without a hint of judgment in her countenance. "You were innocent, Heather. Surely your family and friends would not consider *your* behavior scandalous."

"Oh, how I wish that were true. As it turned out, Ross had learned of Robert's marriage before I did. Unbeknownst to us, Ross and Robert's business dealings concerned Ross' gambling debts. Robert represented the owner of a substantial note Ross had signed. When Ross found out about Robert's marriage he, well, he used it to his advantage." She shook her head. "Ross accused me of being taken in by Robert and bringing shame on our family. My father, already in ill health, was furious. He was so disappointed in me. Nothing I said in my defense seemed to help."

Maggie shook her head. "How did Robert think you would not find out, particularly if you moved to Edinburgh? What was he thinking?"

"A few weeks after Robert's wife's visit, I received a letter from him. His wife had told him of her trip to Perth to see me. He said that by the time he formed an attachment to me he was reluctant to tell me of his marriage for fear of losing me. He was very apologetic.

He explained that he had a marriage of convenience with little love or affection. He said he hoped his wife and he would reach an agreement or settlement. But she was satisfied, if not content, with having the facade of a marriage." Heather wandered to the window. "I know, Maggie. I sound so foolish. It was something at the end of his letter that opened my eyes to Ross' involvement. Robert said he regretted the deception and involving Ross in it, and that he was as desperate in his way as Ross was in his."

Maggie joined her at the window. "You were betrayed by the man you loved and your brother. It is no wonder you closed your heart."

"My father had died before I got the letter explaining Ross' involvement, so my father went to his grave believing I had brought scandal on the family. I felt abandoned by everyone. The main pursuit of my life, caring for my father, was gone. Now, all I had was my family's home and shop. But Ross robbed me of that also."

"How? I would think he would be ashamed of his complicity."

"Two days after Father's burial, Ross approached me to tell me that he had sold the shop, our home, and all its contents. He had used the money to settle his debts. His wife's father offered him a position in his firm and invited Ross' family to live in his large home. I was without a job, home, and resources. Given the growing scandal, leaving Perth, and even Scotland, seemed the best option."

Their discussion halted when Adam and the children came into the house in search of dinner. Heather quickly wiped the tears from her cheeks. It had been difficult to share her shame with Maggie, but it seemed less a burden now that it was addressed. Besides, that was behind her now, finally. Today she just wanted to enjoy her friends.

The conversation at dinner was constant and jovial. More than once Randolph sent everyone into gales of laughter. At one point, the rabbit crawled into Adam's folded waistcoat left on the hearth, only to begin hopping around the room in an effort to get free.

Mary seemed unusually quiet and pale. Heather hoped it was only because the Duncans' departure was drawing near and not because she was feeling ill.

After the dishes had been cleaned and put away, Maggie put an arm around Heather. "You have many choices ahead of you. We want only the best for you, whether you stay or go. You know where we are if you ever need help or friends."

"Thank you, Maggie, and thank you for your prayers." She embraced her friend.

Within moments, Adam announced the family's departure. "We have a bit of a journey ahead of us." He faced Heather. "We will be back before long. Matt and I plan on doing some hunting."

The Stewarts said their farewells and waved to the Duncans as they got situated in their wagon.

Adam called out to her as they began rolling along the path. "We shall expect to see all of you in Alexandria before too long."

By evening, she had finished her chores. Mark, now bored with Randolph's antics, begged her to read to them.

"Please go and get your primer. We shall read from that for a while." Was Mary overtired? She seemed distracted and moody.

"It has been a busy day. Perhaps we should just eat a light supper and go to bed. We can read tomorrow." She got up to prepare a snack.

With their prayers said and the children under their quilt, she knelt beside the pallet.

"Are you well, Mary? Is something wrong?"

"No. I am fine." Her voice was barely above a whisper.

She kissed them both. "Pleasant dreams."

She checked on the animals one last time, came inside, and secured the cottage.

It had been a good visit, the best yet with Maggie and Adam. There was comfort in their presence, and now, a new openness. She wrapped the shawl around her shoulders and stood staring out the window, glancing around the moonlit farm. So why was she still not truly at peace?

As she climbed into bed, she fluffed the pillows and wrapped the cotton shawl more securely around herself. Not yet ready for sleep, she propped herself up and gazed out the window at the stars beyond.

Please help me through this, Lord. You know my intentions to forgive Ross, but I still have resentment and bitterness. How do I keep those thoughts from returning? She wiped a tear from her eye and continued gazing at the evening sky. *I have made a confusing muddle of my life. Lord, I want and need your guidance.*

She sat there a few minutes more, thinking about the choices she would make in the days to come. *You know what path I should take, Lord, so incline my heart to hear and follow after You in everything that lies ahead. I trust You. Thank You for the love and the grace You continually extend to me.*

She put the shawl aside, slid down into the warmth of the bed, and fell asleep.

She had not been asleep long when the sound of her name being called slowly brought her to consciousness. Mary stood beside the bed.

"What is wrong, child?" she rasped.

"Donald Duncan told me that you are going to leave because you are not happy here. Is that true?"

CHAPTER 26

"Here, crawl into bed where it is warm, and I will try to explain." Heather held back the covers, coaxing Mary under them.

Mary hesitated, and then slid into the bed beside her. "It is my fault. You are unhappy because I did not want you here."

"Nay, Mary. It has nothing to do with you." She cradled her, and with her free hand, brushed back the young girl's hair from her face.

"Then why are you going?"

"Your father has offered me my freedom. I signed a seven-year indenture, an agreement that I would work for seven years to pay for my passage here from Scotland. He has been generous and gracious enough to offer me my freedom six and a half years early."

Mary sniffled. "Does that mean you have to go? You are married."

Her heart ached as she suddenly tried to avoid Mary's questioning eyes. "Well, dear, I am not sure this arrangement has worked out as your father had hoped it would. I think he believes a different situation would be better for all of you. Trust him, Mary. He loves you and Mark very much. He will always do what is best for you."

"But I do not want you go. I am so sorry I was mean to you. I cannot even explain why I did not want you here."

Heather held the sobbing child close.

"Please do not go."

She remained silent. *Believe me, I do not want to go.*

"We will talk more tomorrow, Mary. Right now, we both need

sleep." When their tears finally subsided, they slept.

The next morning, she woke before Mary and silently slipped from the warm bed to dress. By the time Mary got up, Heather and Mark were out in the henhouse, gathering eggs.

"Good morning." She smiled at the child. *Best not to bring up last night.*

"I slept late." Mary joined in with the egg gathering. "Do you want me to help you with the milking?" Mary seemed more cheerful this morning. The young were so resilient.

"Nay. The milking has been done. Thank you, though. There is a jug of milk cooling in the water bucket if you want some. And I set out some cornbread for you."

Mark handed Mary his basket and left. Mary placed the few eggs she had found in it.

"Heather …"

"Aye, child?"

"Please do not tell Mark yet about leaving. Tell him later, after Papa comes home."

She studied the pleading brown eyes. It was a small favor to honor if it would cheer Mary. "I suppose it can wait until then."

Several days went by without reference to Heather's departure. It was a busy interval, filled with the routine chores required of a household and farm. They were good days; the best she had experienced in many months. It was as if a burden had been lifted from her shoulders. She slept more peacefully, and when awake, she was filled with a newfound energy and enthusiasm.

Heather washed their clothes and was wringing them out, a mundane chore that always invited her mind to wander. She needed to plan her future. Was she purposely avoiding thinking about her eventual departure and other things she would rather not address?

Mary came outside, beaming. "See, I finished Mark's shirt."

She took the shirt and examined it. "You did an excellent job. The stitches are nice and even. Your father will be proud and impressed with your work." She draped the rest of the wet clothes on the shrubbery. When she again glanced at Mary, the child was seated on a large boulder, shucking corn for the stew.

"That is probably enough corn. Thank you. You can set it inside and help yourself and Mark to some of the ham and bread. When I am done, I will be in to finish the stew."

Two hours later, it was a race to see if they would be able to gather the clothes and get them into the cottage before an approaching storm reached the farm. Mark laughed. He was caught up in the excitement as he followed along with the basket, catching the clothes she and Mary tossed his way.

They all ran into the house just as the downpour began. The repetitive sound of the refreshing rain hitting the roof, and the occasional popping of the pine logs in the fire, made the cottage feel like a safe haven. Heather approached Mark as he stood near the simmering stew pot hanging in the hearth. "Not too close, Mark."

He stepped back. "It smells good, and I am hungry."

Mary set the table for supper. "Do you think Papa will be back soon?"

"Perhaps. It is difficult to say when he shall return. It will depend on whether he finished his business or if there were any delays." Her heart longed for the answer as well. He might be with Caroline at this very moment, asking her to become his wife once Heather left. Caroline would be happy here, make the children happy … make Matthew happy. She shook her head. Why did she allow her mind to dwell on such things?

Later, after settling the children down for the night, Heather poured herself some tea and sat by the hearth. She had purposely tried not to think of Matthew's eventual return. It was the only painful subject she had not resolved. Now, anticipating his homecoming, a variety of conflicting emotions filled her.

She wanted him to come home—he was missed by all—yet she was uncertain what would happen when he returned. She stoked the dwindling fire in the hearth and wrapped her shawl tightly about her. It had grown chilly. She studied the room, wanting to memorize every detail. She walked to the window and peered out at the approach to the farm. The rain had passed, and the sky was clear. Someday he would come up that drive. Then what? For the better part of an hour, she paced through the small cottage, trying not to make any noise that would wake the children. Emotionally exhausted, she poured herself more tea and once again sat in the chair before the fire.

What do you want, Matthew Stewart? Did he want to forgive her indenture so that he could be free himself? She sighed and sank deeper into the chair, gazing at the dying light from the fire, and wiped the tears now rolling down her cheeks. She would not blame him for that. Their marriage had not been one of love, despite the few moments when they reached out to one another in their loneliness. Nay, they were brought together by their separate tragedies. They were both seeking solutions to their own difficult situations. She finished the tea and slowly got up to take the tankard to the table. *I cannot help but wonder, Matthew, had we met under different circumstances, would we—nay.* It was foolish to even speculate.

She scanned the room again. Caroline would fit in well here. Everyone loved her. She would be the loving wife Matthew deserved and the caring mother these children needed.

Heather Douglas—Stewart. Stop imagining Caroline here.

Studying the star-filled sky, she pondered her future. She would hire out. Surely there were families in need of someone to care for their children. Or perhaps she would find a position as a seamstress. Where, though? She had only been to Alexandria. Maybe Maggie would know how she should go about obtaining that kind of work. But how would she get to Alexandria? She tried to sort it out. Would Matthew tell her to find her own way? Nay, he would not do that. They would go into town to see the Duncans, but she would stay there, never to return to the farm.

Sobbing, she glanced down to the shirt she had made him. Lightly, she ran her fingers over the coarse, creamy fabric. "Matthew Stewart, I do not want to leave. I love you."

Her declaration startled the rabbit. He immediately began hopping about.

"I am sorry, Randolph. I did not mean to frighten you." She picked up the quivering ball of fur, held it close, and stroked it. She sat in the chair by the hearth.

"Randolph, you could have left any time you wished. Have you stayed only for food and shelter, or was affection also a consideration? You are so trusting with those dark little eyes." She placed him back in his crate.

Later, as she undressed and crawled into bed, a sense of renewal filled her. The past could not be changed. She needed to press on to what was ahead, to trust again and not fear being hurt, and to have faith that those she cared for would not betray her.

She thought of Sara, missing her wisdom and encouragement. The gift of Sara's friendship during those difficult months on board the ship had blessed her at such a crucial time in her life. Sara had shared so much with her—the power of forgiveness, the shelter of faith, and the richness of an ongoing relationship with God. They were not empty words Sara had spoken but a deep faith that she lived out in her own life.

Maggie and Amelia also came to mind, newer acquaintances who also offered friendship.

She smiled. *Lord, You have provided me with all that I ever needed. I do not know what is ahead of me, but I trust You and want to be ready to follow wherever You choose to lead me.* She drifted off to sleep.

CHAPTER 27

Heather set towels down by the large wooden barrel and arranged the screen around it. "Check the water, Mary."

"The water is still too cold."

"I will go see if the other kettle has heated up enough yet." Heather walked back into the cottage, only to return a few minutes later, carrying more steaming water to add to the tub. "That should do it." She bent over to check the temperature. "Aye, that is plenty warm, lass. Be thankful that you get to take yours first. Now be quick so Mark can get in and out of there too."

"May I wear my blue dress to church tomorrow?" Mary stepped out of her chemise and into the warm water.

"Aye, and I shall wear mine also." She filled the kettle again from the rain barrel and started back toward the steps. "Praise God for all the rain the past few days."

Once the children were bathed and occupied inside, she took her turn in the tub. The warm water relaxed and refreshed her. How different the farm was now, compared to when she arrived. The most startling contrast was the change in seasons. Until recently, vibrant greens covered almost every tree and shrub. Now, the holly and pine trees remained green, but the leaves on the remaining trees were brown, gold, and rust. The ground was a colorful carpet of dead and dying leaves.

As pleasant as it was basking in the tub, it had gotten cold. It was time to rinse off and get inside. With a cloth wrapped around her damp hair, she quickly dried and dressed.

Inside, she huddled in front of the fire, where Mark and Mary were playing with Randolph.

"Are you two warm enough?"

"I am now." Mary nodded.

"I am plenty warm, but I am hungry." Mark's eyes searched the table.

"Well, as soon as I comb out my hair, we can get the supper on. The hot soup should warm our insides."

They teased and joked about their half-drowned appearance during supper.

"Did you hear something, Mary?"

"No."

She got up from the table and went to the window. Someone was out there. "It is probably Mr. Whitcomb." She tried to sound calm but glanced to where the gun was perched, praying she would not need it. Where was the moonlight tonight when she needed it? It finally appeared from behind a cloud.

There it was—a horse. "Oh, my." Her hand went to her throat. She gasped. "Matthew."

Heather lifted the bar that crossed the door. "It is your father." Her heart raced. *Calm yourself.* She took her apron off and put her hands up to her hair. She shuddered. It must be a sight, still damp and hanging loose. *Stop fretting. Thank You, Lord, for bringing him home safely.*

The children shot through the open door. Once Matthew dismounted, they flew into their father's arms.

"Whoa, you almost knocked me off the step." Joy was etched on his face at the sight of his children.

She stood back, clutching the door handle until her knuckles grew sore. She greeted him with a nod of the head.

"I hope I did not give you all a start." He pried himself loose from the small, grasping arms. "I was close enough that I did not want to stay away another night. Children, let me unload this poor tired beast. Here." He handed them each some of the smaller parcels.

Heather intervened. "Carry those inside, children, and give

your father a chance to take care of the horse. I will set another place at the table." She struggled for the right words to say. "I hope your journey went well. It is good to have you home." How much more should she dare say? She placed a bowl of chowder and some biscuits at his place.

Matthew set the remaining bags by the door, looked up, and seemed to search her eyes. "Thank you, Heather. I think it was a fruitful trip, and it is very good to be back." His smile was reserved, not as full as it had been a few minutes earlier. He had more than a full day's growth of beard. The sight of him filled her with joy. She reached for the back of a chair to steady herself. Had he noticed the flush in her cheeks?

During the meal, she watched the excitement generated among the three. It was difficult to take her eyes off him. She was content simply to observe him eating and engaging in the children's chatter. Across from her sat strength, tenderness, integrity—everything she would want in a husband. She pushed her soup bowl away, almost untouched. *If he looks into my eyes now, he will know that I love him. I must wait to learn what he is thinking.*

He finished his chowder and biscuits. "I brought you each a little gift."

The first item he handed to Mark. It was a small tri-cornered cap, similar to the one he wore.

Mark beamed as he strutted around the room with an air of authority. Everyone laughed at the tiny image of Matthew.

"And Mary, this is for you." Out came a doll with a lovely dress and the most beautiful china head. Mary stared at the doll in awe, then at her father as if he had performed some miracle.

"How did you know?" She looked astonished.

"How did I know what?"

"That my doll was broken. Mark broke its head while you were gone." A glance at her brother caught the concern on his small face. "It was an accident."

"I was unaware your doll was broken, Mary. But when I saw

this one, I kept thinking of you and how much you would enjoy it."

"Oh, Papa, thank you." He opened his arms again, and both children filled them.

Heather pressed her lips together. She must keep her emotions at bay. She went to the kettle at the hearth and prepared the tea.

"Papa, we have something for you." Mary was full of glee.

"Well now, wait another moment, please. I have something for Heather also."

By the time she brought the steaming tankards of tea, he found the parcel and handed it to her.

She barely met his eyes as she took the wrapped package and retreated to her chair. Inside were two cakes of soap with the unmistakable scent of violets. At last, she lifted her head and met his smiling eyes. "Thank you." She glowed with pleasure.

"I am acquainted with your desire for cleanliness, and the fragrance, well … it suits you."

When she picked up one of the cakes to smell it, she saw another smaller wrapped item. Perplexed, she glanced at him, noticing he continued to watch her. She lifted the small packet and slowly opened it. Inside was a comb to be worn in her hair. A closer study revealed tiny thistles etched in the silver edge.

"There is another one under the other cake." He pointed to the other package.

She opened the other packet. It was a matching comb. She swallowed, but the words would not come. *Take a deep breath and do not cry.*

"The thistles are what caught my attention. I saw them and knew they belonged in your hair."

"Thistles, Papa?" Mary looked confused.

"Yes. It is a flower, a symbol of Scotland."

She sighed and walked to the hutch. "They are beautiful. What a thoughtful gift." She placed the combs in her loose damp waves and picked up the silver plate to see her reflection. The combs adorned a face glowing with love. "Thank you. I shall treasure them always." She choked back the tears.

"Papa, now we have a gift for you." Mary ran to the hutch where the new shirt was neatly folded, and to the cupboard, where Mark's was stored.

Matthew held up the shirt and examined it critically.

"Heather made it, and I made this one for Mark."

"This is beautiful, Mary." Matthew held up the smaller shirt.

"Heather showed me how." The child climbed on her father's lap, radiant in his praise.

Matthew held up his own shirt. "Thank you, Heather. It is a very nice surprise, and it will be a pleasure to have a clean shirt tomorrow."

"We planned on going to the evensong service tomorrow at six." She poured him some more tea.

"Fine. I have not been to church since I left Philadelphia." He got up from his seat and faced the children. "Now, I think it is time the two of you got to bed."

"Oh, must we, Papa?" Mary shook her head.

"Yes, you must."

Once the children were prayed with and tucked into bed, he returned to the hearth and began unpacking his clothes from his saddle packs.

"I am afraid I have some wash for you here."

"I rather expected you would." She gathered up the soiled garments and put them in a basket.

"I am anxious to see the place in the light of day." He motioned for her to sit down as he took a seat in the cushioned chair near the hearth. "Have you had any problems?" He sounded serious—all business.

She sat down across from him. "Nay. None." She was pleased to tell him that. "The Duncans came for a visit almost a fortnight ago."

"Did they? Good." He leaned back in the chair and studied her.

"Aye. We had a very nice day."

"And George, did he check on you?"

"Aye. And they had us over for dinner one day."

Matthew appeared amused as he leaned forward and smiled. "And how did that fare?"

"I behaved admirably." She smirked, lifting her eyes to meet his.

They both laughed, eyes still locked. They grew silent.

"There is much to discuss, Heather. But tonight, I only want to crawl up there and sleep. We can talk more tomorrow." He rose and went outside for a few minutes before returning to the cottage and climbing to the loft.

With an exhausted groan, he fell on the mattress. She smiled. What would tomorrow bring? *Thank You again, Lord, for returning him safely to us.*

CHAPTER 28

Everyone was up early the next morning and in high spirits. Heather glanced out the window. What a beautiful fall day. Observing Matthew and the children, with their smiles and laughter, filled her with joy. Would she feel that way at the end of the day?

Mark and Mary babbled all through breakfast, filled with tales of their pursuits during Matthew's absence.

Matthew glanced at the rabbit. "Randolph makes himself quite at home here in the house. When did that start?" He did not appear angry, but amused, as he ate some ham, eggs, and stewed apples.

Mary jumped right in. "Right after you left, Papa. He was lonesome out in the barn. And Heather said it would be allowed."

"He missed us." Mark reached for more of the stewed apples.

Heather rolled her eyes and smiled. "I did say it would not hurt while you were gone. His presence in the cottage comforted them the first few rough days. Randolph is really no trouble. He goes outside to do his business."

"Well, I suppose I should not be surprised he is still here, with the three of you spoiling him so." Matthew got up and went over to where Randolph was chewing on pieces of carrot and apple. He bent down and stroked the brownish gray fur. He chuckled. "I guess I should be thankful that you are a Randolph and not a Rebecca."

When he went out the door, Heather continued to watch him through the window, hoping he would be satisfied with the condition of the farm. If she accompanied him on his survey, he would think she sought praise, which probably bore some truth.

He did not return to the cottage until dinnertime. She and the children were preparing a meal of roast chicken, stove tatties, sausage-filled squash, and apple pie.

Matthew came through the door grinning. "Something smells good." He joined them at the table and offered the blessing. Matthew's eyes locked on hers. "I must compliment you, Heather. The farm is quite sound. There is plenty for me to do, but you all have done a remarkable job of taking care of the place."

"Thank you. We worked well together." She smiled first at him, then at the children.

After dinner, she cleaned the dishes. "You may want to take a rest, Mark, so you will be fresh for church, dear."

"Mary." Matthew motioned for his daughter to come to him.

"Yes, Papa?"

"You are such a responsible young lady. I would like you to stay here with Mark while Heather and I go out for a walk. Would you do that for me?"

"Yes, Papa." A worried frown etched her face.

"Thank you. We shall be back in a while. Oh, and lest I forget, I do not think I mentioned to you how becoming you two are in your new dresses."

The child's frown was replaced by a grin before Matthew held the door open for Heather. They walked outside.

She remained silent as she walked beside him.

He took her arm and led her west. "Shall we go this way a while? I would like to see how high the run is."

At another time, the silence between them might have been comfortable and pleasant, but as things stood, it produced an uneasy sensation in the pit of her stomach. There was so much she wanted to tell him, so much she wanted to ask, but she didn't want to interrupt him. He seemed preoccupied.

"I meant what I said earlier, Heather."

She braced herself walking on the rocky path. Was he going to address canceling her indenture?

"You have done a fine job of taking care of the place."

She sighed. "I am glad you are pleased. I was fortunate that nothing went wrong."

"I have confidence that you would have handled any problem wisely."

They continued walking. The only sounds were those of birds and the rustle of leaves beneath their feet.

She both hoped and dreaded he would get to the purpose of the walk soon. Her stomach churned at the silence—and the waiting. "Were you able to stop and see Caroline Taylor as you planned?" There, it was out in the open now. Would he tell her that Caroline would come and replace her once she was gone? *Please do not tell me you love her.*

"Yes, I did. I gave her your letter, and somewhere I have one she sent for you. She and her father were very gracious. They invited me to stay there while I was in Baltimore."

"Aye, very gracious." Of course they would ask him to stay.

"Caroline is an amazing woman."

She kept her eyes forward, on the path. As much as she longed to read his face, she dared not let him read hers.

"With all Caroline has been through, losing Samuel and Seth, she has remained cheerful and interested in the well-being of others."

"A remarkable woman." She bit her lip.

"Caroline spends three days a week at a home established to care for waifs and orphans."

Another saint. Determined to get through this ordeal, she looked away from his now shaven and sun-darkened face.

"Caroline Taylor is an admirable and kind woman with many fine qualities." Her voice sounded shrill. Where was her self-control? *Take a deep breath.*

He looked taken aback.

"Heather, I did not ask you out here to talk about the farm or Caroline." The tone of his voice had changed. It was serious and determined. "I want to talk to you about your future, your freedom. Please hear me out."

Nay, please not that. Not now. "Aye, Matthew." She dreaded this and wished there was some way to prevent the inevitable discourse. Should she say something, tell him? But what if it was too late? What if he only wanted her to leave so he was free to move on with his plans?

Matthew reached up and plucked some golden leaves from a tree. "When I was twelve years old, my parents and I left England and settled in Philadelphia. Fifteen years ago, they died in an accident, leaving me their home. I sold off most of the furnishings but arranged to have the house let. When I married Elizabeth, we chose to keep the house. It was an investment in case we decided at some point to leave the farm, or sell it and use the funds to expand this home and make it into an ordinary. At the very least, we would have that home if some disaster struck."

Why was he telling her of his home in Philadelphia? Where was all this leading?

"The only disaster was Elizabeth's death. Even then I did not sell the house, thinking that someday there might be a need for it."

Was he thinking of leaving the farm and moving to Philadelphia?

"I went to Philadelphia to sell the house, and I was able to get a fair price. While I was there, I also made some inquiries for possible positions for you if you want to relocate there. A friend said that you would easily find work as a housekeeper or governess. There are enough affluent families there who would pay a reasonable wage for a woman with your skills. The funds I provide you with should be adequate so that you would have some flexibility in selecting a position. Of course, you need not be limited to Philadelphia. You might find something in Alexandria or Baltimore."

She stopped walking and stared at Matthew. Why was he doing this? He owed her nothing.

Matthew motioned for her to sit on a fallen tree trunk. "I shall need to keep a portion of the proceeds for Mark and Mary, which

I am sure you understand."

Apparently finished speaking for the moment, he walked a few feet away, picked up a flat rock, and skipped it into the brook they had been walking alongside.

"I am stunned. Why would you sell your property to assist me?" His generosity humbled her.

"Well, I had promised you your freedom. I would not have you leave without help, to be an object of charity, or worse yet, to have someone take advantage of you. Your freedom is important to you. I was never as sure as when I saw you practically give yourself to a man you loathed, simply to free yourself of your indenture."

"Nay. You are wrong, Matthew. How can I convince you that I only acted that way to escape the barn and get to the safety of the cottage?"

His brow furrowed as he threw another pebble. "Heather, you cannot deny that you saw yourself only as my bondservant, and it ate away at you."

She rose from the log. "No one wants to be a slave or a servant, Matthew." She started to walk away as she wiped a tear that rolled down her cheek.

He reached for her arm and turned her so she faced him. He looked irritated. The veins stood out on his neck. "Did I ever treat you like a servant? Did I ever refer to you or introduce you as my bondservant?"

Ashamed, her face grew warm. "Nay. Nay, you did not." He had only treated her with respect, and he always referred to her as his wife when speaking to others. Would she ever stop misjudging people?

He walked away, obviously frustrated, and skipped another stone into the creek.

She had been honest with Maggie, and even Mary. Now it was time to be honest with him. She swallowed hard before continuing. "You were kind to me and treated me with respect." She wanted to remain calm. Eyeing another large log, she sat. She knew what she wanted to convey and took a deep breath. "I was very confused, Matthew, about many things that happened before I ever arrived in Virginia. And you were right. I continued to carry around my past, and I never found closure. I have let a great many things hurt me over the years. Some of it was entirely unnecessary."

He came over and sat on the same log, but a safe distance away. His eyes fixed on hers.

She searched for the right words. *Be completely honest, and trust the outcome.* "I was wrong, Matthew. I am ready to tell you why I left Scotland."

His eyes widened at her remark. His frustrated expression was replaced by one of concern. "I want to understand, Heather, but not if it will cause you more pain." He never took his eyes off her.

"Nay, I must. You were right. It was a mistake to keep it inside, never coming to terms with it. I shall not go into all of it at this time—it is too long a story. But some of it may help you to understand me a bit better.

"My mother died when I was a wee lass, and from that time on I tried to take her place as she had asked me to do, mothering my younger sister and even my older brother and father. Through my own choice, I never married." She told him about her father's debilitating illness and her brother's lack of interest in the family business. "I acted imposed upon. Not a very admirable character trait." She shuddered but saw compassion in his eyes.

"Around two years ago, I met a man, a barrister from Edinburgh, who was in Perth for some business with my brother, Ross. Over time, our friendship grew into love. He inferred we would marry." She had his attention, but what thoughts were behind those penetrating eyes? "Robert said he had some family matters to resolve before my father and I were to join him in Edinburgh."

Matthew got up from the log and began pacing restlessly. "Go on." He threw a couple of stones into the creek.

"My father died of his infirmity, but not before we all learned that Robert already had a wife ... and children."

He sat back down on the log, disbelief written on his face.

She needed to get this finished. "The shock for me was tremendous, but I am afraid it hastened my father's death. In the midst of my shattered world, I learned that Ross had been aware, almost from the start, of Robert's marital status." She told Matthew of the debts and the arrangement Ross and Robert had made. "When Robert's wife learned of our relationship, she came to visit me, to inform me, on her way to Aberdeen. It was not a pleasant scene. She was also badly used."

Matthew shook his head. "I know there are men who are rakes. What he did was disgraceful, Heather, but to also be betrayed by your own brother. Unconscionable."

"My father died believing I had dishonored the family, never aware of Ross' part in it." She told him of the opportunity Ross had with his father-in-law, and that he sold their shop and home to pay his debts. "I had nothing and no one to turn to. I was filled with shame, and the scandal was spreading. I acted impulsively. When I saw a chance to start a new life, far from the ugliness around me, I took it. I signed an indenture."

She studied him while he considered her revelation. "I feared Robert would find me if I stayed in Perth or Edinburgh. Penniless, and with no one to turn to, I did not want to accept his help and risk putting my virtue further in jeopardy." She took a deep breath. She had bared her soul. How would he respond?

"Heather. I cannot imagine a woman like you being mistreated so—and by all the men in your life. It is no wonder that you distrust us. I am so sorry you have been used and hurt." His face distraught, he got up and walked to the edge of the creek, his back to her.

She closed her eyes and folded her hands on her lap, weary, but relieved to have finally revealed what she had kept hidden for so long. When she glanced up, he was facing her, compassion etched on his face.

He motioned toward the cottage. "There is more we need to

address, Heather, but I think we had better head back."

This time, the silence as they walked was comforting. They each needed to digest what the other one had shared.

When they returned to the cabin, there was just enough time to clean up and prepare for church.

❧ ☙

After the service, the family returned home. They had a light supper before Matthew and Heather saw the children off to bed. As she cleaned the kitchen, Matthew approached and placed a hand gently on her shoulder. "Might we have some tea on the porch? It is cool, so you may need your shawl."

His touch made her heart skip a beat and brought a warm sensation to her cheeks. "Aye. I shall be right there." What was on his mind now? Hopefully, it was not to set a date for her departure.

Matthew took a lantern and went out to sit on the steps while she steeped the tea. In the bedroom, she chose the Douglas tartan shawl. It was fetching with the new blue dress. As she was about to leave the room, she spotted the combs. She hesitated a moment. Should she? Smiling, she put them carefully into her hair and carried the tea out to the porch.

When Matthew took the tankard she offered, she noticed a difference in his demeanor. He appeared far more at peace than he had earlier, less tense.

"Heather, I have been thinking about what you told me today, and I think I understand why you kept it to yourself for so long. It means a great deal to me that you have finally felt comfortable, trusted me enough to tell me about your life before coming here."

"It was difficult, but I am relieved to have gotten it all out. It is a memory, but I no longer want it to enslave me."

"I spoke with George Lamont while I was in Alexandria. If you remember, he was the solicitor who assisted me at the dock the day we met. He sees no real difficulty in securing an annulment under

❧ 250 ☙

the circumstances." Resignation was etched on his face. "You will be free ... and go with my blessing to pursue a life that I hope will bring you joy."

She bit her lip. *Whether I lose him or not, I must confess to him how I have changed. And if it is right, tell him that I love him.* She slowly got up from her chair and sat down on the step beside him. "While you were gone, Matthew, I did a lot of thinking, mostly about my life before coming here. The choices I made, the people, and how I responded to them. When I prayed and sought God's help, I was freed of years of resentment and guilt. I see myself as I truly am for the first time." She took a sip of her tea and studied his face. Was she expressing what was in her heart in a way he would comprehend?

"I was relying on my own strength to overcome my difficulties. I was drowning in a sea of hopelessness. It was not until I reached up and received the help that has always been extended to me that I was able to rise above all that has kept me in bondage. It was only by the grace of God."

She set her teacup down beside her and folded her hands on her lap, experiencing a peace and joy that surprised her. "*I am free*, Matthew. You freed me from physical bondage when you married me. But it has only been in these past few weeks that I have been freed from so much emotional and spiritual bondage."

Matthew smiled but remained silent.

She would say no more yet. To do so might bind him—not what she wanted. Nay, it was up to him now.

"I see the peace in your countenance, Heather. I pray the future gives you everything you desire. After Elizabeth died, I came to understand God's love and provision in a deeper way, too. Loss and tragedy can do that. We have each experienced sorrow, Heather, and now some healing by God's grace." His smile was disarming. "I am gratified that you have been able to throw off the barriers and receive His grace and love."

"I am forgiven, Matthew. I had only to accept it." As she gazed up into his dark eyes, she saw him studying her intently.

"If you must go, Heather, you shall go with my aid and my blessing. But I cannot let you go without telling you that I have loved you … a long while."

Tears filled her eyes, joy filled her heart, and peace filled her soul. She placed her hands on his. *Thank you, dear Lord.*

"Matthew, I love you also, though I have not always known it or admitted it."

He wiped away her tears and brought her hand to his lips. He kissed it and drew her to him, his lips to hers. Their kiss was a long-sought-for release. She backed away slightly.

"What about Caroline?"

Matthew looked perplexed. "What about Caroline?"

"I wondered if you were planning on marrying her and bringing her here."

He frowned. "Where did you get that idea?"

"You said that you had someone to care for Mark and Mary. You told me you were planning on seeing her in Baltimore." Now she was confused.

"The children were to live with Maggie and Adam until they were a little older. Some of the funds from the sale of the property were to be used for Maggie to hire a girl. And, Heather, if you were traveling through Baltimore, surely you would also stop to see Caroline and her father. She was a friend of ours." His words were gentle, his eyes kind.

"Aye. I guess I would."

"Anything else you care to ask about?" He grinned and pulled her onto his lap.

She bit her lip. "Elizabeth?"

His brow furrowed. "Elizabeth? I explained my relationship with Elizabeth. Heather, she shall not be a ghost between us. My love for her does not diminish my love for you. It enhances it. So much of what I have learned about sharing and giving is to her credit."

She put her arms around his neck and gazed into his eyes. "Matthew, I fear you are married to a silly woman, and one who is only now learning to dispense with her doubts."

"You shall not have doubts of my intentions for long." The twinkle in his eyes was visible in the lamplight.

Their kisses were filled with an unquenched longing and an unmistakable joy, as if they had each been lost a long time and only now found themselves home.

"I have wanted you a long time, Heather. I confess, at times I battled with myself to keep my hands off you. But I would not take what you were not willing or ready to give."

Exhilarated, she ran her fingers through his dark waves. "I love and admire you, Matthew, more than I can put into words. And you already know I love the children. My prayers are truly being answered. God is giving me all the desires of my heart."

He drew back and motioned for her to stand. As he stood facing her, he took each of her hands in his. "I have come to an important decision, Heather."

The intensity of his gaze and subtle smile was intriguing. "What is that?"

"I want my bed back." His teasing eyes captured hers. "And I would like it back tonight."

"Hmm …" She smiled coyly. "And what of Mr. Lamont and his annulment papers?"

With an arm around each other they walked back into their home. He whispered in her ear. "They shall not be worth much by tomorrow."

❧ ❧

The next morning, she and Matthew teased and laughed all through breakfast, with the children joining in the fun.

Several times, Mary appeared suspicious as she observed each of them. Finally, she climbed onto her father's lap and asked, "Does this mean Heather is going to stay? I want her to stay."

Heather winked at the little girl and smiled as Matthew hugged her.

Matthew pulled at a strand of Mary's hair. "Oh yes, my sweet, we shall not let Heather get away. She is here to stay. She is our captive—our beautiful, dear captive. Somehow, children, somehow over these past months, we have managed to capture her heart."